Music of Ghosts

"Bissell's fifth Mary Crow novel is an eerie tale that skillfully weaves folklore, Cherokee tradition, and familial angst." —*RT Book Reviews*

Legacy of Masks

"An amazing adventure … Fans of rich mystery will enjoy this book, as will anyone interested in the complexities of humanity." —*Fresh Fiction*

"Skillfully interweaves Cherokee lore and human nature at its best and worst." —*Booklist*

"[Mary Crow is] a kickass Atlanta prosecutor." —*Kirkus Reviews*

"Mary proves a captivating protagonist. The mystery and suspense are eerily entrancing." —*Romantic Times*

"Readers will take a few deep breaths … A fascinating mix of Cherokee customs and folklore plays an important role … Sallie Bissell has created a set of characters that are realistic and full-bodied." —*Mystery Scene*

Call the Devil by His Oldest Name

"A deftly written thriller that grips you from beginning to end. Sallie Bissell's protagonist, Mary Crow, is one of the toughest and sharpest investigators in the genre and totally captivating. A riveting read with a conclusion that shocks even the most intuitive reader."—Nelson DeMille, *New York Times* best-selling author of *Word of Honor*

"*Call the Devil by his Oldest Name* has it all—nail-biting suspense, poignant human drama, non-stop action, an intriguing locale, and no small doses of humor. Heroine Mary Crow's spirit and guts make her impossible not to love. Once again, Sallie Bissell delivers herself a magnificent novel."
—Nancy Geary, author of *Regrets Only*

"Ties with *The Narrows* by Michael Connelly as the best mystery of the year so far." —*Nashville City Paper*

"Tightly wound … offers a disturbing look into contemporary Appalachia; very well done." —P.T. Deutermann, author of *The Last Man*

"Bissell's strong writing and clever, didn't-see-that-coming denouement will keep readers enthralled... She may soon be keeping company with the likes of Tami Hoag and Sandra Brown." —*Publishers Weekly*

"An extremely exciting crime thriller about an obsession taken to extremes … a pulse-pounding, adrenaline-pumping novel that the audience will remember long after finishing the last page." —*Midwest Book Review*

A Darker Justice

"[A] fast-moving story, elegantly told, in which Bissell … weaves a palpitating web of sinuously deadly suspense." —*Los Angeles Times Book Review*

"For thriller fans who value action." —*Booklist*

"Bissell's Mary Crow is one of the most intriguing characters in today's mystery genre." —*Tulsa World*

"At the end of this book, I felt I had read a masterpiece." —*Deadly Pleasures*

In the Forest of Harm

"A top-notch thriller … the pressure builds steadily … [in] this taut debut … [a] solid page-turner." —*People*

"Hair-raising … harrowing." —*Publishers Weekly*

"Bissell tightens the screws slowly and expertly … A shrewdly imagined female actioner, tailor-made for audiences who would've loved *Deliverance* if it hadn't been for all that guy stuff." —*Kirkus Reviews*

"In the mode of Patricia Cornwell … Bissell masterfully drives the plot with … gut-wrenching suspense." —*The Ashenville Citizen-Times*

SALLIE
BISSELL

A Novel of Suspense

....

Deadliest of Sins

MIDNIGHT INK
WOODBURY, MINNESOTA

FIRST EDITION
First Printing, 2014

Book format by Bob Gaul
Cover design by Lisa Novak
Cover photo: 136554325 © Santiago Bañón/Flickr Open/Getty Images
Editing by Nicole Nugent

Midnight Ink, an imprint of Llewellyn Worldwide Ltd.

This is a work of fiction. Names, characters, places, and incidents are either the product of the author's imagination or are used fictitiously, and any resemblance to actual persons, living or dead, business establishments, events, or locales is entirely coincidental.

Library of Congress Cataloging-in-Publication Data
Bissell, Sallie.
    Deadliest of sins: a novel of suspense/Sallie Bissell.—First edition.
        pages cm.—(A Mary Crow novel; #6)
    Summary: "Mary Crow's new job as western North Carolina's special legal counsel leads her to a string of possible homophobic hate crimes tied to an extreme preacher as well as a boy searching for his missing sister"—Provided by publisher.
    ISBN 978-0-7387-3622-8
1. Crow, Mary (Fictitious character)—Fiction. 2. Public prosecutors—Fiction. 3. Cherokee women—Fiction. 4. Women lawyers—Fiction. 5. Hate crimes—Fiction. 6. Human trafficking—Fiction. I. Title.
    PS3552.I772916D43 2014
    813'.54—dc23
                                    2013029779

Midnight Ink
Llewellyn Worldwide Ltd.
2143 Wooddale Drive
Woodbury, MN 55125-2989
www.midnightinkbooks.com

Printed in the United States of America

The Mary Crow Series
In the Forest of Harm
A Darker Justice
Call the Devil By His Oldest Name
Legacy of Masks
The Music of Ghosts

My thanks to Susan Blexrud, Jeanne Charters, Jennifer Holmes, Cynthia Perkins, Madeena Spray Nolan, and Beth Robrecht—good friends and fine writers who read this manuscript in its earliest incarnation. Thanks also to Susan Walker, RN, MSN, ACNP-BC. All made it a much better book.

Special thanks to Robbie Anna Hare, friend and agent extraordinaire.

PROLOGUE

"You gonna be okay, driving this bad boy home so late?" Ray Atkins stood in an instinctive cop stance, arms folded, legs wide. He smelled of bourbon and cigarettes, remnants of his evening at the Boot Scoot Club with Kathy, his wife.

"I'll be fine, thanks." Samantha Buchanan tugged the heavy car door open. The overhead light came on, revealing the Lincoln's dark maw—black leather seats, black dashboard, an inky interior so spotless that the car could have come from a dealer's showroom rather than her stepfather's garage. Gudger lovingly called the car Suzie Q. She and her little brother Chase called it The Hearse.

"I didn't think Gudger let anybody drive this car." Atkins lurched forward to shut her door.

"He didn't until a couple of weeks ago." Sam put her purse in the passenger seat, where she used to sit, enduring Gudger's hand on her knee, his awkward brushings against her breast as he wiped some imaginary spot from her window. "I don't know why he decided to start letting me drive."

"Maybe he thought you'd grown up enough to do it." Ray Atkins's eyes lingered on her legs as she buckled her seat belt. He, too, apparently thought she was grown up enough to do a lot of things that had nothing to do with babysitting his children.

"I guess I am, then." She turned to the man who'd just given her a five-dollar tip on top of her hourly fee. "Your boys were awfully good tonight, Officer Atkins. Both asleep by nine thirty."

"Then you must have the magic touch." Weaving on his feet, he gave her a tipsy wink. "Maybe you can come and touch 'em again next week."

"Just give me a call." Tired of woozy, middle-aged daddies who still considered themselves studs, she turned the key in the ignition. Suzie Q's engine roared to life.

"Whoa!" Atkins jumped as she gunned the motor. "Are you sure you're okay driving this thing? You want me to follow you home?"

"I'm fine," she assured him. "Just hit the gas a little too hard."

"Well, take it easy. It's mighty dark on these roads."

She smiled, then put Suzie Q in Reverse. With Officer Atkins watching, it took her three tries to maneuver the car around their sprawling patio, but she finally got the big Lincoln pointed in the right direction. With a brisk wave at Atkins, down the driveway she went, veering only briefly into his wife's row of yellow forsythia bushes.

When she got to the end of the driveway, she paused, releasing the breath she'd been holding. "Thank God," she whispered. "No half-drunk cop following me home." She turned left, driving slowly, figuring he would watch her taillights until he couldn't see them anymore. Half a mile down the road she lowered the car windows and sped up, turning the radio to a rock station out of Charlotte. Pink's old "Blow Me" came on; she turned it up loud. As the song blared forth, she pressed the accelerator harder. The massive car leapt forward, gobbling up the pavement like a hungry animal. A cool night breeze whipped through her hair, teasing her with the summery scents of honeysuckle and fresh alfalfa. *Right now I could go anywhere I wanted*, she thought. *Charlotte, to see that fancy South Park Mall. West Virginia, to visit my old house. Even Florida, where I could finally see the ocean. I could drive down there, sell this old car, and just live on the beach*, she told herself. *I'd never have to look at Gudger again.*

As she flew past battered rural mailboxes, Florida suddenly seemed like a real possibility. They must have children down there who needed babysitting. She could take them to the beach. Smear their little noses with coconut suntan lotion, play Frisbee in the sand, then let them nap under a palm tree, the waves lulling them to sleep. At the intersection of Cordell Cove Road and State Route 19, she actually stopped and considered it. A left turn would take her home, a right would get her to Charlotte. From Charlotte she could find her way to Florida—people did it all the time. She started to turn the steering wheel to the right when she realized it was crazy. Gudger was a retired cop; all his friends were working cops. If she drove this car a mile out of Campbell County, he'd have her arrested and put in jail. Or worse, take it out on her mother.

"Some other time," she whispered, her dream of Florida vanishing as she turned left. "Some other life."

Now she drove slowly, wanting to stretch out the minutes before she pulled up in Gudger's driveway. He would, of course, be watching for her, his figure dark in the light of the kitchen door. Probably by now he'd be pacing by the mailbox. Before he'd driven her to her jobs, jingling his keys in front of the kitchen sink. *Where are we going tonight?* he'd growl. *Remember, you've got to pay me for gas.* But lately he'd changed, preferring to sit in front of the TV, staring at a baseball game, a cooler full of beer cans at the ready. Tonight he'd even entrusted her with an errand.

"Stop by the Gas-n-Go on your way home," he'd told her, pulling a five-dollar bill from his wallet. "I want some Jo-Jo chocolate milk. They only sell it there."

She knew then that he meant to do some serious drinking. Gudger only drank chocolate milk as a hangover preventive. She shot her mother a warning look as she headed toward the kitchen door.

"Be careful, honey." Her mother perched like a little sparrow in the chair next to Gudger, still wearing her gray work uniform.

"I will, Mama," she replied. "You be careful, too."

"Don't forget his chocolate milk," Chase had whispered, looking up from his book as she passed by the kitchen table. "There'll be trouble if you do."

She drove on, thinking what an asshole Gudger was, wishing she could go back home, load up Chase and her mother, and just drive away, leaving him to his beer and his Barcalounger and his stupid chocolate milk.

"Like that's ever going to happen," she whispered. She was stuck at Gudger's one more year, until she finished high school. Chase would be stuck for five more beyond that. How long her mother would endure Gudger was up for grabs. "He'll give us a safe home," her mom had told them when she and Chase asked why on earth she was marrying this bald-headed creature who strutted around in a police uniform. "We won't have to worry about being on the street." At first Sam had understood that; lately she thought they'd all be better off on the street.

As the car floated down the road, almost steering itself, she wondered where she would be two years from now. They had no money for college and though her grades were good, they weren't scholarship-good. More than once she'd considered joining the army. Fort Bragg was fairly close—if she could get stationed there, then Chase and her mother could come and live with her. They'd never have to see Gudger again. Warmed by that thought, she pulled to the corner of Route 19 and Potato Branch Road. She was halfway through her turn, picturing herself saluting people in a snappy army uniform, when she realized she'd forgotten Gudger's stupid Jo-Jo milk. Sold only at the Gas-n-Go, a good ten miles in the other direction.

"Shit," she whispered, her fingers tightening on the steering wheel. Forget the army, forget everything. Her first night with a mission and she'd already screwed up. For a moment she just stopped in the middle of the road, wondering what she should do—if she drove home now she wouldn't be late, but she wouldn't have the milk. If she arrived late, she'd at least have chocolate milk to mollify Gudger. Being late would be bad enough, but showing up without the milk would be much, much worse.

"Come on, Suzie Q," she said. "Gotta go the other way."

She turned around and sped south, driving along a divided four-lane that sliced through acres of farmland—wide-shouldered, with cornfields growing on both sides of it. In the morning it would be crowded with commuters heading to Charlotte and Gastonia. Now, Suzie Q's headlights flashed along a deserted road, skittering through tall, ghostly-looking stalks of corn.

A few minutes later, she pulled into the Gas-n-Go, a small puddle of neon light in the darkness. A Hispanic man stood at the gas pump, filling up a battered red station wagon that seemed to hold at least ten squirming children. She got out of her car and hurried into the little store, where a bored-looking black man sat behind the counter, playing a game on his cell phone.

"Have you got Jo-Jo chocolate milk?" she asked.

"Back wall, next to the beer," the man replied without looking up.

She found it quickly—*Jo-Jo Choco* read the label. *Chocolate milk from chocolate cows.* She grabbed two small cartons and ran to the cash register.

The clerk looked up from his game and gave her a sly grin. "You got a jones for chocolate milk tonight?"

"Yeah," she replied. "I do."

He rang up her purchase. "$3.79."

She gave him Gudger's five-dollar bill and raced for the door.

"Want your change?" called the clerk.

"No. You keep it."

She hurried back to Suzie Q. The Hispanic family had gone, leaving the parking lot empty. She turned around in a single large swoop and headed back the way she'd come, plunging into the cornfields. She drove fast, praying that no deer or raccoons would dart out in front of her. The last thing she needed was to come home with roadkill smeared across Suzie Q's grille. With her tires hissing along the pavement, she'd gotten halfway home when she saw something moving on the side of the road. She swerved into the left lane, blowing her horn. As she flew past, she glimpsed what she assumed was some animal. But as she hauled down the highway, she realized it wasn't an animal at all. It was gray, but tall, with angular edges.

"Oh my God!" she whispered. "That looked like a baby's car seat."

She drove on, telling herself that it was a box, or a crate, or even some suitcase, flown out the back of someone's truck. *But it was moving*, a voice kept saying in her head. *It was a car seat, and it was moving. Those Mexicans have dumped one of their kids.*

"It was just a box," she said, gripping the steering wheel harder. "The car going by made it move." She told herself that for another mile, then she could stand it no longer. She jammed on her brakes and turned around, driving over the grassy median that divided the highway. Suzie Q bucked and lurched in the rutted ground, but regained her traction as her tires hit the pavement again. Sam sped up to ninety. Whatever Gudger might do to her when she got home, she couldn't let this go. If there was a baby in that car seat, she'd never forgive herself for not stopping.

She raced on, watching for the car seat on the opposite side of the road. She saw nothing for so long that she wondered if she hadn't imagined the whole thing, then suddenly, there it was—a car seat, still wiggling, still facing the cornfield. She pulled over to the median, but a large culvert ran down the middle of this section, impossible for Suzie Q to ford. She would have to go down to the nearest access road and approach the thing from behind.

She zoomed down the road, finally finding an access road that bridged the culvert another mile away. She jerked Suzie Q to the left, made the turn on two squealing tires, then tore up the road in the opposite direction. Flipping her headlights on bright, she peered into the darkness. Then it came into view—the dim, wiggling thing she'd first thought was a possum, was, in her bright lights, clearly a car seat. She braked hard, pulled to the shoulder of the road. Her first instinct was to run and grab this child who'd been dumped like so much garbage. But what if whoever had dumped this baby changed their minds and came roaring back to pick it up? If they found her here, they would realize how much trouble they were in. Or worse, accuse of her of trying to steal their child.

"Don't be an asshole," she told herself, unconsciously adopting Gudger's tone of voice.

Twenty feet away, she put Suzie Q in Park but left the motor running. Quickly, she got out of the car. The road was devoid of cars, of trucks, of everybody but her. As she left the comforting purr of Suzie Q's engine, her footsteps echoed on the pavement and she felt as if she were the only person in the world.

Just think of how that poor baby must feel, she told herself, disgusted at her own cowardice. She walked on, getting closer. As she did, the car seat seemed to move more vigorously. "Honey?" she called, her voice thready. "Sweetheart? Did somebody drive off and forget you?"

She cocked her head—did she hear a whimper of response? Was that a tiny bit of pink blanket poking out from one side of the car seat?

"Oh my God," she whispered. "It's a little girl!"

She hurried forward. Only a few more seconds and she'd be back in the car, with an abandoned baby! Anxious to turn the car seat around, she was reaching for the top of it when she felt a sharp sting on the back of her neck. Instinctively she tried to slap at whatever insect had bitten her, but her knees suddenly grew weak, then crumbled. Still trying to get to the car seat, she collapsed by the side of the road, thinking of her mother and the warm sand of Florida as the hum of Suzie Q's engine faded into silence.

ONE

PATSY KING HAD JUST aimed her right foot at Mary Crow's nose when the Rolling Stones blared forth over the grunts and groans of the karate class—Mick Jagger, singing "Start Me Up!"

Startled, Mary jumped back from Patsy's oncoming foot and scrambled to grab her gym bag. "Start Me Up" was the only ringtone she'd ever purchased—and she'd dedicated it solely to calls from the Honorable Ann Chandler, governor of North Carolina.

"Sorry," Mary apologized to Patsy, who was now hopping on one leg like a wounded stork. "I've got to take this call."

Hurrying past scowling old Yamamoto, the renegade sensei who gleefully taught women every forbidden kick and illegal hold in all of karate, Mary grabbed her bag and went out into the hall. She fumbled with the phone, finally cutting Mick Jagger off mid-chorus. "Governor Chandler?" she said, her voice echoing in the empty hall.

"Hello, Mary. How are you?"

"Fine, thanks."

"Are you in your office?"

"No ma'am." Mary felt her face grow hot, as if the governor had caught her goofing off in a woman's self-defense class when she should be working. Then she realized it was a foolish reaction—though she was on retainer as the governor's special counsel, she'd had no directives from Raleigh, nothing much to work on at all. So she'd filled her empty hours with learning eye gouges and how to release her inner tiger.

"Can you get to someplace private?"

Mary glanced down the hall. The lower floor of the downtown Y held the ladies locker room (which was private but could get noisy) and a deserted dance studio, empty until the noon Zumba class. She ducked into the dance studio. "I'm in a private place now."

"Mary, we have a situation in Sligo and Campbell Counties that I'd like you to look into. Are you aware of the Bryan Taylor case?"

The name rang a distant bell, but nothing specific. "No ma'am, I'm afraid not."

"Bryan Taylor was a gay man who was found beaten to death in Campbell County last month. A year ago, another gay man was similarly killed in neighboring Sligo County."

"That's terrible," said Mary.

"Have you heard of Homer Trull, North Carolina's latest embarrassment?"

"You'd have to live in a cave not to have heard of Homer Trull." Mary recalled the infamous YouTube video of a fiery preacher advocating that gays and lesbians be imprisoned behind electric fences. It had gotten over half a million hits; only a handful had been positive.

"Do you know how many CEOs have cancelled meetings with me since that moron went viral?" The governor's voice crackled with anger. "I'm sitting here looking at a ten percent unemployment rate and this Reverend Trull is yammering about creating a concentration camp for gays!"

"It did make the state look pretty bad." Mary wondered where the governor was going with this. "How can I help?"

"I want to find out if Reverend Trull had anything to do with these attacks against those young men."

"You mean beyond preaching about the evils of homosexuality?"

"Yes. He certainly hasn't backed off any of his statements, and I happen to know that he started a legal defense fund for the young man who was ultimately acquitted of the Sligo boy's murder."

Mary frowned. "That's pretty risky territory, both legally and politically. Aren't the local DAs looking into this?"

"Not to my satisfaction," said the governor. "They claim they're hamstrung because there's no law against gay hate crimes on the books, and all this nonsense goddamn Trull spouts is protected speech."

"They do have valid points, ma'am."

"They also don't have any balls, if you ask me. They're just scared of losing their jobs. They've both got real Bible-thumping, conservative electorates."

Mary walked over and looked out the tall windows that looked out on the mountains that surrounded Asheville, her current home base. "So what's my part in this, Governor?"

"Mary, next week I've got a meeting with the Ecotron Corporation that'll put five hundred new green jobs in Campbell County— *if* I can assure them their gay employees won't get clubbed to death by religious lunatics. I already have the votes in the state house to add homosexuality to the hate crimes act, but that won't happen until the legislature reconvenes this fall. It would ease Ecotron's mind considerably if I can tell them that I've got my special prosecutor investigating anti-gay conspiracies down there."

11

"But…"

"It's all set up, Mary. The DAs know you're coming, and they're on board with it. With you there, they won't have to take any more calls from me."

I bet they're just tickled pink, Mary thought, knowing that DAs guarded their little fiefdoms like junkyard dogs.

"You have the full authority of my office, Mary. That means backup if you need it—the SBI, the AG's office."

"I see."

"Get down there right now and you can attend Reverend Trull's prayer meeting tonight," said Ann Chandler. "I need a report on my desk next week. I need to show Ecotron that I'm serious about protecting their people. Gay might be the new black in the rest of Dixie, but it's not going to be in North Carolina, at least not on my watch."

———

Mary changed into her jeans and hurried out of the Y, glancing at Yamamoto, who now had the class sitting on mats visualizing the invisible, protective tiger that lived inside them all. Thinking that an extremely visible tiger in Raleigh had just sent her on a mission, she walked quickly through downtown Asheville, heading back to her office in the Flat Iron building. That day the town seemed awash in teenagers—hordes of them came out of the Civic Center, wearing different-colored camp T-shirts—green for Camp Altamont, red for Camp Ridgetop, other colors denoting camps she did not recognize. Tourists who normally clogged the sidewalks were taking refuge in the outdoor cafes, sipping lattes while they stared grumpily at all the shrieking campers. As Mary turned down Haywood Street, a trio of street musicians played, while another young woman had sprayed herself silver and was posing as the Statue of Liberty. Mary had to smile. It was too bad Ecotron didn't want to put their jobs in Asheville. People wouldn't blink an eye at anybody being gay, and the city could use the tax revenue.

She hurried past her favorite bookstore, then turned up Battery Park. Her office was in a building built in 1925. Its dark woodwork and frosted-glass door panels reminded her of old Humphrey Bogart movies. She'd managed to get a small office on the top floor that had a spectacular view of the western mountains. The only drawback was the elevator. One of the few remaining that required an operator, its pilot was Franklin, a rail-thin man with sleepy eyes whom she suspected spent much of his shift on the top floor smoking weed. Most of the time it was faster to walk up the six flights than to wait for Franklin. Today, though, she lucked out. Franklin was letting an old woman out just as she turned the corner.

"Going up?" asked Franklin as Mary skidded into view.

"Can you get me to five faster than I can walk?" asked Mary.

"Depends how fast you walk."

Sighing, Mary got in the ancient cage. Franklin closed the brass gate, then turned the crank. With a shudder, the elevator began to rise.

"You having a good day?" asked Franklin, his tone laid-back and dreamy.

"Too early to tell yet," Mary replied. Her assignment in Campbell County seemed dubious, but she would do as the governor directed. Anyway, it wasn't as if she had anything else going on in her life right now. "Lots of kids in town today," she said.

"Summer Camp Tour of Asheville today. Eighty jillion campers running around," Franklin replied. "I just took one up to your floor."

"My floor? What for?"

"Probably a dare. One or two sneak in here every year. They all think this building's haunted."

Sometimes Mary thought the same thing, given the odd creaks she'd heard late at night. But ghosts were not her concern today; hate-mongering preachers were. "Thanks," she said as Franklin opened the gate on the fifth floor. "Have a good day."

"It's all ups and downs for me," said Franklin.

Suffering Franklin's bad pun with an inward groan, Mary hurried toward her office, quickly negotiating the maze-like series of sharp turns and half-staircases that led there. She passed the communal ladies' restroom, then an architectural practice, then she was there, at her own little office—MARY CROW, SPECIAL PROSECUTOR lettered on the pebbled glass door. The only thing amiss was the small boy hunkered against her doorway, pale, skinny arms gripping blue-jeaned legs, looking up at her like some waif from the streets.

"Well, hello," said Mary, surprised. "Can I help you? Did you get separated from your group?"

"I'm not with a group," the boy replied. "I'm looking for Mary Crow."

Mary frowned at the child. "I'm Mary Crow. How can I help you?"

He stood up, dug in an old blue backpack held together with duct tape, and pulled out the front page of a newspaper. "I read about you here," he said, his voice high, his accent rural.

Mary fumbled with the newspaper, her own backpack, her purse, and her office keys. "Come on in," she said. "It's too dark to read anything in this hall."

She unlocked her door, threw her stuff on the small sofa that sat beneath her windows. The boy stood there, watching as she scanned the article from the *Campbell County Clarion*. "Governor's Special Prosecutor to Open Investigation" read the headline.

"What the—" she said. She turned to the kid. "Where did you get this?"

"Gudger brings it home sometimes. He likes to look at the car ads."

Mary read the rest of the article, which delineated Ann Chandler's concerns about anti-gay sentiment in the area. "However you may feel about homosexuality," the governor was quoted, "gay people are citizens and citizens have rights. Nobody in North Carolina should fear for their lives because of their sexual orientation." The article went on, citing Chandler's position that anti-gay activity was costing the state jobs, and that she was sending her special prosecutor, Mary Crow, to look into whether any of this activity was illegal. Mary read the article, then checked the date. It had come out a week ago.

"Damn!" Mary whispered, forgetting that a child was within earshot. "She set me up."

She started to walk over to her desk to call Ann Chandler on her landline when she remembered the little boy standing in the middle of her office, staring at the toes of his sneakers.

"So who are you?" demanded Mary. "Why did you bring me this article? Are you gay? Did someone try to beat you up?"

The boy looked up at her, wide blue eyes horrified. "N-No ma'am. I'm only eleven ... I'm not nothin' yet."

Mary's anger evaporated. She realized she was peppering this child with questions as if he were on the witness stand. He was just a little boy. A scared little boy, at that. "I'm sorry," she apologized. "This article just took me by surprise. What's your name?"

He stuck out his hand, formal and serious. "I'm Charles Oliver Buchanan ... Chase, they call me."

She shook his hand. It was shaking and cold, like some little thing that'd been left out in the weather too long. "What can I do for you, Chase?"

"I need you to help me. Somebody stole my sister."

TWO

"Stole your sister? What do you mean?"

"Everybody says she ran off with her boyfriend, but I know different. She would never go anywhere without telling me. She promised me that, right after we moved in with Gudger."

Mary frowned. "Who's Gudger?"

"Mama's new husband. Here." He reached into his backpack again, this time handing Mary two folders. One held a thick collection of newspaper articles pasted on lined notebook paper. All pictured a beautiful young girl with long blond hair, who'd apparently gone missing after a babysitting job. The boy's second folder had "EVEDINSE" printed on the cover. It held pages of drawings and torn-apart maps, timelines scribbled in green markers.

"Everything's in there," the boy told her. "Everything they've written about Sam, along with what Gudger's done since she's been gone. He's bought a motorcycle and new tractor and a—"

"Wait." Mary held up one hand to stop the tumble of words that flowed from this pint-sized Sherlock Holmes. "I'm sorry about your

16

sister, but this is a job for the police. I'm a lawyer. I work for the governor, on special cases. Your local sheriff should be investigating this."

"He thinks Sam ran off with her boyfriend!" the boy cried. "Gudger told him so."

"And the sheriff believed Gudger?"

"Gudger used to be a cop. Everybody believes him. The sheriff says I used up all my brownie points with him months ago." The boy's chin quivered. Mary realized he really was a child—blond hair still baby-fine, the back of his neck velvety looking. It would be years before his cheeks would know the bite of a razor.

"So you're in trouble with the sheriff a lot?" asked Mary.

Shrugging, he mumbled his reply. "I used to call 911 some, back when we lived in the duplex. The sheriff thinks I'm a sissy."

"How'd you get up here?"

"Hitched a ride."

"*Hitched a ride*? With whom?"

"I don't know. Some old man bringing a load of peaches up from South Carolina."

Mary blinked. Eleven-year-olds hitching rides on peach trucks with wild tales of familial kidnapping was a new page in her book. Though the kid wore faded jeans and a too-big white T-shirt, his clothes were clean and he didn't smell nearly as ripe as some of the campers she'd passed. He just looked scared and hungry, as if someone had sent him to bed without supper for the last couple of months. *Watch out*, she warned herself, thinking of Lily Walkingstick, *kids have a million ways to break your heart.*

"Well, I don't think hitchhiking is the smartest thing to do," she finally told the boy. "But it doesn't sound like something a sissy would do."

He pulled out a funny little homemade purse with an owl appliqued on the front. "I brought money to pay you," he said. "It's Sam's money, but I don't figure she'll care." He counted out an array of bills, some loose change. "Ninety-four dollars and seventy-one cents. I know lawyers cost a lot more than that. I can pay you more as we go along."

"How would you do that?"

"Cut grass, trim hedges," he replied, looking at her with such serious innocence that she didn't know whether to laugh or cry. "This fall I hope to get a paper route."

Mary handed the creased, limp bills back to the boy. "Thanks, but I can't take this. Like I said, I'm not a lawyer for hire anymore." She glanced at her watch. Almost two. She hadn't eaten since early morning and a headache was beginning to lick around her temples. "Have you had lunch?"

"No ma'am."

"Are you hungry?"

"I've been worse off."

"Well, I'm famished," said Mary. "Let's go get something to eat. You can tell me more about your sister over lunch."

She'd planned to get a quick bite at the Indian restaurant on the ground floor of her building, but she didn't think young Sherlock would go for Bhel Puri or Papri Chaat. Instead, she took him to the homey restaurant across the street, where they served traditional American fare.

"You like cheeseburgers?" she asked, as they stepped up to the counter.

"Yes ma'am," he whispered, his eyes wide at the size of the burgers coming out of the kitchen.

"Good. So do I." Mary put two cheeseburgers, fries, and sodas on her credit card and then led the boy to an outside table. She noticed he looked at every passing car, as if one of them might hold his sister.

"So have you lived in Campbell County all your life?" she asked as they waited for their food.

"No ma'am. Just two years. We lived in West Virginia until my daddy died. Then we went to live in Gastonia. Mama got a job there, taking care of Cousin Petey."

"And that didn't work out?" asked Mary.

"It was great until Cousin Petey died. Then her kids came and made us move out. But I got to take all of her books, and she gave me her granddaddy's army pistol, until Gudger made Mama sell it to Dr. Knox."

Mary nodded as a waiter placed two cheeseburgers and a basket of fries on the table. The boy fell to, attacking his burger as if he hadn't eaten in days.

"So then you came to Campbell County?"

"Mama got a job in a nursing home," the boy said, his mouth full. "We moved into this duplex. The men next door were drug dealers. They used to hassle Sam all the time. That's when I got out my pistol and started calling the police."

"What do you mean, hassle Sam?"

The boy wiped his mouth with his hand, sucked down half his Coke. "They'd knock on the door, scratch on our windows. They used to holler terrible things... about how they wanted to take her clothes off and do stuff to her. Mama made us lock ourselves inside the house until she came home from work."

"Why didn't you move?"

"We were going to, but then the car needed a new gasket and Sam got bit by a dog and had to have a lot of stitches. After all that, we didn't have the money to move. Mama said as bad as the duplex was, it beat living in our car."

Working poor, thought Mary. Staying afloat, then one or two unexpected bills come along and they're sunk. "So how did this Gudger get in the picture?"

"He was still a cop, then. He came over once when I called. Then, after he met Mama, he came over every time I'd call. He'd go over and talk real mean to the druggies. Things would get better for a few days, then it would start all over again."

"He never got a warrant to search the other side of the duplex?" Mary wondered if the cop had ignored standard procedure because he liked seeing the boy's mother.

"No ma'am." The boy licked his fingers. "He said he never found any possible cause."

"Probable," corrected Mary. "Probable cause."

"Yeah," he said, swirling a French fry in a pool of ketchup. "That's it."

"So why do you think Gudger stole your sister?"

The boy looked at her with blue eyes that seemed far too old for his peach-fuzzed face. "Because Sam stood up to him one time too many. Gudger sold her to someone—you know, to be their slave."

Mary almost choked. "That's a pretty serious charge."

"But it's true!" Chase dug in his backpack and brought out the EVEDINSE folder again. "Look," he said, turning to a page that looked like some kind of connect-the-dot puzzle. "Gudger always said she was too big for her britches, that Mama spoiled her, that she needed to be taught a lesson. But then one night, for the first time ever, Gudger loans Sam his car. Lets her drive, all by herself, to her babysitting job. That's the night Sam disappears. Gudger pretends to be all shook up—he calls his old cop friends, is real nice to my mom, tells everybody Sam's run away with a boy. But you know what I caught Gudger doing, the morning after Sam disappeared?"

"What?" asked Mary, intrigued in spite of herself.

"Looking at motorcycles, on the computer," said Chase, triumphant. "A week later, he rolls up on a brand-new Harley, smiling like he's never even heard of Sam, while my mom's inside crying her eyes out. Then he got mad because nobody wanted to go on a ride with him."

Mary didn't know what to say. This child had concocted an entire kidnapping theory based on his dysfunctional family and possibly abusive stepfather, then hitchhiked up here to tell her about it. Whatever else he might be, he had grit and a prolific imagination.

"I've known hundreds of police officers in my career," she finally said. "Most are good, courageous people, who want to do good jobs. Maybe Gudger bought the motorcycle just to take everyone's mind off your sister."

"But Sam promised she'd tell me if she ever left," he said, blinking back tears. "She swore on the Bible!"

"Honey, sometimes when teenagers are really unhappy, they do crazy things … things they don't mean. Don't give up on her yet— she'll probably come back before school starts. Nobody wants to miss their senior year."

He shook his head, adamant. "No. She's gone. And she didn't run off with a boy, either. The one boy she liked moved to Charlotte, and he didn't even have a driver's license. If you don't help me, I'll never see her again."

"I'm so sorry," Mary said, "but this isn't what I do anymore."

There seemed nothing more to say, so Mary asked the waiter for a to-go box and packed up half of her hamburger and the rest of the French fries. "Look, I've got to get going," she told him. "How are you going to get back home?"

"I dunno," he whispered, growing even smaller in his seat. "I hadn't thought about that yet."

She looked at him, seeing him with his bitten nails and scrawny neck riding in the back of truck load of peaches, full of hope and ninety-seven dollars, coming to hire her to find his sister. That had taken some nerve—too much nerve to leave him here at Kats N Dogs with only his thumb to provide him a ride home.

"What did you say your name was again?" she asked.

"Chase Buchanan."

"Well, Mr. Chase Buchanan, you picked the right day to hitch up here. I happen to be heading down your way this very afternoon. Would you like to ride with me?"

"Oh yes ma'am," he replied, his voice shaking with relief. "That would be awful nice."

"Then take the rest of this food. You might get hungry watching me pack."

———

She took the little boy over to the condo she'd sublet, parking him in front of the television while she threw clothes in a small suitcase. She had no idea what to take on a homophobic preacher conspiracy hunt, so she packed jeans, a skirt, and her beige linen jacket that went with everything. She was about to close her suitcase when she saw her Glock 9, gleaming dully in its shoulder holster at the bottom of her underwear drawer. As an afterthought, she threw it in her suitcase, along with a box of ammunition. Though she doubted she'd need to pack heat at a prayer meeting, she *was* going where two young men had been beaten to death.

"Ready to go?" she called as she hurried down the stairs, where Chase was sitting in front of the TV, watching a movie where zombies were threatening to eat both houses of Congress.

"Yes ma'am." He stood quickly, as if embarrassed to be caught watching such a silly movie. "I'm ready."

"Then let's get moving."

She turned the TV off and headed down to the basement of her condo. Chase followed, backpack strapped to his shoulders. Mary opened the garage door and turned on the lights. The Miata she'd driven for the past ten years gleamed, its new paint job reflecting like obsidian glass.

"Wow. This is way cooler than any of Gudger's cars."

Mary smiled as she put her small suitcase in the space behind the roadster's two seats. "She gets me where I need to go. Hop in."

"Could we ride with the top down?" he asked, gaping at the little roadster.

"You'll have to hold my suitcase."

"I don't mind." He got in and buckled his seat belt, putting his backpack between his feet and holding Mary's suitcase in his lap.

Mary unclamped the roof, pushed it into the well behind the seats. A few moments later they were driving through downtown Asheville, heading for the county where girls disappeared, little kids brought the heat down on drug dealers, and ministers of the gospel advocated the extinction of homosexuals.

THREE

AT FIRST GLANCE, CAMPBELL County could have been the cover of a Norman Rockwell calendar. In the deep green blush of summer, it was a bucolic land with cornfields plowed so straight that they reminded Mary of the lined paper in Chase's EVEDINSE folder. A small church sat at practically every intersection. Mary noticed they were never Methodist or Catholic or Presbyterian congregations, but independent outposts of Christianity: Living God Chapel, Holy Spirit Meeting House, Mount Nebo Assembly.

"Where do you go to church here?" Mary asked her small passenger as they drove along a four-lane locally known as Jackson Highway.

"Different places, and only at Christmas time," said Chase. "Mama has to work Sundays, and Gudger says all churches want is your money."

They'd just passed a sign marking the city limits of Manley when Chase pointed to the right at an intersection with a blinking yellow light. "Turn here."

Mary did as he directed. The road took them into what was apparently suburbia, for Campbell County. Modest houses sat far back from the road on plots too big to be mere yards, but too small for any real farming. The homes were well kept, with vegetable gardens and swing sets, tree houses and an occasional trampoline. They went on for several miles, then, as Mary turned around a wide curve, she noticed that Chase was clutching the door handle, his brows knotted in a frown.

"I can get out here," he told her. "It's close enough."

"How far away is your house?" Mary asked.

"I don't know … maybe a mile."

"That's no problem." Mary kept going. The boy leaned forward in the seat, now biting his lower lip. As they crested a small rise, Mary saw a man raking out a ditch beside a mailbox that was bedecked in yellow ribbons—the old symbol of someone waiting for a loved one's return.

"Oh no!" the boy cried. Quickly, he lifted Mary's suitcase to hide his face. "Gudger's out by the mailbox!" he whispered. "I can't let him see me." He looked over at her, pleading. "Please just drive on by—and drive fast!"

Mary started to tell him that Gudger would probably be relieved that he was home and safe, but then she saw the look of utter terror on the boy's face. "You got it," she said softly. "Hang on."

She pulled her baseball cap lower on her head and downshifted into third gear. The little car whined as she pushed it up to sixty, then shifted into fourth. Easing over into the middle of the road, they tore by the beribboned mailbox. As they passed, a fiftyish-looking man with a dark moustache and a bad combover jumped back from the road and shook his rake at them. She watched in the rearview mirror as he yelled something, his mouth square with anger.

A mile past the mailbox, she slowed down. "You can sit up now," she told Chase.

"Did he see me?" the boy's voice trembled.

"Nah. He was too busy yelling at me." She pulled into the parking lot of a convenience store and stopped the car. "What's the deal here?" She turned to the boy, her tone serious. "What would that guy have done if I'd pulled up and let you out of the car?"

Chase shuddered. "He'd have been awfully mad."

"Would he have hit you?"

The boy looked down. "No. He's too sneaky for that. He'd have gotten even in different ways."

"Like how?" pressed Mary.

He started to speak, then it seemed that a kind of shutter came over his face. "It doesn't matter. Gudger isn't so bad ... he just gets mad when he thinks things are out of control."

Mary sighed. She'd seen this behavior before, back when her case log was full of domestic abuse cases. Kids would show up with broken ribs or cigarette burns on their legs and still insist that life with their abusive mom or dad was just peachy. She'd finally realized that the lousy parents they had were always preferable to the worse parent they might get from the DHS.

"Okay," she finally said, "what now? Where do you want me to take you?"

He pointed straight ahead. "There's a road down here that circles Gudger's property. If you let me out there, I can walk home. I can sneak through the back yard and get inside before he gets back in the house."

"Okay, buddy." She drove as he directed, knowing there was little she could do to help this boy. Until he made his own complaint or his mother got the courage to leave, Chase was stuck. The sister had apparently caught on early and took off the first chance she got. What a shame she hadn't bothered to tell her little brother good-bye.

"Here," he said, as they neared a reedy little creek that went under the road. "I can follow the creek to Gudger's back fence and crawl under it." As Mary rolled to a stop, he grabbed his backpack. "Thanks for everything," he said.

"Wait a minute." Opening her purse, Mary dug out a couple of her business cards. She knew it was folly, but she couldn't stand the idea of this little boy feeling so helpless. She handed him two cards. "Listen—I've got to go to a church service tonight, but tomorrow I'm going to be talking to some local cops. How about I ask them if they've got any new leads in your sister's case?"

"You'd do that?" He looked like she'd given him a shiny new bike.

"Only if you promise that if it gets bad—if this Gudger starts hitting you or your mom—you'll call me."

He shook his head. "I can't. Gudger won't let anybody but him use the phone."

"Then go call from a neighbor's house, or from that convenience store. If you hitched all the way to Asheville in a peach truck, I know you can get to a telephone."

"Yes ma'am." The boy frowned but took the cards and stuffed them in his backpack. "How will I know if you hear anything about Sam?"

Mary got a pen from her purse. "What's your mother's name? Where does she work?"

"Amy Gudger. She works at the River Bend Rest Home."

Mary scribbled the name on the back of an old parking ticket. "If I find out anything about your sister, I'll contact your mom. Gudger will never know we met."

For the first time, the boy truly smiled—a smile that mirrored his sister's from the photos—open, bright, as if they had the whole world to look forward to, for the rest of their lives. "Thanks," he said. He opened the door, hopped out of the car, then scampered off the bridge and down to the creek. Mary gazed after him as he slipped through a weedy growth of cane, his EVEDINSE folder in his backpack, gnats buzzing around his head like a filmy gray halo.

"Watch out for snakes!" Mary called. She watched until he disappeared, then she turned around, thinking that she was a fool to get even remotely involved with another kid—a fool to buy into, for a single minute, another troubled child's version of reality.

———

Chase waited until the growl of Mary Crow's little car grew faint in the distance, then he took off his shoes, rolled up his pants, and stepped into the creek that would, eventually, lead him to Gudger's property. Though the water was icy cold and he hated the slimy feel of the rocks beneath his feet, Cousin Petey had told him it was always safer to walk in a creek rather than follow one.

"Copperheads like to hide along the banks," the old woman had told him one day as she poked her walking stick into the mint that grew along her own little back yard stream. "So do snapping turtles. Better to walk in the middle of the water; not much can ambush you there."

So he waded on toward Gudger's house, his feet freezing, his brain on fire with the day's activities. That Mary Crow had turned out to be nice. He'd been scared of her at first—her eyes had lasered into him as if he were telling lies. But then she'd looked at his EVEDINSE file and paid attention when he talked about Gudger. When he told her about riding on the peach truck, she'd actually smiled—after that, she seemed to think he was okay.

Though she hadn't promised to help him find Sam, she'd bought him a big hamburger in a fancy restaurant and then given him two of her cards. All together, it had been a good day. Now, though, he had to get back, and fast. The afternoon sun was sinking behind the trees. When he slipped out this morning, he'd left Gudger a note saying he was going fishing in the creek. But that had been almost twelve hours ago, and he doubted that the shallow little creek had enough fish to hold anybody's attention for that long. Still, if he could sneak back home without Gudger seeing him, he might get away with it.

He hurried through the water, mosquitoes whining in his ears while dragonflies hovered low over the water. At one point he slipped on a rock and almost fell, but he caught his balance and continued on. The cane on the banks finally began to thin out, allowing him a glimpse of the rose bushes in Mrs. Carver's back yard. He was tempted to leave the creek and walk to Gudger's through Mrs. Carver's property, but Gudger had forbidden any contact with the old woman. They had a long-standing property dispute that came to a head when both parties drew weapons on the other—Gudger his service pistol, Mrs. Carver her late husband's shotgun. Gudger had claimed victory, but he'd never forgiven the old woman for making him look like a fool. The battle lines, as well as the property lines, were still clearly drawn.

Chase waded on, deciding it was better to stay in the creek than to risk Mrs. Carver's wrath. His pants were now wet to the knees, his T-shirt sticky with dirt and sweat. Maybe if he timed it right, he could just reappear at the exact minute his mother came home from work. Or if his mother wasn't home, maybe he could sneak through the back yard and jump into the swimming pool that Gudger had set up earlier this summer. *That's it,* he told himself. *Just get in the pool and wait until Mom drives up. Then go in and tell them that when I got back from fishing I went swimming all afternoon.* Of course he didn't have his bathing suit and would have to swim in his underwear, but Gudger wandered around in his underwear half the time anyway, his gut hanging over his jockey shorts like a watermelon.

Energized by his plan, Chase scrambled out of the creek at Gudger's back fence. He slipped between two loose barbed wires and hid behind some bushes while he put his shoes back on. *Maybe this won't be so bad*, he told himself. *Maybe Gudger had just been out getting the mail earlier and had gone back inside the house to watch one of his stupid ball games. Maybe he's in there now, passed out, not giving a shit about me.*

"Yeah, right," he whispered. He crept through the wild honeysuckle that grew along the fence line. Gudger's entire back yard was clearly visible—the house with its big picture window, the patio, a brick toolshed where Gudger kept his new tractor and his yard tools. Between the toolshed and the patio, hidden from his view, was the swimming pool. If he could get to the toolshed without Gudger seeing, he could take off his clothes, run around the little building, and just hop in the pool. Float until his mom got home. It was perfect!

He held his breath, watching the back of the house. Except for a squirrel that scampered along the roofline, the place was still. Gudger wasn't tinkering with his new motorcycle, nor did he see the glow of the TV screen through the picture window in the den. Just to be safe, though, he dropped his backpack on Mrs. Carver's side of the fence. If she found it, she'd just throw it away. If Gudger found his EVEDINSE file, though, he'd kill him.

Filling his lungs with air, he gave the house a final check, then he raced for the toolshed. As he reached the cool shade of the back wall, he hunkered down, listening for the scrape of the back door opening, Gudger's harsh *You, boy!* But again, he heard only the bird-chirp sounds of a summer afternoon. Weak with relief, he unlaced his sneakers, pulled his T-shirt over his head. As he took off his jeans, he thought how good the swimming pool was going to feel. Even though it was one of those above-ground things that Gudger put up so he could ogle Sam in her bikini, they loved it, nonetheless. The water was as cool as the creek, but without the dangers of water moccasins and snapping turtles. He could dive under the water and hide from Gudger for a whole thirty seconds, or at least until he had to breathe again.

He folded his clothes into a small pile and stood there in his underpants. He felt horribly exposed, but he had no choice. He could explain taking his clothes off to swim; swimming in his thick, heavy jeans would be a much harder sell. A mosquito with striped wings landed on his belly, just below his navel. If he didn't get in the water soon, he'd be eaten alive.

"Come on," he told himself, slapping at the bug. "Don't be a sissy."

He paused in the concealing shadows of the toolshed for another second, then he made his move. Digging his bare toes into the ground, he ran down the side of the toolshed as fast as he could—arms pumping, head down, his eyes on the ground. He turned the front corner of the toolshed, then raced for the bright blue plastic pool that had stood there since May. Only today, it wasn't there. Today, only jagged pieces of plastic lay in a jumble, while a swarm of mosquitoes hovered over the soggy ground.

He stopped, stunned, gaping at the wreckage of the pool. Suddenly, he heard a howl of laughter behind him. He turned. Hidden inside the toolshed, Gudger sat on his new motorcycle, his cell phone to his ear.

"Oh, man, you ain't gonna believe this," he told whomever he was talking to, his voice cracking with glee. "I figure Shithead's run off, so I bulldoze this stupid pool so I can plant some tomatoes. Now here comes Shithead running up in his skivvies, all ready to dive in it! Hang on a minute. This is just too fucking good."

Red-faced with laughter, he aimed his smart phone at Chase. "Give me a big smile, Olive Oyl. I'm gonna put that big ol' rig of yours on YouTube! All the fifth grade girls will go crazy!"

Chase stood there paralyzed. There was no pool. There was no great trick he'd managed to pull on Gudger. There was only Gudger, sitting there laughing, taking a video of him nearly naked. Soon everybody—all of Gudger's friends, all of the kids at school—would see him pigeon-chested and skinny-legged, wearing only a ragged pair of underpants. He turned and raced toward the house, his cheeks flaming with embarrassment.

"Aw, don't run away, Olive Oyl," called Gudger. "Come back and make a muscle for the camera!"

As Gudger's voice echoed over the yard, Chase opened the back door and ran to his room. He threw himself on the bed, tears of humiliation stinging his eyes. Of all the things Gudger could have done, why this? Why not just ground him? Or beat him? Or even kill him? Anything would be better than having those pictures on the Internet. He felt sick inside as he pictured himself on YouTube, stripped to his underwear, running away from a dead swimming pool. The kids at school would laugh at him for the rest of his life. And why had Gudger destroyed the pool in the first place? He and Sam loved it—even his mother liked to float in it at night, after supper. The pool had been the only good thing about this place and now it was gone.

A rage filled him. He got up and started pacing in front of his window, staring at Gudger who was still on his stupid cell phone. How he hated him! How he wished he could pound his stupid face into mush. But Gudger had at least a hundred pounds on him, plus he always carried that Taser on his belt. If he raised a fist at Gudger, the jerk would probably shoot him with that thing and then tell his mother he'd had a kiddie heart attack.

"But it won't always be like that," he whispered. "Someday I'll be grown up. Someday I'll be as big as Daddy." He pictured himself tall, with his father's big hands. He would be in the Marines, but he'd come home to visit his mother. There Gudger would be, sitting in his stupid chair, watching his stupid baseball game. He'd walk up and lift him up by the collar and punch him out. *That's for the swimming pool*, he'd say. *And for the time you put me on YouTube.* And then when Gudger started to cry, he would hit him so hard his teeth would fly out of his mouth. *And that's for selling my sister, you bastard!*

FOUR

SAMANTHA OPENED HER EYES when the girls started leaving for the night. The black girls came first, their voices high and raucous. *I ain't going in that Bekins truck tonight. That white boy's dick is like sucking on a straw! And then that little ol' piddle of kum!*

That one came back what's gonna put me in the movies … I'll let y'all know when I get to Hollywood. They started to laugh, cackling like crows, then a rough male voice cut them short. *You bitches shut up. At least them boys got dicks. All y'all got's fat asses and big mouths.*

Others began to hurry past her room. The one who always cried for her mother went by, softly wailing *mama, mama, mama* as if it were a kind of prayer. The one they called Dusty came by full of piss and vinegar. *You just get a load of me tonight, Clifford!* She said, her voice coarse, her accent strange. *I'll bring you back two grand!*

I'm banking on it, baby, cooed a different male voice. *You were made for that casino. We are one kick-ass team!*

Sam got out of bed and went to the bathroom. Afternoons, when the girls went out, weren't so bad. They'd eaten and slept, been given their drug of choice. Twelve hours from now it would be different. Their footsteps would be heavy and defeated, much like her father's mine crew at the end of a shift. The black girls would be angry, calling everybody a motherfucker. Dusty would bounce off the walls either high or drunk or both; others would come home crying about the trick who hit them or the cop who made them blow him for free. Always she waited to hear the one who cried *mama, mama, mama*. It surprised her that she came back at all.

She flushed the toilet, then turned on the water to wash her hands. She knew that once the others left, Ivan would come with her tray of milk and cornflakes. In a month she'd never seen anyone else, never eaten anything but cereal for breakfast and a fast food meal for supper. Ivan had let it slip, though, why no pimp had taken her and herded her out with the others. "Word from the boss," he whispered. "You're special... you're a virgin."

How they'd found that out, she didn't want to think about. She assumed it had been when she was knocked out, after she'd gone to check out that car seat by the side of the road. She had a wisp of a memory of hands plucking at her clothes, but even that notion swirled away in a miasma of barely recalled dreams and sensations. When she finally woke up for real, she was in this small, boarded-up motel room with a bed, a bathroom, and a collection of old cartoon VCR tapes to play on a battered TV.

She went back to her bed and waited. Five minutes later she heard a key at her door. Ivan stepped into the room bearing a tray of cornflakes. From Moscow, he had a lupine face and the long, lean body of a ballet dancer. They'd struck up a curious friendship during the past month—he'd taken pictures of her, given her little snippets of information while she'd taught him how to put his long blond hair up in French braids. Today he was dressed all in black, with glittery purple eye shadow that made his green eyes glow. In the outside world, he would have frightened her. In here, he was her only friend.

"Good morning, Kiska," he said, his English thick with Russian. "How are you today?"

"Okay." She sat cross-legged on the bed. "Considering all the racket outside."

"You hear Dusty bragging?"

"It was hard not to."

He tucked a stray curl into his beloved French braid. "She's proud of the money she brings to Clifford. I warn her—shut your mouth, you'll have trouble if you make the black girls mad."

"What would they do?"

"Who knows? Cut her face up, kill her. You never know what women will do. Anyway," he sat down on the foot of her bed. "You need to forget about Dusty. Today is big day for you."

"What do you mean?"

"Tonight Boyko comes with doctor, to examine you."

She tried to keep her voice steady. "What for?"

"To make sure you are virgin. If doctor says okay, they will send you someplace much nicer than here."

"Where?"

"Far away. You will never see here again."

"But where is *here*, anyway?"

"That I cannot tell you."

She looked down at her bowl of cornflakes, the squat little carton of grade-school milk. Her heart began to beat like a drum. If she never saw here again, then she'd probably never see her mother or little brother again, either. She started to tremble, fighting back tears.

"Ah, Kiska, do not cry. Is not so bad. A wealthy man will take care of you. You will have good food, pretty clothes. You will never have to work the casino or the streets."

"But I'll never see my family again!" She looked up at him, tears finally spilling down her cheeks. "Don't you know what that's like? Don't you miss your family in Moscow?"

"I miss them, but they don't miss me." He wiggled his fingers, showing off the purple nail polish that matched his eyelids. "In Russia, they hate pretty boys like me."

His words made her cry harder. How had she ever wound up here? How could she ever escape?

"Kiska, please." Ivan ran to the bathroom and spooled off a handful of the rough toilet paper. "If they see you've been crying, they'll know I've told their secrets." He thrust the toilet paper at her. "Please—dry your eyes."

She wanted to tell him she didn't care if they found out—she didn't care if he got in a lot of trouble. Then she realized that he was truly scared—not for her, but for himself. Instead of drying her eyes, she sobbed louder.

"*Ne plach'*, little Kiska!" he cried, sitting down close beside her and putting his arm around her shoulders. "You mustn't be crying when Boyko comes. I was teasing about the doctor—just telling you foolish gossip."

She knew his words weren't gossip—weeks ago he had told her exactly what awaited her if the doctor pronounced her pure. She kept on crying.

"Shh!" He tightened his grip and shook her, as if that might staunch her tears. When it didn't, he slid to the floor and beseeched her like a frightened puppy. "Kiska, please. How can I make you quit crying? What can I do to make it better?"

"Fuck me," she whispered. "Make me not a virgin anymore. Then at least I'll be able to go outside."

He shrank back, his eyes wide with terror. "That would be *bezumnyj* ... suicide."

She started to beg him to have sex with her, then she noticed he was wearing a little holster that held a cell phone. Suddenly, she saw her chance. "Let make a call on your phone. To my mother."

He looked as if she'd suggested sex again. "Boyko would kill me if he found out."

"He won't find out! I'll never tell him. I won't even talk long. I just want to tell my mother good-bye!"

He shook his head. "I'm sorry, Kiska. Is not possible."

"Please!" She scooted off the bed, sitting on the floor, nose to nose with him. She took his face in both hands and kissed him, gentle as a sister. "*Pozhaluysta*, Ivan," she begged, using one of the Russian words he'd taught her. "I love my mother. Please let me talk to her—just one last time!"

For an eternity she gazed into his eyes. They flashed green beneath their purple lids, emotions rushing across them like clouds in a stormy sky. His own tears welled up, running his mascara into thin black streams. Finally, he gave a hopeless sigh and reached for his phone.

"For the French braid, Kiska. One minute. And only to your mother."

She grabbed his phone and hurried over to the window. Turning her back to him, she started to punch in her mother's work number. But suddenly her hands started to shake and she couldn't remember the proper sequence of 4s and 2s that made up the nursing home number—was it 242-4244? Or 424-2424? She couldn't remember—her brain seemed frozen on the mere fact she was finally holding a cell phone. Finally, she gave up and punched in the number Gudger had them memorize the day after they'd moved into his house—the landline to his archaic black phone in the den. Though Gudger was the last person she wanted to talk to, he was better than nothing.

The phone rang once, twice, three times. Was there an answering machine attached to this line? She couldn't remember. She gripped the cell harder as the phone kept ringing. "Answer," she whispered, hearing the rustle of silk as Ivan got up off the floor. "Somebody please hurry and answer!"

The phone rang on, then, suddenly, a child's voice said, "Hello?"

"Hello?" she cried. "Chase?"

"Time to get off," said Ivan. "She knows you're alive."

"No, wait!" She shrugged away from Ivan and turned to the corner of the room. "Chase, I'm in trouble," she whispered. "I'm scared. You need to tell Mama."

"What did you say?" Chase asked over some loud pounding in the background. "Sam, is that you?"

She knelt down in the corner and went for broke, yelling as loud as she could. "I don't know where I am, but tell Mama some men are going to send me away!"

Before she could hear Chase's reply, the door burst open. She looked over her shoulder as two men strode into the room. One had a shaved head, but the same high cheek bones as Ivan; the other hulked like an ape and carried a rifle. Ivan turned toward them, holding his hands out in supplication.

"Boyko! *Zhdat!*" were the last Russian words he uttered. The huge man aimed his rifle and fired. Ivan slammed into the wall beside her, sliding to the floor, his face and torso torn open. Blood gurgled from a ragged hole in the middle of his throat, while another had ripped off most of his lower jaw. His pretty French braid was now peppered with bits of tissue and white chunks of bone.

"Ivan?" she cried, as a new coppery smell mingled with his jasmine perfume. His green eyes looked at her in surprise for moment, then the light in them died, suddenly overshadowed by the fluorescent magenta smear on his eyelids.

"Ivan, come back!" She reached to touch him, reached to shake him back to life, but before she could the two men were on her. The bald man wrenched Ivan's phone from her grasp, while the other one slung her over his shoulder like a sack of potatoes.

"Mama, please help me," she whispered, sounding a lot like the girl who'd just gone off to work, calling for her mother in a helpless and unanswered prayer.

FIVE

After Mary left Chase at the creek, she continued along Jackson Highway through the town of Manley, then on to the larger city of Gastonia, where she presented her state credit card to the clerk at the Holiday Inn. It was safer, she'd been advised, to stay outside the county you were investigating. "Always watch your car," warned Tom Ruffing, her counterpart in the eastern part of the state. "I once found a dead squirrel stuffed in my exhaust pipe." After a quick supper at the motel café, she headed back to Campbell County, where, according to Governor Chandler, the One Way Church's Wednesday night prayer meeting would soon begin.

It looked similar to the other little churches that dotted the county. A small brick building topped by a squat steeple, it had signs asking God to bless our troops, warning sinners that the path to hell was easy and wide. What made the One Way Church unique was the parking lot. That evening it overflowed with cars, protestors waving signs, a couple of media trucks with rooftop satellite dishes aiming heavenward. Mary pulled up to the policeman who stood at the entrance of the lot, directing traffic. "Any room for me?"

The cop eyed her Miata with suspicion. "You a reporter?"

"Just a churchgoer," she said, smiling.

Frowning, the cop scanned the crowded parking lot. "Pull over there," he said. "You can wedge in between those Dodge Rams."

"Thanks." Mary drove where he'd pointed, nosing her little roadster in between the two monster trucks. Reminding herself to check her exhaust pipe for dead squirrels before she left, she walked to the front of the church, where a large knot of protestors chanted *Real Christians don't hate!* Mary walked through the din, passing a reporter doing live news feed from WRAL in Raleigh. She wondered if Ann Chandler was watching from the statehouse; if so, she hoped she saw her on camera. As she neared the entrance of the church, a gray-haired man poked his head out the door.

"Ma'am, are you here for services?" he called.

"Yes sir."

"Then come on in." Glaring at the shrieking protestors, he held the door open wide. "Welcome to One Way Church."

She stepped into a small lobby, where another man began wanding her like an airport security guard. When he determined she wasn't carrying any weapons, he asked if he could look in her purse.

"Of course," she said, handing him her bag, thankful she'd left her Glock in the motel room. "Looks like you've got some security issues tonight."

"Oh, somebody put Brother Trull on YouTube. Now nobody can come to service for those queers out there, protesting something that ain't none of their business to begin with."

"I see," said Mary.

He pawed through her purse, took out her cell phone. "I'm not going to confiscate this, ma'am, but I have to ask you to promise not to record any of the service."

"I hadn't planned to."

"I know you weren't. You just can't hardly trust anybody these days." Smiling, he returned her purse. "Welcome to One Way. I hope you enjoy the service."

She was tempted to tell the man he'd just conducted an illegal search and violated her first amendment rights, but decided not to. Reverend Trull was the issue tonight, not his security guard.

She went inside the sanctuary and took a seat in a back pew. The One Way sanctuary looked a cut above what she'd expected—there was bright red carpet on the floor, padded pews, a big wooden cross hanging over the altar. Though the congregation ranged from lap-held babies to white-haired grandmothers, she saw no people of color, and very few who, like her, sat alone. As she studied the congregation, two men stepped up to the altar, plugged electric guitars into amps, and started singing a zippy hymn about Jesus being THERE FOR YOU. People clapped and sang along, and when the song ended, they waved their hands in the air, index fingers pointing toward heaven. After the guitarists left the stage, an older man got up and made some announcements—the women's circle was collecting food for the needy, old cell phones for our soldiers overseas, gently worn sneakers for people in the Sudan. Warriors for Christ would meet Sunday afternoon, rather than tomorrow night, due to the rescheduled baseball game.

The man bowed his head for a brief prayer, asked God to bless the proceedings, then Reverend Trull took the pulpit. He looked as Mary remembered from YouTube—a short man with a potbelly, going gray at the temples. He wore a dress shirt with the sleeves rolled to his elbows and thick glasses that darkened his eyes. The congregation seemed to hold its collective breath as Trull stepped up to the lectern.

"First, let me say how proud I am to see so many of you out there. I know it was probably a little scary tonight, coming to church and having reporters taking pictures and then having a bunch of sign-waving sinners saying you're bigots and full of hate. But you know what? I don't care. If living our lives according to the Bible makes us bigots, then I say so be it! If believing the Holy Scriptures makes us full of hate, then I say so be it!"

"Amen!" shouted several people from around the room.

"You know," said Trull, warming to his audience, "those people hollering and carrying signs outside think that God loves homosexuals just as much as He loves us. That Jesus loves them and so should we. Well, you know—those people are right. God does love homosexuals, and so do we. We love them enough to try and stop them from going down the wrong path! We love them enough to tell them that God is just and righteous and they are going to burn in hell if they don't start obeying His commandments!"

"You tell 'em, brother!" said an old man sitting on the row in front of Mary.

"Now if you went outside right now, those folks with the signs would tell you that Jesus never said one word about queers and dykes. And that's true, too—he didn't. But do you know why he didn't? Because he didn't have to! The Old Testament covers homosexuality in Genesis, Leviticus, Judges, Isaiah. Jesus would have thought only complete knuckleheads wouldn't know that men having sex with other men was evil and wrong!"

The congregation laughed. Mary had to admit that Trull was more than the blustering demagogue she'd expected. He was skillful with words, used humor to get his message across. She watched as he unbuttoned his coat, loosened his tie.

"But you know something else, brothers and sisters? The Bible is a wonderful book." Trull hoisted a Bible the size of the Atlanta yellow pages. "It tells you how to solve just about any problem you have. Just look at Proverbs 22, verse 15. *Foolishness is bound in the heart of a child; but the rod of correction shall drive it far from him.* Now you probably think that's talking about if your son or daughter won't clean their rooms, or sasses you when you tell 'em to go to bed. Well, you're right—it does mean that. But I think it means something else, too. I think it means if you've got a little boy mincin' around with a limp wrist, then you take him to the woodshed. Do your duty as the Bible clearly tells you, and he'll man up right smart. You got a girl wearing jeans and holding hands with other girls? Same prescription. Take her to woodshed, pull those jeans down, and give her a lickin'! She'll put her skirts back on pretty fast."

Mary's stomach turned as the congregation murmured their approval.

"Now those folks outside would probably say I've told you to beat your children. But you know that's not true. I'm just saying that God has given us clear directions on how to raise a child up right. He's also given us directions on how to deal with queers."

Trull paused, as the congregation seemed to catch its breath. "I know some of you think that if a homosexual sidles up and bats his eyelashes at you, then you're going to hell just like they are. Before our blessed Lord came to earth, that was probably true. But I'm telling you, our sweet Jesus does not want anyone to go to hell, and He's even got a plan to save the queers." He leaned forward on the lectern and grinned. "You want to know what it is?"

For an awkward moment, his question hung unanswered in the silent air, then a woman reluctantly asked, "What?"

"Sisters and brothers, as much as you might not want to go any-where near these people—as disgusting as you might find them, it's your duty, as Christians, to tell them you love them. Tell them they need to quit their evil ways, for the sake of their immortal soul! All they have to do is accept Jesus as their personal savior. Once they do that—once they truly and honestly accept our Lord—a miracle will happen. He will change them into normal people! Instantly! Right before your eyes! So, brothers and sisters, don't be afraid of these poor people outside the church. Go out there, put your arms around them, and tell them how much God loves them! Stand up for what you know is good and right and true, and when your own day of judgment comes, you can look at Jesus with pride, knowing you tried your best to bring all His sheep back into the fold!"

Everyone stood up. Cheers of *Amen, brother* and *Praise Jesus* came like waves, caressing Trull's grinning face. The guitarists reappeared, striking up another Christian rock anthem as ushers began to pass collection plates. With the congregation digging deep into their wallets, Mary slipped out of the pew and down the aisle. Grabbing a program that she'd missed on her way in, she hurried out the door and down the front steps of the church, eager to get away from Trull's brand of Christianity. As she walked toward her car, she passed a fresh crew of young men who were chanting *God made me gay and I'm okay!*

Watch out guys, she was tempted to tell them, *a miracle is about to occur. In a very few minutes about two hundred people are going to come roaring out of that church, determined to pray every one of you into being straight.*

SIX

SMILEY SECRETLY HATED THE Russians. He didn't like the way they muscled into a territory, knocking back their vodka, assuming that America was now theirs for the plundering. In particular he didn't like the fact that their local lieutenant, Boyko Zelinski, was now glaring at him with the butt of a Makarov pistol protruding from the shoulder holster under his pricey linen jacket. *No respect,* he thought to himself. *Not an ounce of deference for me and my people, the ones who'd been plundering America back when his ancestors were growing turnips for the Czar.*

Boyko's pale eyes narrowed. "You always allow your girls cell phones, *moy drug?*"

"Ivan was one of yours, Boyko. Not mine."

"Ivan was here to help you, Smiley. Feed the girls, dole out their drugs, don't pop any of their cherries. He was not to loan his cell phone out for calls."

Smiley stepped aside as the walking side of beef they called Volk carried Ivan's corpse down the dark hall. "Then I guess Ivan screwed up, didn't he?"

"Yes, he did. And it's too bad, too. I hate to kill Russians." Boyko glared at Smiley. He'd started to say something else when another man joined them in the hall. Short and stocky, he had his slicked-back brown hair curled over the collar of his white lab coat. Smiley noticed he carried a tattered black doctor's bag. Boyko nodded at the man, then returned his attention to Smiley.

"But enough about Ivan," he said. "Tell me about this girl … this treasure who's already cost me a man."

"You saw her, before you whacked Ivan," Smiley replied. "Sixteen. Beautiful. And she's a virgin."

Boyko laughed. "Sixteen is old to be virgin."

"This one really is, as far as we could tell. She's not strung out or crazy like these others. She's clean—a country girl. Just wants to go home to her mother."

The Russian gave him a cold look. "How did she wind up here?"

"Doesn't matter," said Smiley. "She's here now. Jersey told me to call you—the Seattle market's good, but they thought there could be an even bigger payoff overseas."

Boyko snorted. "Overseas is lot of trouble. But let's go look."

He motioned for the doctor to follow him but paused before they entered to the girl's room. "Smiley, if this girl is not a virgin, it will not go well for you. Russians I hate killing; Americans mean less to me than dogs."

———

Samantha lay in her room, trembling, covering her nose against the sickly sweet smell of Ivan's blood. The last half-hour had passed in a dream. She'd actually heard Chase's voice, asking her where she was, then the phone, Ivan, the room—everything exploded. Every time she closed her eyes, she relived it all over again.

"I can't do this," she whispered, her teeth chattering. She was cold, so cold. Even though it was July and not a breath of air stirred in the boarded-up room, she felt like she was adrift on an iceberg. She wished she were home; she wished she were dead. She wished she were out there with Dusty and the others, sucking men off at the truck stops. She wouldn't be so cold, then. People would be alive. Nobody would have their brains oozing out their ears. She heard footsteps, a soft knock on her door. She sat up, pulled her knees under her chin, and pressed her back against the wall. Maybe they were coming to kill her. In a way, it would be a relief.

As she watched, the door opened. The bald man who killed Ivan peeked inside the room.

"*Dorogoy*? Kiska? Are you okay?" He sounded so much like Ivan, she wanted to cry all over again. "May I come in?"

She was too scared to answer, so he came in anyway. As he neared her bed, she saw that he was not bald, but wore his blond hair shaved so close to his head she could see the veins crisscrossing his skull. His eyes were of a dark, indeterminate color that reminded her of the little chips of coal that her father tracked in from the mine. She shrank back closer to the wall.

"You have had a bad time today, little Kiska, and I am sorry. I did not mean for you to see such a terrible thing. I know Ivan was your friend." He took several steps closer to the bed and withdrew a Hershey bar from his coat pocket. "Nothing can replace him, but please know that we mean you no harm."

She watched him. He dropped the chocolate bar on the bed, then backed away, as if she were a wild animal that might come at him with teeth and claws.

"We are very concerned about you, Kiska. We have called a doctor to make sure you are okay."

Her heart began to beat wildly. This was the man Ivan had told her about—Boyko, who was bringing a doctor to attest to her virginity. She looked around the room for something she could jam up inside her. If she wasn't a virgin, maybe they would let her just go out and be with the others. But the room held nothing. She could not lose her virginity to a candy bar.

"No need to be frightened," Boyko murmured as he motioned for another man to enter the room. "This is Dr. Petrov. He is going to examine you."

She watched as the doctor came into the room. He was older than Boyko with yellowish-gray hair greased back from his forehead. He wore a long white coat that had brown stains on the lapels and rimless glasses that magnified his eyes, giving him a strange owlish appearance. A third man followed the doctor into the room but stayed by the door, watching the other two with dark, unreadable eyes.

The doctor walked over and dropped his bag on the side of the bed. He looked at her dispassionately, as if she was some lab rat in a cage. In a way, she guessed she was.

"Have you ever had a physical examination?" His English was formal, but awkward, as if he seldom spoke it.

She gulped, her mouth dry as a cracker. She'd been to doctors to get shots for school and once to get a dog bite stitched up. Beyond that, her mother had taken care of her.

"Do not be afraid," said the doctor. "It will be painless."

Her heart thudding, she watched as he opened his bag and withdrew a pair of latex gloves. As he shoved his plump fingers into the gloves, he turned to look at the two men who stood by the door.

"Do you need to watch this?"

"I do," said the man Boyko, whose coal-chip eyes now gleamed.

The doctor shrugged, then turned back to Samantha. He pulled a flashlight and wooden tongue depressor from his bag and tapped her chin with the little wooden stick. "Open, please!"

She opened her mouth. Immediately, his fingers began a rough probing, feeling her gums, pulling her tongue up to peer underneath. Finally, he withdrew the tongue depressor and stuck his own tongue out, motioning for her to do the same. He shined the flashlight down her throat, then stuck another instrument up her nose and into her ears. As he turned her head, she saw Boyko watching her with hungry eyes.

When the doctor had finished with her head, he took out a stethoscope and listened to her heart. His pale eyes gleamed moistly behind his thick glasses and he smelled of the same disinfectant that sometimes clung to her mother's work uniform. As he worked, he breathed heavily through his nose, the air whistling through his nostrils.

Done with her heart, he straightened up. *"Razdeváysya."*

She didn't understand what he wanted. When she didn't move, he made another motion, crossing his arms over his chest and then lifting them up. "Remove your clothes."

She looked past him, at Boyko and the other man who stood gaping at her from across the room. "No."

The doctor frowned. "If you don't, they will," he warned her in a whisper.

She lowered her head. Tears rolled down her cheeks as she realized that she was one of their girls now—no longer a person—just a thing to examine, use, and then discard.

"Bystro!" the doctor finally cried. Impatient, he reached behind her and pulled her T-shirt over her head, her bra down to her waist. As she moved her arms to cover herself, he pushed her flat on the bed. Suddenly, his latex-covered fingers were feeling her breasts, making large circles around the outer edges, smaller circles around her nipples.

She turned her head and saw Boyko, his thin lips parting as he watched the whole procedure.

The doctor's hands left her breasts. She thought—prayed—for a moment that he might be done, that this might be the end of it, but faster than she could imagine, he pulled her shorts and underpants to her ankles, then off entirely. He pushed her knees up and spread her legs wide. Then suddenly, the same fingers that had catalogued her teeth were now inside her, probing and feeling. At that point, she closed her eyes and took herself away. Down, down into a soft darkness that she imagined her father's mine must have been like. Suddenly, he was there, scooping her up in his strong arms.

Sam-I-Am, he whispered, just as he had when she was little. He still looked the same—his face sooty up to his forehead, then pale white where his miner's helmet had covered his head. He smelled of cold and metal, and she could feel his outrage—his desire to come into this room and smash the doctor's head in, strangle Boyko like a rag doll. But he made no move to do that. Instead she simply felt his warmth around her as he whispered, *It's all up to you, Sam-I-Am. Now it's all up to you.*

SEVEN

Miles away, Chase Buchanan lay in bed, reliving the call that had come this afternoon on Gudger's precious and forbidden telephone.

"Chase?" Though the young female voice had been faint, his heart nearly stopped. It was Sam calling.

"Sam?" he'd cried. "Where are you?"

She said something; he couldn't hear it. Pressing the heavy black receiver to his ear, he turned. Gudger was banging on the glass panes of the door next to the fireplace, his face now contorted with rage instead of laughter. "That's my private phone, you little ass-hole!" he shouted from the other side of the door. "Hang that up!"

He ignored Gudger, listening as Sam's words came sketchily over the old receiver. "Trouble…scared…Mama."

"What did you say?" He gripped the phone harder. "I can't hear you!"

"Tell Mama…men…want…"

"What?" he cried. "What—"

Then he heard no more. Rough fingers ripped the phone from his grasp as a hand pushed him so hard he fell down. "I told you never to answer this phone, you little bastard!" Gudger cried, his upper lip curling in a snarl.

"But it was my call," he'd cried, tears streaming down his cheeks. "It was for me!"

———

"At least I didn't tell him who it was," he whispered now, staring at the cracks in his ceiling. He'd barely been able to stand it until his mother came home; then when she walked in the kitchen door, his head began to swim with doubts about what he'd heard. The voice had sounded like Sam, but why had she called Gudger's landline? If she were in trouble, why not call 911? Or even his mother, at work? That made him think maybe it wasn't Sam—maybe it was just someone playing a trick. But who would do that? One of those snotty high school girls who used to call Sam the Coal Miner's Daughter? Or somebody from his class, Ms. Norman's fifth grade? He tried to figure out who it might have been, but he couldn't come up with anybody. He and Sam were new to their school, uncool outsiders from West Virginia. They weren't important enough for anybody to play a trick on. He turned over, crumpling his pillow. As he did, it occurred to him that maybe Gudger had hired someone who sounded like Sam to call. But why? To raise his hopes? To see if he would tell his mother? To drive them both crazy? Gudger was mean enough to do that, but Gudger was also cheap. He'd never pay someone to make a fake phone call.

"No," he told himself aloud. "It was Sam—I know it was. The landline must have been the only number she could remember."

But where was she? What had happened to her? Why hadn't she called back? He got up from bed and turned to look out the window. The blue plastic shards of their ruined pool glowed in the patio lights. In the shadows beyond stood the toolshed where he'd taken off his clothes. Behind the toolshed was the fence that enclosed Gudger's property, and behind that, in Mrs. Carver's yard, was his backpack with Mary Crow's business card.

Mary Crow would know what to do, he decided. She was the governor's cop. She could trace the number, find out where Sam was calling from. But why had he put the card in his backpack, instead of his pocket, or even in his shoe? How could he have been so stupid?

"Doesn't matter," he told himself. "You'll just have to go get it." Of course he would have to wait until Gudger and his mother went to bed, but that was no problem. He would just sneak out to the toolshed, grab one of Gudger's flashlights, and retrace his steps along the fence line. Once he found the backpack, he'd hurry back here. If Gudger was snoring as loudly as he usually did, he would call Mary Crow immediately, from the forbidden phone in the den. Who cared what Gudger thought?

He got up from the window and cracked open his door. The late news theme song blared from the television. That meant his mother would be heading to bed. Gudger would linger to watch the weather and sports, then he would follow. Their bed might squeak for a few minutes, then they would go to sleep. Softly, he closed his door and got back into bed. All he had to do now was wait. Once he heard Gudger snoring, he could go and get that card.

———

Hours later, he opened his eyes. He bolted upright, blinking, ready to sneak out of the house and retrieve the card, but something was wrong. It was light outside. Birds were chirping. He was dressed but sock-footed, his shoes still peeking from under the bed. He realized that while he'd been waiting for Gudger to go to bed, he'd fallen asleep.

But maybe I can still do it, he thought. *Maybe I can sneak up there if they think I'm asleep.*

Quietly, he got out of bed, opened his door. Though he smelled fresh coffee, the house was silent—he heard no TV commercials, no cabinets slamming as Gudger fixed his usual Cheerios and milk. His mother had probably gone to work, but where was Gudger?

He crept into the hall, tiptoeing past the master bedroom. The door was open, revealing a made-up bed, a dresser clean of Gudger's normal paraphernalia (wallet, car keys, Taser). Chase had a wild moment of hope—Gudger had been promising to take his mother's car into the shop for months—had he dropped her off at work so he could take the thing to the mechanic?

Emboldened by his possible good luck, he padded through the den and into the kitchen. The coffee was still warm in the pot and Gudger's cereal bowl lay in the sink, but the house was empty. Chase's heart leaped. Gudger was gone!

Quickly, he headed for the back door. He wouldn't need a flashlight now. Now all he had to do was get to the back fence, grab his backpack, and get home. He hesitated a moment, remembering yesterday, when Gudger had appeared from nowhere and snapped those pictures of him in his underwear. The man was mean, and sly as a fox. But as he scanned the back yard, he saw that the patio was empty and the door to Gudger's shed was closed and locked.

"Come on," Chase told himself. "Don't be such a nelly. Gudger's not here."

He took a deep breath and stepped out into the already hot morning. Feeling strangely exposed, he ran across the patio and headed toward the toolshed. He'd just jumped over his mother's sad little patch of marigolds when a voice rang out.

"Well, if isn't Olive Oyl, done with her beauty sleep!"

His heart caught in his throat as he turned to see Gudger sitting under the eaves of the house in an aluminum lawn chair, drinking coffee as he read the paper. Chase closed his eyes. He should have known better. There was no way of escaping Gudger.

"Where are you going in such a hurry, boy? You look like your head's on fire and your ass is catching."

"N-nowhere." Chase felt as if he was standing there naked, even though he'd slept with all his clothes on.

"Well, nowhere must be a pretty exciting place, if it's got you out of bed with so much piss and vinegar."

He didn't know what to say. Sam's phone call had gotten him out of bed; saving his sister had filled him full of piss and vinegar.

"I've been wanting to talk to you anyway, Olive Oyl. Who the hell were you on my phone with, yesterday?"

"A computer," he lied. "It said we'd won a cruise to Jamaica."

Gudger frowned. "I'm on the Do Not Call list, Olive Oyl."

"Well it called, just the same."

"Then why'd you say it was your call?" asked Gudger.

"I thought it might be Mom," he replied.

"She doesn't call on that line. She always calls my cell."

"Well, she could have forgotten." Riding a sudden swell of defiance, he said, "She could have just wanted to talk to me!"

"You're lying, Olive Oyl," Gudger said. "Just like you lied about going fishing yesterday. I'm gonna straighten you out, boy. I can stand a lot of things, but not a liar. Since you're so bright and bushy-tailed today, how about you go and grub out that poison ivy along the back fence?"

He couldn't believe what he heard. Was Gudger actually sending him to the very spot he needed to go? "Over by Mrs. Carver's?" He pointed over his right shoulder.

"Naw, I don't want you near that old witch. I want you over there." Gudger pointed to the opposite corner of the yard—a football field away from where he needed to go.

"I-I'm not sure what poison ivy looks like," Chase said.

Gudger spread three fingers. "Three green leaves on one long stem. It's a vine, coils up around things. Go get a hoe from the shed."

"But—"

"Get up there, boy." Gudger snapped his paper back open. "I'm tired of your lying nonsense."

Chase turned, fighting back tears. Whatever you did, however hard you tried to get past him, Gudger was always there—grinning, leering, grinding him down into something that felt mostly like a fool.

———

Miles away, Mary Crow was walking into the office of Richard Drake, district attorney for Campbell County. He was a tall, thin-faced man who buttoned his suit coat as he rose from his chair.

"Ms. Crow." He nodded, extending his hand. "How nice to meet you."

She shook his hand, wondering what you should say to someone you were supposed to light a fire under. *Sorry I have to be here? I know you're a good lawyer, but the governor thinks you have the balls of a chipmunk and is less than pleased with your performance?* She couldn't decide, so finally she just settled on, "Nice to meet you, too."

"Please have a seat." He offered her a chair, then got right to the point. "I understand that the Honorable Ann Chandler is unhappy with our lack of an indictment for Bryan Taylor's murder."

Mary smiled, grateful that the man was brave enough not to shilly-shally around. Still, she tried to be diplomatic. "The governor is always troubled when murder indictments are overly long in coming. But I think she's even more dismayed by the anti-gay sentiment in this county. She thinks it sullies the state's reputation and she's particularly concerned that this Reverend Trull is feeding the flames with all his sermons against homosexuals."

"I don't like Trull any more than Ann Chandler does," said Drake. "He's a fanatic who's embarrassed the county with that ridiculous video. But Trull notwithstanding, the majority of people in this county are conservative Christians. They believe homosexuality is a choice and a sin."

"And does this belief extend to violence toward gay people?"

"Of course not. Most folks here take 'love the sinner, hate the sin' to heart."

"Well, clearly, *someone* beat Bryan Taylor into a very early grave."

"But we don't know whether his killer had any connections with Reverend Trull."

"But you don't think Trull has upped the ante here? His YouTube video advocates an internment camp for gay people. Last night I heard him advise parents to use corporal punishment should their children show any homosexual tendencies."

Drake shook his head. "Ms. Crow, you know as well as I do that I can't charge Trull with anything. A sermon is protected speech, and the current hate crime statute doesn't even include sexual orientation. Even the great Ann Chandler can't regulate what people say in church."

Mary sighed. This is exactly what she'd told the governor—Trull hadn't broken any law, the way the current law was written. Shifting in her chair, she switched the subject from the theoretical to the reality at hand. "Then what's the status of the Taylor case?"

"It's a priority. We are moving with due diligence."

"Any arrests?"

"No. I advised Chief Ramsey that I'd need a totally airtight case, so he and his staff are going slowly."

Mary frowned. "Why would you need a totally airtight case?"

"Like I just told you—the folks who put me in this office believe homosexuality is a sin. If I go to trial without a smoking gun, they won't convict. They didn't in Sligo County, and they won't here. It's time to walk softly, Ms. Crow. Tempers are hot. Everybody hates all these outsiders with their picketing and their YouTube videos and, frankly, they're not real crazy about Ann Chandler sending you to whip us into shape."

"I'm sure Governor Chandler would have preferred sending me elsewhere," said Mary, "except Reverend Trull is about to cost this county hundreds of new jobs. Ecotron is a Dutch company that doesn't discriminate against gays. They won't come here if their gay and lesbian employees might be in jeopardy."

"Corporate bucks get the governor's attention right fast, don't they?" Drake gave a tight smile.

"This county's twelve percent unemployment rate gets it faster," Mary snapped back.

"Tell your boss to get Raleigh to add sexual orientation to the hate crimes statute and I'll go to town down here. Until then, I can't prosecute people for breaking laws that aren't on the books."

Drake pulled a sheet of stationary from his lap drawer, scribbled something on it. "I've told you all I know, Ms. Crow. I suggest you go down to the police department and talk to Victor Galloway. He's a new hire, working undercover on the Taylor case. Maybe he can convince you and the governor that even here, in Bible-thumping Campbell County, we still believe in equal protection under the law."

EIGHT

Detective Victor Galloway was law enforcement's yang to District Attorney Drake's cool, intellectual yin. Galloway wore a tattered Atlanta Falcons T-shirt instead of a suit, red Asics running shoes instead of leather brogans, and kept his police badge fastened on his belt rather than pinned over his heart. When Mary knocked at the entrance of his cubicle, he had his feet up on his desk, sipping a bottle of orange Jarritos soda.

"Victor Galloway?" she asked, not seeing any name plates or name tags or name anything.

"*Sí, senorita.*" He grinned and winked. "*Que pasa?*"

She smiled. Away from the mountains of Western North Carolina, people often mistook her Cherokee black hair and olive skin for Latina. "I'm Mary Crow," she said, stepping into his office. "From the governor's judicial task force."

Gulping his soda, Galloway whipped his long legs off the desk and stood up. "I'm sorry," he sputtered, his face turning red. "I haven't worked here long enough to know who to salute yet."

"Well, you don't have to salute me." Mary handed him the carte blanche letter the DA had written for her. "I'm looking into the Bryan Taylor case."

As Galloway scanned the sheet of paper, she scanned Galloway. Like her, he had olive skin and black hair. Unlike her, his eyes were a fierce blue, his body rangy and muscular. She felt, oddly, that she'd seen him somewhere before.

"Okay." He looked up from Drake's letter. "Have a seat and I'll get you up to speed."

She lifted a heavy packing box from his one chair and pulled it up to the desk.

"Sorry about all the clutter," he said. "I just moved up here from Georgia."

"Really? Where in Georgia?" asked Mary.

"Cobb County. I got my detective shield in Marietta."

Mary smiled. "I used to be a prosecutor in Deckard County. How'd you wind up here in Carolina?"

"Got tired of Atlanta traffic and Marietta politics." He laughed. "When two newer guys got promoted over me, I saw the writing on the wall. This little force put out a call for a detective who could *hablo Español*, so I answered the ad. Took a big cut in pay, but at least I'm not spending three hours a day stuck in traffic."

"Why *Español* here?"

"Lots of Latino-on-Latino crime along Jackson Highway. The chief got tired of his conviction rate sinking because his cops had misunderstood the Spanish." He shrugged. "*Aquí estoy yo.*"

She nodded, wondering if Galloway shared the same macho distaste for investigating gay crimes that most cops did. "So they put you undercover, in the middle of a gay murder investigation?"

Galloway smiled. "I was perfect to go deep—too new for anybody to recognize."

"Okay—what can you tell me about this case?"

He rifled through a stack of papers on his desk and pulled out a thick envelope. "You can read it, or I can tell you the basics."

"Let's do both," said Mary. "You start first."

Galloway opened the file. "Bryan Taylor, twenty-seven-year-old white male, found dead along Jackson Highway. He was a resident of Brooklyn, New York, here visiting his parents."

He handed Mary two photographs—one of a handsome young man with sandy brown hair and several days' worth of beard on his cheeks. The second was a crime scene photo where that handsome face was bloodied beyond recognition. "Geez," said Mary. "Did someone take a tire iron to his head?"

"We think it was a baseball bat. He'd just subbed in a church league softball game. Bryan had played on St. Alban's team before and was a pretty good short stop in high school."

"So did he make the winning play at second base and then get beaten to death?"

"Actually, his team lost," said Galloway. "After the game they went over to Clancy's Grill—it's a popular place with ball players. His teammates said Bryan ordered a hamburger, drank a couple of beers, and then left. We think somebody followed him, killed him, and dumped his body a couple of miles down the road."

"He wasn't killed at the scene?" asked Mary.

"No, he was dumped. Wasn't a shred of evidence along that highway."

"Had he hit on anybody at the bar?"

Galloway shook his head. "According to his teammates, he ate, drank his beer, and left. Said he had an early flight back to New York the next day."

"Where was his car?"

"Here's the odd part … his car was parked at an I-85 truck stop, twenty miles east of his home. And no," he continued, answering the question Mary was about to ask, "it hadn't been wiped. It was lousy with his and his mother's fingerprints … it was her car. There was also a partial print of somebody who isn't in the system. And a single black hair was found on the driver's seat."

"Pubic hair?"

"Nope. Head hair. But we didn't get any of the root, so no DNA there."

Mary asked, "You think he drove to the truck stop for a brief encounter and got more than he bargained for?"

"That's a possibility," admitted Galloway. "Except he never showed up on any of the lot security cams. Didn't buy gas or go in the store, or go to the men's room."

"So maybe he just got lucky in the parking lot. You know, in the back of a semi."

"That was my first thought, except for this." Galloway pulled another picture from the file—this one of Bryan with his arm around another young man. "This is Leo Maiello, Bryan's husband. They got married in New York six months ago. Bryan was a newlywed and, according to his parents, very happy."

"Too happy to go prowling around truck stops?"

"He texted Leo at nine thirty-four that night, saying he was on his way home. *Can't wait to see you* was his last message."

"And Leo was in New York, equally thrilled that Bryan was coming home?"

Galloway nodded. "Leo checks out. He's the stage manager at some Broadway theater. He was at work that night. No less than Bernadette Peters backed up his story."

"You really talked to Bernadette Peters?" Mary was impressed—on her last trip to New York she'd seen the red-headed actress bring down the house in a Stephen Sondheim play.

"I did," said Galloway. "She was really nice. Sympathetic, you know?"

Mary flipped through the file, looking at the crime scene photos, notes of the interviews with Taylor's parents and friends. She stopped at a group photo of the ball team, grinning at the camera. "All of his teammates check out?"

"They do. The rest of them stayed at the bar until the Yankees game ended, then they went home. A typical night in church league ball."

Mary frowned at the picture. "Who was St. Alban's playing that night?"

"This is where it gets interesting." Galloway grinned. "Reverend Trull's One Way Saints team. I happen to be their newest left fielder."

Suddenly, she remembered where she'd seen him. At church last night, sitting toward the front, along with some other broad-shouldered young men. "You were there last night, at the church service, weren't you?"

His brows lifted. "How do you know?"

"I was there, too. The governor called me yesterday and I booked it down here in time for the Wednesday night prayer meeting."

"Can I ask why the governor is so interested in this one particular crime? Is she a friend of Taylor's family?"

Mary wondered what she should tell him—she wasn't sure how much of her agenda Ann Chandler wanted known. "The governor's concerned about the number of crimes against gay people in this state. Since that Trull video went viral, businesses are starting to look elsewhere to expand, simply because they fear their gay employees won't be safe."

"They sure as hell wouldn't be safe around here," said Galloway.

"Do you think Reverend Trull has anything to do with that?"

"I think Reverend Trull has a lot to do with that, Ms. Crow. I grew up Catholic, thought I'd heard every weird interpretation of Christianity on the planet. But this guy spins it in ways that would make Jesus blush."

"What's this Warriors for Christ group?" asked Mary. "They mentioned it last night at church."

"From what I can gather, they're God's own shock troops of mercy. Anything bad happens—a flood or a tornado or a blizzard—they load up this van and take food and medical supplies. You're supposed to be able to drop everything and leave at a moment's notice."

"What about people who have jobs?"

"They need to have jobs they can leave," said Galloway. "It's a pretty elite group."

"So you don't think there's a connection between them and Bryan Taylor?"

Galloway shook his head. "The demographic's wrong. The Warriors are older—men and women established enough in their careers that they can take time off, or retirees with nothing but time on their hands. The baseball team's more likely to hide a killer."

"Tell me about that," said Mary.

"They're young, full-of-fire guys who played in high school and probably could have played in college, if they'd been smart enough to get in. They hunt, fish, distrust strangers, and—"

"Hate gays?" Mary interrupted.

Galloway studied his orange Jarritos bottle. "Let's just say a gay person would not be welcome on their team. Whether or not Reverend Trull spurred one of them to kill Bryan Taylor is still up for grabs."

Mary realized Galloway had just returned her to the gray area of law that Ann Chandler considered black-and-white: whether a preacher who advocated action against a particular group could be held responsible when and if one of his flock took matters into their own hands. She reached for the thick file that lay on Galloway's desk. "Would you mind going over this with me?"

"I'll get you a soda and tell you everything I know," he said. "I've got nothing to do until the baseball game tonight."

NINE

THAT THE POISON IVY was payback for the day before did not surprise Chase; Gudger's favorite means of discipline usually involved scrubbing or painting or picking bugs off his tomato plants. What gave him pause was the enormity of the task. The poison ivy draped kudzu-like over Gudger's back fence for half the length of a football field, seemingly sending out even more hungry tendrils as he stood there looking at it. All morning he'd worked, yet he'd only cleared about a yard of growth. Now the sun was high and blistering; sweat stung Chase's eyes as mosquitoes whined around his ears. When he stepped back and looked at what he'd accomplished, he realized that it would probably take him the rest of the summer to grub out this fence.

Mindful of the sticky poisonous sap that covered his gloves, he pulled them off finger-by-finger, then took off his shirt. As the breeze cooled his sweat-soaked back, he sat down in the shade of a non-ivy-contaminated tree. All morning he'd kept an eye on Gudger, or at least on Gudger's car. He'd decided if it ever left the driveway, Chase was heading for the other end of the fence to get his backpack and Mary Crow's card. But Gudger, apparently, had no travel plans. Suzie Q just sat like a big black beetle, baking in the sun.

He stared at the car, remembering the night Sam didn't come home. They'd started worrying when Jay Leno went off—his mother pacing in front of the windows, Gudger first calling Sam's cell phone, then his cop buddy Crump, then making an official report to the police. Hours later the cops had called back on the landline, saying they'd found Gudger's car but not a trace of Sam. They'd brought the car back, after the forensic team had gone over it. For days afterward his mother had gone out and sat in it, touching the steering wheel, stroking the upholstery, as if Suzie Q might be coaxed into telling what had happened.

"I bet the car knows," Chase whispered, staring as the heat shimmered from its black roof.

"Knows what?" the voice came over his shoulder, out of nowhere. Chase jumped, turned. Gudger stood there, dressed in khaki pants and a white polo shirt, Taser hanging from his belt. "Are you talking to yourself now, Olive Oyl?"

"Uh-huh." He'd learned it went better if he just agreed with Gudger, regardless of whatever stupid thing he said.

"Well, yourself better tell you to get back to work." Gudger tossed him an apple and a can of Coke. "I've got to go to the hardware store. When I get back, I'd better see a lot more fence cleared than I'm seeing now."

"Yes sir." Chase lowered his head, trying to hide his excitement. The hardware store was ten minutes away! Gudger would be gone long enough for him to get that backpack!

He gulped the Coke, watching as Gudger walked down to the car. Suzie Q's motor roared to life as her brake lights came on. A moment later, she and Gudger rolled down the driveway. Chase waited until they turned down Kedron Road, then leapt to his feet. Ten minutes to the hardware store, ten minutes in there, then ten minutes back. He'd have half an hour to find the backpack, get the card, and call Mary Crow.

He raced along the fence line, ignoring the branches of poison ivy that slapped against his bare chest. The back of Gudger's house came into view, then the stacked up remnants of the swimming pool. Finally, he reached the toolshed. The clothes he'd taken off the night before still lay in a pile. For an instant his cheeks flamed as he wondered if Gudger had truly posted those pictures of him on YouTube. Then he shrugged it off; nobody would laugh at him until school started in August. Right now all he wanted was to find that backpack.

He slowed, retracing his steps, searching the deep green underbrush that crowded up from Mrs. Carver's back yard. He remembered dropping the backpack close to the fence, near a fallen tree, but he couldn't remember exactly where. Walking slowly, he searched the thicket all the way to the end of the fence without seeing a thing. A moment of panic gripped him—had Gudger found his backpack? Did he now have his EVEDINSE files? *Please no*, he prayed. *Please anything but that.*

He took a deep breath and turned to retrace his steps again. Now he was going in the same direction as he had yesterday—maybe that would make it easier to find. Inching along the fence line, he peered into the underbrush. He saw a squirrel dart through the leaves, a mottled rock that could have been a snapping turtle, then he saw something shining through the branches of a bush. He hurried toward it. It was his backpack! His dad's old blue carabiner clip glinted in the dappled sunlight.

He leaned over the fence, pulled the thing to him. Cradling it like a football, he raced for the house. It had taken him far longer to find the backpack than he could have imagined. Gudger would be coming home any minute. He ran past the toolshed, over the ground still wet from the slaughtered swimming pool, across the patio, and into the house. He headed straight for his room, throwing his backpack on the floor. He held his breath as he unzipped it. To his great relief, his EVE-DINSE file lay undisturbed, along with Mary Crow's business card. He grabbed the card, stashed the backpack on the floor of his closet, and raced for the den. He had only moments now to reach Mary Crow before Gudger got home.

He glanced out the window, to make sure no black car was rumbling up the driveway. All he saw was the white fence that surrounded Gudger's front yard, and two small goldfinches pecking at the bird feeder his mother had put out. He hurried to the phone, dialed the number, awkward with the process of sticking his finger in seven different little holes and letting them spin. The phone seemed to work okay, though. After a few clicks, Mary Crow's number began to ring. He turned toward the window to watch for Gudger when his heart sank. Suzie Q's chrome grille glittered like a menacing smile as the car slowly rolled up the driveway.

"Answer," he whispered, his legs beginning to tremble. "Answer now!"

The phone rang again. He ducked to the floor as Gudger drove past the house and pulled the car into the garage. In just a minute he would be inside the house.

"Please," he cried, begging now. "At least let your answering machine pick up!"

The growl of Suzie Q's engine stopped. He heard her door open. He was just about to put the heavy black receiver back in the cradle when a voice said *hello*. Not an answering machine, but a real person.

"Miss Crow?" he gasped, fighting tears.

"Yes?" She sounded puzzled, as if she didn't recognize him.

"This is Chase Buchanan, from yesterday?" He hopped on one leg as he watched Gudger get out of the car.

"Well, hi, Chase. How are you doing?"

"Miss Crow, my sister Sam called last night!"

"That's great!" Mary replied. "I told you she would."

"No!" he cried, breathless. "You don't understand. She called on Gudger's landline. She's in trouble! She needs help!"

"Did you tell your mother? Call the police?" asked Mary.

"No, Gudger came in and grabbed the phone out of my hand." He looked out the window. Gudger was heading straight for the back door. "I gotta go. Please call the cops for me—its Sam's only chance!"

———

Before she could answer, the little boy had hung up, his voice replaced by a dial tone. Mary clicked off her cell phone, ashamed that the child had not crossed her mind all morning.

"Everything okay?" Galloway asked softly from behind his desk.

"I don't know," she replied. "This weird little kid came to my office yesterday—said he'd hitchhiked up to Asheville on a peach truck. He claimed his stepfather had sold his sister and wanted to hire me to find her. He's from this county—you may have heard of the case."

"What's the name?" asked Galloway.

"Buchanan. The kid's name is Chase, he calls his sister Sam."

"Samantha Buchanan," said Galloway. "She was the big story before Reverend Trull stole the show."

"So what's the deal?"

"She vanished on her way home from babysitting. They found her car over on Jackson Highway—lights on, motor running, purse and wallet intact. Everything intact except Samantha, who wasn't there at all."

"Do they have any leads?"

"I don't know…I came on board here after that happened." His blue eyes flickered toward his open door. "Hey, Crump," he called to someone out in the hall.

"Yeah?" A tall man with graying hair stuck his head in the door. A sergeant's chevron decorated the sleeve of his uniform.

"Come tell this nice lady from the governor's office what you know about Samantha Buchanan."

Crump stepped inside the office and basically repeated the same story Galloway had told her. "We're pretty sure she met up with a boyfriend," he added. "Nothing else makes sense."

"That's not what her little brother thinks," said Mary, relating what Chase had told her. Crump listened, then shook his head.

"That little Buchanan punk is probably one of the reasons his sister ran away. The kid's a nut case."

"Oh?" Mary thought of the hungry little boy who'd inhaled a half-pound hamburger before she'd gotten her napkin in her lap.

"Yeah. He used to call in a couple of times a week. One day it would be a robber trying to break in the house, a few days later it would be the people next door, cooking ice. He had some kind of old Civil War pistol—it's a miracle he didn't shoot himself in the ass."

"Did you respond?" asked Mary.

"Every time—Ralph Gudger would usually lead the charge. He was dating the boy's mother and thought maybe some of his old collars were harassing the kids, but that never materialized. Then, after Gudger married the kid's mother, the calls stopped."

"Did you know the boy's terrified of Gudger?"

"Wouldn't surprise me," said Crump. "Gudger always said the kid needed to man up—I imagine he's trying to make that happen."

"This Gudger sounds like a real piece of work," said Mary, remembering how the boy had huddled in her car, quivering like some animal caught in a trap.

Crump nodded. "Gudger's tough. I've known him for years. He's an ex-army MP, a no-shit kind of guy. Life with him was probably too tough for the girl. The boy'll likely run away, too, if he ever grows the nuts to do it. You know how these blended families are."

Mary winced at the memory of her own failed blended family. Yeah, she knew how exactly how those families were.

"You playing ball tonight?" Crump turned his attention to Galloway.

"Right field for the Saints," said Galloway. "Come on out and cheer for me."

"No thanks," said Crump. "I've worked security for that durn church for the last five nights. I'm parking my ass and a six pack in front of TV tonight and watching a real game. No pussy church league for me."

Galloway lifted a hand. "I hear you, brother. Thanks for stopping by."

As Crump ambled out the door, the new detective turned back to Mary. "So how come this Buchanan kid's gotten under your skin? I thought you were the governor's hired gun."

"I don't know—you've got to admire any eleven-year-old who hitches to Asheville to hire a lawyer to nail his stepfather. It sounds to me like he's got plenty of moxie already."

Galloway laughed. "Tell you what—let's make a deal. I'll check out this Gudger's phone records if you'll come cheer me on at the baseball game."

She looked at him as if he'd gone crazy. "You want me to cheer for you and the One Way Saints?"

"It's not just my fragile male ego," he said. "I need better cover. I've been knee-deep in Trull's church for three weeks, solo. They're going to start thinking *I'm* gay if I don't show up with a girl at some point."

"So you want me to be your beard?"

"You could call it that."

Her first inclination was to tell him she had a busy evening of washing her hair planned. But then she realized Victor Galloway was her only inroad into what was really going on at Trull's church. It would be nice to report back to Ann Chandler with some inside information.

"Okay." Mary smiled. "Where do I go?"

"Armory Park, diamond two. Just sit in the One Way bleachers and cheer whenever I do something right."

TEN

MARY LEFT VICTOR GALLOWAY's office with directions to the base-ball field. Since she had several hours before the One Way Saints were scheduled to take the field, she ate a quick lunch and drove over to Sligo County. According to Richard Drake, Sligo had indicted some-one for the murder of a homosexual, but couldn't get a conviction. Mary wanted to find out as much as she could about the person ac-cused and how they'd managed to walk away from a long stretch in prison. Killing was killing, regardless of whom the victim liked to sleep with.

John Kephart was District Attorney of Sligo County. He seemed more of an old-school politician than the self-important Richard Drake—shaggy gray hair, glasses on the end of his nose. He greeted her in a short-sleeved shirt, with a pencil stuck behind one ear.

"Hello, Ms. Crow," he said, smiling. "It's nice to finally meet you ... the governor really sings your praises."

"Thanks," said Mary. "If you've spoken with the governor, then you must know why I'm here."

Kephart reached for a thick manila folder lying on the credenza behind his desk. "Alan Bratcher," he replied, dropping the folder in front of Mary. "A gay kid who made a pass at a guy named Buck Honeycutt. Honeycutt took a very dim view of Bratcher's affections."

Mary opened the file and looked at the autopsy photo. As in the other case, it looked like a handsome young man had gotten his face caught in a buzz saw.

"It was basically a bar fight that went way overboard," explained Kephart. "We went after Honeycutt for manslaughter, but the jury wouldn't convict."

"Was this your case?" asked Mary.

"I gave it to Penny Morse, our new hire out of Carolina."

Mary frowned. "You gave this case to a rookie?"

"She requested it … she'd done some pro bono work at Chapel Hill for a gay student alliance."

"Could I get a transcript of the trial?"

"Absolutely." Kephart reached for the phone, then said, "But wouldn't you rather just talk to Penny? She could give you all the details and you could give her a pep talk—she's been pretty glum over this whole thing."

Mary remembered her first capital case. A basic slam-dunk, but she'd still lost ten pounds getting her argument together. The fifty-minute jury deliberation had felt like fifty years. "It would be tough to lose your first case."

"I told her to play it straight—go for simple Man One. Defense opened the gay door, and the jury bought it. Like I told your boss, we can't convict someone of a crime that isn't on the books. Add sexual orientation to the hate crime statute, and we'll start prosecuting accordingly."

"That's a tough sell in the current legislature," replied Mary. "The rainbow flag doesn't fly so high in Raleigh."

"It doesn't fly at all in Sligo County," said Kephart. "The majority of folks here believe in that old bromide about Adam and Eve, not Adam and Steve."

"Then what do gay people do here?" she asked.

"If they're smart, they leave." He rose from his chair. "Come on, I'll introduce you to Penny."

He led her down the hall, knocking once before he opened a closed office door. A thin young blond woman looked up from her desk, startled. She wore a navy jacket and pearls, and reminded Mary of a doe flushed from the underbrush. "Yes sir?" she asked.

"Penny, I'd like you to meet Mary Crow. She's from the governor's judicial task force. She'd like to talk to you about the Alan Bratcher case."

The new hire from Carolina stood up, the color draining from her face.

"Hi, Penny," Mary said, wanting to put the young lawyer at ease. "It's a pleasure to meet you." She stuck out her hand. Penny shook it with icicle fingers.

"I'll let you two talk," said Kephart. "Ms. Crow, if you need anything more from me, I'll be in my office."

"Thanks." Mary smiled as the DA disappeared down the hall. Then she closed Penny Morse's door and sat down across from her. The woman still stood like someone facing a firing squad.

"Mr. Kephart said you were coming to town, to look over the Honeycutt case." Penny gulped. "I blew it, didn't I?"

"I don't know," said Mary. "Why don't you sit down and tell me about it?"

Penny sat down, reciting the details of the crime—in a crowded bar, Alan Bratcher had put an arm around Buck Honeycutt's shoulders. The action infuriated Honeycutt, who later beat Bratcher up in the parking lot of the bar. Three eyewitnesses testified to the whole thing; brain-dead Bratcher lived for three days until his parents pulled the plug.

"That's horrible." Mary grimaced at the viciousness of the crime. "And the jury still wouldn't convict? Even for Man One?"

"I was feeling pretty good about it. Then the defense counsel got up and claimed that Bratcher had made a pass at Honeycutt."

"And the jury went sour?"

"No, I figured the defense would go there. So I entered testimony that established Honeycutt as a homophobe with anger-management issues. I subpoenaed witnesses who testified Honeycutt had made similar gestures to them." Penny's eyes grew moist. "I even showed an old video of a Sligo County High football game where Honeycutt had patted several of his teammates on their butts—far more intimate touching than Bratcher's arm around his shoulders."

"That's terrific work," Mary told the girl. "I'm truly impressed."

"I felt like I was doing okay," Penny said. "Then Honeycutt took the stand."

"Defense counsel let the accused testify?" Mary asked, surprised.

Penny nodded. "Wayne Snodgrass just turned Honeycutt loose. Under oath he admitted he'd had way too many beers, that Bratcher had scared him."

"Scared him?" Mary checked the case file in her lap. Bratcher was slightly built, boyish. Honeycutt had shoulders like Man Mountain Dean.

"That's right. Honeycutt claimed he was a born-again Christian. He quoted some Bible verse that said if you were even touched by a homosexual, you'd go to hell just the same as the homosexual would."

"So he bashed Bratcher's head in to keep from going to hell?"

Penny nodded. "Honeycutt swore he never meant to kill Bratcher, just to teach him a lesson. He cried as he apologized to the poor guy's parents. In his summation, Snodgrass said Honeycutt had a moment of 'gay panic' and simply defended himself to save his immortal soul."

"That sounds as idiotic as the Twinkie defense," said Mary.

"Yeah, but it worked. The jury deliberated less than an hour," said Penny. "I polled them; each one said *not guilty.*"

"What was the jury makeup?"

"Six men, six women. I thought I'd done a good *voire dire*—weeded out all the homophobes."

"But twelve snuck in anyway?"

"I guess so. I just feel so bad for Mr. and Mrs. Bratcher. Alan was their only son—an ophthalmologist, in Charlotte." She looked at Mary, her pale brows drawn. "Is this going under judicial review?"

"Not at all. It sounds like you ran an excellent case. The governor is just concerned that in certain counties, gay people are not getting equal protection under the law. Could I ask you a few more questions?"

"Sure." Penny brightened now that the threat of judicial review had been lifted.

Mary pulled a notepad from her purse. "Do you know if this Buck Honeycutt belonged to the One Way Church, in Campbell County?"

"Reverend Trull's church?" Penny shook her head. "I can't remember his having any particular religious affiliation, other than rabid fundamentalism."

"Any minister visit him in jail?"

"I don't think so. Most of the guys sign up for Sunday church service just to get out of their cells for half an hour. I don't recall Honeycutt's name on that list."

Mary made a note on her pad. "Has he got any family here?"

"He and his girlfriend live with his mother."

"Does he have a job?"

"As far as I know, he still works as a tree topper for the Douglas nursery." Penny sighed. "Other than six months in jail, not too much bad happened to Buck Honeycutt."

Mary clicked her pen, pondering her notes. "Did he seem sincere when he apologized to the boy's parents?"

"He squeezed out a couple tears on the stand. I heard some snickers from the back of the courtroom. I noticed he walked back to the defense table red-faced, with his head down."

Mary took another look at Honeycutt's mug shot in the case file. His eyes were defiant, the curve of his mouth arrogant. Nothing about his features indicated any capacity for sympathy at all. She closed the file and gave it back to Penny Morse.

"I've got to tell you, Penny, defense counsel must have eaten his Wheaties during this case. That 'gay panic' thing was a stroke."

"He sure had an answer for everything I brought up."

"Don't beat yourself up about it. You just ran into a jury with concealed prejudice. It isn't fair and it isn't right, but sometimes it happens."

Penny frowned. "There was one weird thing about Buck Honeycutt."

"What?"

"You know how most defendants, when they're acquitted, show some emotion?"

"I do."

"Honeycutt just stood there, fists clenched, looking mad as hell. When the judge dismissed the case, he just turned and stalked out the door. Didn't even bother to shake counsel's hand."

Mary chuckled. "Maybe he thought shaking a lawyer's hand would send him to hell too."

———

Mary left Penny Morse reassured that she'd done a fine job, that Mary herself could have done no better. The two women exchanged cards, Penny telling Mary she could call anytime if she had further questions about the Bratcher case. As Mary drove back to Campbell County, she wondered if Penny could have gotten a conviction even if homosexuality had been in the hate crime statute. Somehow, she doubted it. The injunction against homosexuality was Scriptural; not even Ann Chandler could rewrite the Bible just to bring more jobs to North Carolina.

She drove back to her motel. If she was going to this baseball game as Victor Galloway's girlfriend, she needed to change clothes. Showing up in the One Way stands dressed in a skirt and heels would cause more notice than she wanted. She changed into jeans and a T-shirt, then checked her messages. One frantic one from Ann Chandler's aide Jake McKenna, wondering what she'd found out. Nothing from the little boy who was so concerned about his sister. Nothing from Jonathan Walkingstick, of course. Nothing from Walkingstick in nearly two years.

"No surprises there," she whispered, running a comb through her hair, wondering if she would check her messages for the rest of her life, always hoping for a call from him. Putting that thought out of her mind, she laced up her running shoes and headed for the door. She had a ball game to attend and a rookie right fielder to cheer for.

———

By the time she found the ball park, the game was in the fifth inning. The One Way Saints were at bat, going up against the Asbury United Methodist Circuit Riders. Mary knew immediately that the Saints were far more into baseball than the Methodists. The Saints wore tight black uniforms, their letters and last names emblazoned across the back. The Methodists just played in jeans and seemingly whatever T-shirts they'd grabbed from their closets. The score reflected the differing attitudes—the Saints led the Circuit Riders 12–0. Mary took a seat in the One Way bleachers and looked for Galloway. She found him, sitting at the end of the bench, intently watching one player who was walking up to bat. She followed his gaze, then caught her breath. The young man who was digging into his stance over the plate wore the number eleven and the name HONEYCUTT on the back of his jersey.

She craned her neck, tried to see if it was the same man in Penny Morse's case file, but the batting helmet hid all but the lower half of the man's face. Still, Mary could see he took his sport seriously. As the Methodist pitcher laughed at some joke from his catcher, Honeycutt just hunkered over the plate, not cracking a smile.

Finally, the pitcher got serious. As he began his windup, two girls several rows down from Mary stood up and yelled, "Come on, Buck! Kick some butt!" The One Way crowd laughed as the pitcher threw a fast ball. It looked like Honeycutt was going to let the thing pass, then, at the last possible second, he lowered his shoulder and swung. The bat cracked as the ball flew just inches over the pitcher's head. Everyone leapt up and cheered as the ball flew past the pudgy Methodist short stop and ripped up center field. Honeycutt raced for first base, then went for second. By the time the hapless Methodists had gotten the ball back to the infield, Honeycutt was standing on third base, his right arm lifted, his index finger pointing toward heaven. Everyone around Mary mirrored his gesture, lifting their arms and pointing their fingers upward. Instead of lifting her arm, Mary touched the smart phone in her pocket. I *should send Ann Chandler a picture of this*, she thought.

The rest of the game went quickly. The One Way team fielded as well as they hit, dispatching the Methodists with a murderous efficiency. Galloway played a credible right field but struck out in the ninth inning. By then, it didn't matter—the Saints were ahead 20–0. After the game ended, Mary again kept her eyes on Honeycutt. Though he bumped fists with the Methodists, his face remained stern. Only when he turned to greet his other teammates did he display any exuberance—leaping onto the catcher's back, again pointing his finger at the heavens. The team trotted off the field together, finally dispersing among the people in the bleachers. Victor Galloway came up to her, sweatier from his chest-bumping celebration than his efforts on the field.

"So what'd you think?" he asked, out of breath.

"I think they put you in the right position," said Mary.

"I really suck, don't I?"

"You did okay, considering you're playing with semi-pros."

"I'm probably lucky they let me play at all." Galloway laughed, un-embarrassed by his lack of baseball skill. "You want to go get a beer? I found out some stuff about your kid."

"Honeycutt?"

"No, your little kid in the peach truck."

"Sure," she said. "Let's go."

———

She followed him to a quiet restaurant far from the church league baseball crowd. They sat at the bar, underneath a television that was airing a soccer game.

"That's my sport," said Victor as the barkeeper put two beers in front of them. "I'm a much better fullback than I am a right fielder."

Mary looked up at the screen. She hadn't watched soccer since Lily played in the nine-year-old league, in Cherokee. The memory was bittersweet—Lily had loved soccer, but back then, Lily Walkingstick had also loved her.

"I played in high school, then some club soccer in college," continued Galloway. "My mother's brother, Alejandro, played forward for Argentina."

He pronounced *Argentina* with a Spanish accent. Until that moment, Mary had forgotten that he'd been hired for being bilingual. "So your mother's Argentine?"

"*Sí, senorita*. Maria DeCampos, *des* Buenos Aires. My father's Pete Galloway, from Brooklyn." He grinned. "I got my mother's charm and my father's hustle."

"Yeah, I saw all your hustle, out there in right field."

Shrugging, he nodded at the TV. "Like I said, soccer's my game … not baseball."

"So have you found out anything about your teammates?"

"Only that they take baseball almost as seriously as they take God."

"I found something interesting on your number eleven. Honeycutt."

"What?"

"He's the guy Sligo County indicted for Alan Bratcher's murder."

Galloway put down his beer. "Are you kidding me?"

"Nope. They were in a bar, after a baseball game. Bratcher was gay, put his arm around Honeycutt's shoulders. Honeycutt took offense and beat the shit out of the guy in the parking lot. He died three days later, after which Sligo charged him with manslaughter. His lawyer got him off with some idiotic 'gay panic' defense."

"Gay panic?"

Mary nodded. "Claimed Honeycutt believed some obscure Bible verse that said if you're even touched by a homosexual, then you'll go to hell along with the homosexual."

"And the jury bought that?"

"Apparently. The prosecutor was too much of a rookie to wiggle out of it. The DA may have set her up, too. Come election day, he won't look like a gay-rights activist."

Galloway gave a low whistle. "So I'd better not pat Honeycutt's ass, huh?"

"I wouldn't if I were you." Mary took a sip of beer. "What did you find out about my little kid?"

"After you left I pulled the phone records on Ralph Gudger's landline. They did get a call from a cell phone about the same time the kid claims to have heard from his sister."

"Oh, yeah?"

"Yeah. But it's from a stolen cell with a 704-999 exchange—that's Mecklenburg County."

"Charlotte," said Mary.

"Exactly where the boyfriend is from, according to Crump. Did the sister sound like she was in trouble when she called?"

"The boy said so, but I think he was scared his stepfather would catch him on the telephone. This Gudger character sounds like a real Nazi."

"Well, that pretty much corroborates what Crump told us," said Victor. "The girl's miserable at home, hates her stepfather, so she gets her boyfriend to pick her up as she's on her way home from a babysitting gig. She leaves her car running, hops in with him, and off they go. She probably felt bad and called home to let her mother know she was still alive. Instead of her mom, she gets her psycho brother."

"But why would she tell her brother that she's in trouble?" Mary asked. "Why didn't she take her purse and her babysitting money? Has anybody questioned the boyfriend? The little brother says he doesn't exist."

"Crump said it was probably an Internet romance she hadn't told anyone about." Galloway shrugged. "It sounds like the girl was determined to leave the stepfather and just took the first way out that came along." He gave a bitter laugh. "I honestly think that after assault weapons and drunk drivers, the most hazardous thing to your health is your own family."

"You might be right." Mary scooped up some cheese on a nacho chip. "Tomorrow I'll call the boy and tell him that his sister was calling from Charlotte, probably just to let them know she was still alive."

ELEVEN

CHASE GRUBBED THE POISON ivy long past sunset, pulling the green vines off the fence, hacking at the roots with a pickax, all the while thinking he'd managed to screw everything up again. Though he'd managed to hang up the phone and run to the bathroom before Gudger came inside, he had a bad feeling that the ex-cop suspected something.

"What are you up to in there, boy?" Gudger had demanded, pounding on the bathroom door.

"I had to go to the bathroom," Chase cried.

"Haven't you heard of pissing in the woods?"

"It's not piss." Chase crouched on the toilet, shaking. "It's the other."

"You can do that in the woods, too, Olive Oyl."

Chase held his breath, wondering if Gudger was going to open the door and throw him off the john, but his footsteps thumped down the hall and into the bedroom. Chase waited a moment, flushed the toilet for show, then scampered back up to the poison ivy.

Now he sat by the fence in the growing dark, arms and legs aching, hiding until his mother returned home from work. Over the course of the afternoon he'd been tortured by the notion that Gudger had figured out that he'd been on the phone. If so, then he'd probably had one of his cop friends trace the call. Gudger would know then that he'd called Mary Crow. That would be bad enough, but what if the cops had also said, "Gudge, you had another call on that line yesterday, and it wasn't from any Jamaica Cruise company, either."

That made him sick inside. He couldn't imagine what Gudger would do if he found out that Sam had called and that he, Chase, had lied to him about it. Beat him, probably. Or lock him in his room for the rest of the summer. Better to stay out here until his mother got home. Gudger wouldn't do anything to him in front of his mom.

He huddled in the shadows, watching the sky turn from pink to a soft, hazy blue. As fireflies began to blink close to the ground, he saw distant headlights threading through the trees along the driveway. He watched as his mother's old Dodge slowed to a stop under the oak tree. A moment later his mother emerged, juggling an armload of packages. She hurried toward the house with her head down and her shoulders hunched, as if she slogged through a private world of frost and despair, instead of the warm summer night that surrounded him. Already he'd seen new wrinkles bracketing her mouth and he often caught her staring out the living room window, as if waiting for Sam to roll up in the driveway and say hello, Suzie Q's radio blaring.

"I should tell her," he whispered. "Tell her that Sam called, that she's still alive."

It seemed mean to keep that kind of secret, but telling her would unleash a torrent of questions—*When did she call? What did she say? Where is she? Why didn't she call me? Why didn't you tell me this the instant she called?*

He knew if he answered truthfully, they'd never see Sam again. His mother would go to Gudger and though he would make a big show about getting the cops involved again, secretly he would make double-sure that this time, Sam would stay gone for good. His sister's only chance of coming home depended on Gudger thinking that she was already far, far away.

"I'm sorry, Mama," he whispered to her as she opened the back door. "I've got to keep this secret."

He waited until he saw the lights come on in the kitchen, then he figured it was safe to go inside. Gudger's attention would be on his mother and supper, rather than him. Grabbing the pickax, he lugged it back to the shed. His arms and shoulders ached from all his chopping, and as he headed toward the house, the skin on his face and shoulders felt too tight for his own body. When he opened the back door, he found Gudger in the kitchen, holding a bucket of fried chicken as if it were dog shit. His stomach clenched; Gudger was already mad, and he hadn't even laid eyes on him yet.

"You roll in here at nine thirty at night?" Gudger was yelling at his mother. "With this for my supper?"

"I'm sorry," Amy replied. "I caught my hand in a door at work—I had to fill out an accident report and have the PA examine it." She held up her right hand—it was purple, her wrist swollen to twice its normal size. "I thought maybe we could just have take-home chicken tonight."

Gudger's face was turning the same color as his mother's hand, when Chase stepped forward. "Thanks, Mama," he said, wrapping his arms around her waist. "I love fried chicken."

His mother looked down at him. Suddenly her eyes grew wide. "Chase! What happened to you?"

"For once he's made himself useful." Gudger looked at him, his mouth stretching in mirthless grin. "I had him dig poison ivy off the back fence."

"Did you make him do it all day?" His mother put a hand under his chin, inspecting his body proprietarily, as if it were still somehow attached to her own. "He's blistered with sunburn. And look at these spots all over his arms!"

"Aw, they're just mosquito bites." Gudger scoffed. "You treat that boy like he was a china doll."

"But he's covered in these things!" She turned to Gudger in a rare show of anger. "Couldn't you have given him some insect repellent?"

"It's okay, Mama," Chase said, not wanting to stoke Gudger's wrath further. "I'll go wash up and put on some lotion."

"Good idea, boy." Gudger said a bit too heartily. "By the time you get back, we'll have a nice plate of fried chicken ready for you."

Chase went to the bathroom, weak with relief. Gudger hadn't been mad at him; Gudger had been mad at his mother not having a hot, home-cooked supper on the table at six thirty. He turned on the overhead light. As he started to fill the sink with water, he caught a glimpse of himself in the bathroom mirror. Suddenly he realized why his mother was so upset. He looked like something out of an old sci-fi movie, where people had been zapped by too much radiation. His skin looked like raw flesh from his hairline to his collar bones, covered in both mosquito bites and smaller, paler pimples that he'd never seen before.

"Wow," he said, barely recognizing the face that stared back at him. "No wonder Mama got mad." He washed the dirt from his face with cool water and dabbed pink Calamine lotion on his bites. He looked cleaner, but slightly comical, spotted in pink and white dots. He went to his room and put on a clean T-shirt, in case Gudger decided it would be fun to post more pictures of him on YouTube.

By the time he got back to the kitchen, Gudger sat hunched over his plate, making short work of three big pieces of chicken.

"Here, sweetie," his mother said, giving him another worried look as she retrieved a plate from the oven. "I kept yours warm."

He ate. Fried chicken, macaroni and cheese, applesauce his mother had canned last fall. Never had anything tasted so good. He was about to ask for another piece of chicken when Gudger scooted back in his chair and tossed his napkin in his plate.

"I'm going to catch the rest of the game."

Chase focused on his plate as Gudger went into the den. Soon the voices of the baseball announcers wafted into the kitchen. As he scraped up his last bite of applesauce, his mother started clearing the table. He could tell by the way she carried the plates that her hand was hurting her, so he got up to help her.

"That chicken was good, but it wasn't as good as yours, Mama," he said, handing her his dirty dishes as she filled the sink with hot water.

"Did you get enough to eat?" She tried to squeeze her swollen hand into a rubber glove, but it wouldn't fit.

"I can wash the dishes," he said. "I'll wash and you dry, just like Sam and I used to do."

For a moment she smiled, then she leaned over the sink and started to cry. "Oh, Chase," she sobbed. "What are we going to do?"

Suddenly, he couldn't stand to see her like this anymore. The words he'd earlier decided not to say filled his mouth. *Sam called yesterday, Mama. I talked to her. She's alive, but she's in trouble. I called Mary Crow about her this afternoon.* They were just about to spill out when Gudger's voice cracked like a whip.

"Chase!" he yelled. "Get in here, boy. You and I need to have a little talk."

His heart stopped. Gudger must have found out about his making that phone call. All night he'd just been waiting for the right moment to spring his trap. "I'm helping Mama clean up," Chase called, stalling for time.

"Your mama can clean up by herself. You come on in here."

"Go on, Chase." His mother wiped her eyes with the corner of her apron. "These dishes won't take long. I'll be in there in just a minute."

He had no choice. Gudger was calling, his mother was telling him to go. His mouth chalky with fear, he walked slowly into the den. Gudger sprawled in his lounge chair, a small pile of beer cans in a wastebasket beside him. Chase approached the man cautiously. Gudger was mean enough sober; drunk, he was ten times worse.

"Yes sir?" Chase stopped well out of range of Gudger's fists.

"I wanted to tell you that I'm proud of you, boy," Gudger said, just beginning to slur his words. "You did a man's work today, and you've earned a man's rest tonight. Come watch this game with me."

He was stunned by Gudger's offer of camaraderie, also distrustful. It would be just like Gudger to pretend to be friends, and then blindside him when he wasn't expecting it. "Thanks, but I'm kind of tired. I'd really just rather go to bed."

"You felt strong enough to help your mama a few minutes ago … are you saying you're now too tired to watch a ball game with me?"

Chase knew he was walking into a trap, but he couldn't tell what kind it was. Anyway, he knew arguing would only make Gudger more determined to spring it. "No sir," he said. "I'll watch the game."

He walked over and sat down on the sofa. On television, the Braves catcher was jiggling his fingers between his legs—some kind of signal to the pitcher. He didn't know anything about baseball—his father had been a Cincinnati Bengals fan. He sat staring at the screen, wishing Gudger would pass out when he felt something cold against his bare leg. He jumped, looked down. Gudger was holding an icy can of Pabst beer against his shin.

"There you go, boy. Working man's reward. Uncork that puppy and knock it back. It'll cure what ails you."

Chase shook his head. He'd had beer before. It looked a whole lot better than it tasted. "No thanks," he told Gudger.

"Aw, what's the matter? You too much of a mama's boy to take a drink?" Gudger's eyes glittered with dark glee, as if he'd discovered some secret Chase had been trying to hide. Again, he knew he was trapped. If he didn't drink the beer, he'd hear about it for weeks, possibly months.

"No, I'll drink it," he said. Slowly, he pulled the can open. White foam gurgled to the top. He took a small sip; bitter, pungent bubbles filled his mouth. Sputtering, he put the can down. Gudger started to laugh.

"Go on, boy, knock it back! Chug it like a man!"

Chase took another sip, choked a mouthful down.

"No!" cried Gudger. "Not like that. Like this." He opened a new can, held it up to his mouth, and poured it down his throat, his Adam's apple bobbing. He tossed the empty in the box and turned to Chase.

Just get it over with, Chase told himself. He did exactly what Gudger did—held the can up high and poured it down his throat. Though he hated the taste, hated the way the stuff foamed up into his nose and sinuses, he managed to gulp the stuff down. When the can was empty, he gave it back to Gudger. "There," he said. "I chugged it like a man."

Gudger was going to say something, but the game on TV caught his attention. Chase sat back on the sofa, belching as one player hit the ball and another player caught, then dropped it. Gudger began screaming at the TV. Suddenly, the men on the screen grew fuzzy— comical pin-striped characters frolicking across a field of green. He blinked—his face felt hot, his skin tight. The room began to tilt as he felt a rolling sensation in the pit of his stomach.

"Did you see that pitch, boy?" Gudger turned to him, excited.

He couldn't answer as his mouth began to flood with saliva.

"What's the matter with you, boy?" cried Gudger.

"I-I think I'm going to be sick."

"Aw, come on," said Gudger. "After one beer?"

Quickly, he stood up. He knew he was going to puke—either here or in the toilet. Tripping over Gudger's feet, he stumbled toward the bathroom.

"Are you kidding me?" Gudger started laughing, then grew silent as Chase lurched into the door frame. "Oh, go on and get out of here, you lying little weasel," he says. "Just see if I waste a good beer on you again."

With the house spinning, Chase managed to get to the bathroom just as the beer erupted from his stomach. He clutched the commode like a man on a life raft as the beer and fried chicken made its way into the toilet. Though the room still spun and his body trembled in a cold, drenching sweat, Gudger's parting words sobered him quickly. *You lying little weasel.* There would be no reason for Gudger to call him that unless he knew that he'd been on the phone, talking to his sister.

TWELVE

SAM COULDN'T REMEMBER IF the doctor had pulled her shorts back on; what she did remember was being flipped over on her stomach, then a sting in her left buttock. After that she floated away, back to Chase climbing high into Cousin Petey's sycamore tree, back to her father waving to her from his truck, back to a strange, lush land where people had wings and dogs walked upright, reciting poetry. For days she traveled through dazzling meadows with a poetry-quoting Airedale, then, when they came to a river that flowed like honey, the dog turned to her, saying, *Little Mary, quite contrary, how does your garden grow? With silver bells and cockle shells and pretty maids, all in a row!*

Grinning at her, the Airedale vanished. She jumped, surprised by his disappearance. She found herself not in a magical land with talking dogs, but back in a shabby motel room. She sat up in the bed, blinking, still looking for the dog and the meadow and the lapping river, but she saw only a gray linoleum floor, a boarded-up window, an ancient television crowned with a rabbit-ear antenna. For a moment she sat there, wondering where the dog had gone; then the edges of reality sharpened. There were no dogs or golden meadows here. Here was only a sweat-stained mattress, a battered bureau all in a concrete-block box.

As she grew more fully awake, she realized she was both thirsty and needing to pee. She lifted the lint-speckled blanket that covered her and stood up. The soles of her feet tingled as they touched the cold linoleum floor. She felt woozy but managed the four steps to the bathroom without stumbling. As she sat down on the toilet, she saw that someone had scratched *this place is a hell hole* at knee-level, on the wall.

"You got that right," she whispered.

As she peed, she closed her eyes, tried to piece her recent past into some kind of order. A horrible old doctor had examined her in front of a man named Boris? Bucko? She couldn't remember his name, but his actions were etched her in memory—he'd yelled at Ivan, and then the man who looked like an ape pointed a rifle at Ivan; flames had come out of the barrel. But why? What had made Boris-Bucko so mad? She put her head in her hands and tried to think—was it something the doctor had done? Some part of her body that he founding lacking? She was filing through hazy wisps of memories when suddenly, she remembered! Ivan had let her use his cell phone! She'd called home and talked to Chase!

Chase, I'm in trouble, she remembered saying. *I'm scared. Please tell Mom.*

What did you say?

She could barely hear him, the connection was sketchy and someone seemed to be hammering in the background. *Tell Mama some men are going to send me away!* she'd finally said, yelling as loud as she could.

Then a huge noise, then blood, then Ivan slammed against the wall right beside her with half his face gone. She covered her own face, trying to block out the memory. Had Chase heard anything she'd said? Had he told Mama? Had either of them called the police?

Sam didn't know; the world had gone crazy after that phone call, becoming a maelstrom of shouts and voices, none of them speaking a word she could understand.

"Oh Mama," she whispered, longing for her mother's arms, the soft shoulders that had blotted so many of her tears. "I am in so much trouble."

She sat there trembling, then she remembered her father speaking to her in another dream—a dream of warm, deep darkness. *It's all up to you, Sam-I-Am.*

"I guess it is," she said. Neither Chase nor her mother could get her out of this mess. This time, she would have to save herself.

She dried her eyes and got to her feet. She pulled the lever that flushed the ancient john with some trepidation, but the tank emptied and refilled, making a curious tapping sound as the water level rose. Grateful to at least have working plumbing, she stepped over to the sink to wash her hands. As a stream of tea-colored water issued from the faucet, she lifted her head to look in the medicine cabinet mirror. Someone (maybe the person who'd written the hell-hole graffiti) had put a fist in the middle of the thing—cracking the glass so that her face looked as if it had been jig-sawed into a puzzle that didn't quite fit together. She traced one of the long shards with her finger. It wiggled in its rusty metal frame, sharp as a stiletto.

Okay, she thought. *If it comes to it, I can take myself out of here. Better that than whatever Boris has in mind.*

Turning away from the mirror, she stepped back into her room. She'd assumed it was her same old room, but as she looked around, she realized it was different. Ivan's blood did not stain the floor, nor did any bullet holes speckle the wall next to her bed. This room had a bureau shoved in one corner, one drawer of which held a tattered collection of old sci-fi paperbacks. The television pulled in a single, fuzzy shopping channel, and when she tried to peek out the nailed-shut window, she saw nothing but a sheet of plywood. She walked over to the door and flipped the switch for the overhead fluorescent. Neither on nor off had any effect; the cold, anemic light that shone now would, apparently, illuminate the room 24/7.

As she fiddled with the light switch, the john began rattling again. The sound reminded her of their scary old toilet back in West Virginia. It had seemed like a living monster when she was four; she was convinced some ogre lived in the thing, just waiting to grab her bottom and pull her down into the dark, watery depths. Then her father explained it was just air in the old pipes.

"Only there probably is a monster in this john," she whispered, thinking of Boris. "It speaks Russian and has a head like a cue ball."

After a moment, the tapping stopped. She paced off the room—twelve feet by twelve feet—the same size as her last one. Something was different here, though. Before, she was aware of a world beyond her locked door—the sounds of girls trooping past her door twice a day, distant music playing, loud arguments usually involving Dusty and the men. Here, she heard nothing. Except for the noisy toilet, this room was as silent as a tomb.

Suddenly she panicked. What if Boris had locked her in here and gone away? What if Chase had called the police and they'd taken everyone to jail, but hadn't searched the place well enough to find her? What if Boris and the doctor were saving her for something worse than the truck stop? What if they'd gone and just left her here to die?

She turned and started pounding on the door. "Hey!" she cried. "Is anybody there? Can anybody hear me?"

She stopped, pressed her ear to the crack, and listened. Nothing.

"Hey!" she called louder. "I'm hungry! I need some food!"

She listened again, praying to hear something—anything—even that *mama, mama, mama* girl was preferable to this. Again, she heard nothing.

"Please!" she cried, banging harder. "Somebody! I need help!"

She listened again. Did she hear footsteps? She pressed her ear to the door as the muffled sounds seemed to grow louder. Then she heard a key fumbling at her lock. Scared, she hurried back to the bed. As she did, the door opened, revealing a short, dark-haired man wearing jeans and bearing a tray of food. He stepped inside the room and kicked the door closed behind him. His brows were knitted above his nose, his mouth a thin, downward curve. His expression was stern but neutral; his dark eyes focused on her face rather than her body.

"You ho-kay?" he asked in heavily accented English.

She didn't know what to say. She wasn't in physical pain; no doctor was stuffing his fat fingers up her crotch. Still, she was about as far from okay as she could get. "Where am I?" she asked. "What day is it?"

"You with Yusuf," the little man said. "You eat, then drink tea."

He put a tray down on her bed. It was not the fast food crap that Ivan had brought her, but real food. Orange-colored chicken stew over rice with little triangles of bread, accompanied by a small teapot that had steam seeping from the spout. As she inhaled the savory aromas, her mouth began to water. She couldn't remember when she'd last eaten.

Yusuf snapped a big linen napkin open and laid it across her lap, then sat down on the floor, keeping his eyes on her the whole time. "You eat. I stay . . . make sure you ho-kay."

She frowned, realizing that he wasn't going away until she finished. She looked for a spoon or fork on the tray, but found none there.

"I don't have anything to eat with," she told him.

"Turkish way." He made a motion of scooping something into his mouth. "With bread."

She picked up a triangle of the flat bread and scooped up some stew. It tasted as delicious as it smelled—chicken and cinnamon and a lot of other spicy-sweet flavors she couldn't name. She shoveled the food into her mouth; never had anything tasted so good.

He watched her as she ate, his gaze never wandering. At first he made her nervous, then she decided to ignore him. This Yusuf seemed another version of Ivan—short and dark instead of tall and blond—but a foreigner, nonetheless. If she could make friends with him, maybe he would tell her where she was, what they planned to do with her. She wiped her mouth with the back of her hand and smiled. "This is good. Thank you."

"Good to eat," he said. "Make healthy."

"Does everybody here eat like this?"

Yusuf shook his head, as if he didn't understand. "Everybody here?"

"Here." She spread her arms to indicate the whole building. "As opposed to the cornflake and Big Mac wing."

"Everybody here special," he replied, his tone guarded.

Yusuf had neither Ivan's conversational skills nor any apparent interest in engaging her in conversation. She returned her attention to her food and, with the last triangle of bread, scraped her plate clean. The moment she finished, Yusuf jumped up and moved quickly to pour her tea.

"Now you must drink." Though his smile stretched all the way across his face, his dark eyes bored into her, glittering in a way that made her go cold inside.

"What kind of tea is this?" She frowned. This man was standing too close, pouring the tea too readily.

"Turkish tea . . . make you feel good . . . sleep."

She remembered her last sleep, where she'd crossed a magic land, conversing with dogs. As wonderful as it had been, she didn't want to go back there—not now, anyway.

"No thanks." She shook her head. "I've slept enough lately."

Yusuf acted as if she hadn't spoken a word. He stood there, staring at her, holding out the teacup.

"No." She shook her head, wondering if he was having difficulty understanding her West Virginia accent. "Thanks, but no tea."

Still he remained there, implacable, tea in hand. "You drink now."

"No!" she repeated. This time she pushed his hand away. He moved the tea quickly out of her reach, then, with his free hand, pinched the fleshy top of her right shoulder. Pain shot up into her face, making her eyes water.

"You drink tea, ho-kay? You no get Yusuf in trouble!"

"But why?" she cried. "Why do you care if I drink tea?"

"My job keep you strong and healthy."

"What for?"

"Soon you will be in new home. Far away."

For a time, she'd forgotten—she was an American virgin … a rare delicacy for a man with enough money to buy her. "No!" she cried, panicky, trying to squirm away from his grasp. "I won't go!"

He stepped closer, giving her shoulder another squeeze, showing her that the pain could get considerably worse. "Yes. When it's time, you will go."

"No, I won't," she cried, as tears began to flow from her right eye.

"Yes, you will." He released her shoulder and pulled out another smart phone. This one he did not offer to lend, but to show her pictures on the screen. As he held the thing up, she gasped. He had a photo of her mother in her work uniform, going into the nursing home. Her head was bent down, her face drawn in sorrow.

"Where did you get that?" she cried.

He grinned proudly. "I take, yesterday." He swiped a finger across the screen and pulled up another image. "This, too."

The second picture showed Chase getting the mail from Gudger's yellow ribbon–clad mailbox. He looked quizzical but timid, as if he were afraid some car might stop and scoop him up, too. Her mouth went dry with terror. "How do you know about them?"

"We know all about you. You give trouble, these people pay."

She closed her eyes. All the time she'd been teaching Ivan about French braiding, she'd talked about how much she missed her mother and her brother. He'd patted her hand, told her he knew how hard it was to be without your family. She thought he'd honestly sympathized—instead, he'd just been pumping her for information. She bit her lower lip—not from the pain in her shoulder, but for the fact she'd been such a fool.

"Come," Yusuf said, putting the phone back in the pocket of his jeans. "Drink the tea. You will not sleep too long—just more happy."

As she gazed at the cup, her heart shriveled. The police were not coming for her. She could tell that by her mother's sorrowful, beaten-down posture. And Chase was getting the mail scared, his gaze fearful of strangers in cars. He must have not heard her when she called. Either that, or Gudger had simply convinced everyone that he was lying again.

She took Yusuf's tea and drank it in two gulps. What did she care how long she slept? Soon they would ship her out as bit of precious cargo. If she fought that fate, her family would suffer; better that they never see her again than that she cause them any more pain. She handed the cup back to Yusuf in slow motion, the room already beginning to spin. As she flopped back down on the bed, she caught a quick glimpse of the shattered bathroom mirror, the shards that would slice a willing vein like razors.

It's all up to you, Sam-I-Am, she told herself as she sank into a frothy cloud of sleep. *You can cancel this deal anytime you want.*

THIRTEEN

MARY SLEPT LATE THE next morning—she'd left Galloway mid-way through his third beer and returned to her hotel, spending the rest of her night studying the case file on Bryan Taylor. For a non-employee to have an active file was irregular, unethical, and probably illegal, but Galloway hadn't blinked when she'd asked him for it. She guessed being the governor's envoy had its advantages—everybody seemed happy to give her whatever she wanted, no questions asked.

So she'd studied the case that had, along with Reverend Trull's video, brought the governor's wrath down on Campbell County. The similarities between Bryan Taylor and Alan Bratcher's murder were striking. Both young men were gay, both had been visiting their families from out of town, had died of blunt-force trauma to the head. Where Bratcher had died in a bar fight, Bryan Taylor's body had been found dumped along Jackson Highway, his car fifteen miles to the east at an I-85 truck stop. His body had not been mutilated, as was the case in some gay murders, nor were there any tears or wounds around his rectum.

"But would a newlywed go looking for love at a truck stop?" Mary had whispered. "After texting his spouse that he couldn't wait to see him? And why dump him so close to town, with all his IDs? Why not drive thirty miles across the state line and drop him in some nameless ditch in South Carolina?"

Now, in the morning light, she was rereading the file, just to make sure she hadn't overlooked anything. The guy she'd met yesterday—Crump—had been first on the scene, then called in a Detective Smithson, who was apparently within a month of retirement. Crump had roped off the crime scene, and Smithson had spent his last month of his career interviewing truck stop employees, truckers who'd bought gas that night, even the driver of a Greyhound headed to Virginia. Nobody had seen anything unusual that night.

"Nobody ever sees anything," Mary said aloud, as she finished her second cup of coffee. "That's what makes police work so much fun."

Still, something niggled at her—Bryan Taylor's death seemed more than just a gay tryst gone bad. She grabbed her briefcase, deciding that a visit to Taylor's parents might be helpful, when she remembered the little hitchhiker who was so upset about his sister. Thumbing through the phone records Galloway had copied for her, she found the number of the boy's landline. Quickly, she punched it into her cell phone. Her news would not be what he wanted to hear—that his sister had called from Charlotte and was very likely with some unknown boyfriend—but at least it would reassure him that his stepfather hadn't sold her to gypsies. As she walked out the door, his phone began to ring. Once, twice, three times—on and on. No one answered, no machine ever picked up. *I'll call back later*, she decided, heading for her car. *Right now, Bryan Taylor is at the top of my to-do list.*

———

The Taylor home was a comfortable red brick rancher, set back from the street among tall maple trees. A twirling copper garden sculpture glittered in the front yard while a rainbow flag hung from the front porch. The house had a settled look about it, and Mary noticed that the door knocker she lifted was cross-shaped, with the inscription *As for me and my house, we will serve the Lord.* She was wondering if everybody in this county wore their religion like a brand-new hat when the door opened. A tall, gray-haired man stood there, dressed in a black shirt with a cross dangling from around his neck.

"Uh, I'm looking for Bryan Taylor's father," said Mary, assuming the man was a priest.

"I'm Bryan's dad."

Mary hesitated, looking at the cross. He smiled gently at her obvious confusion. "Episcopal. Our guys can marry."

"Of course," Mary blushed, thinking she should have take a crash course on religious denominations before she'd stepped foot in Campbell County. "I'm Mary Crow, special prosecutor for Governor Ann Chandler. First let me say how sorry I am for the loss of your son."

"Thank you." His smile faded as his face settled into newly familiar lines of grief and worry. "You're from Raleigh, you say?"

"The governor sent me here to investigate possible anti-gay conspiracies. Could we talk for a few minutes?"

"Certainly." He opened the door wide. "Please come in."

She stepped into a living room that could have been the front parlor of a funeral home. Potted plants clustered around the windows while rainbow-colored Mylar balloons hovered near the ceiling. A dozen fruit baskets stood unopened, the smell of overripe apples rank in the air.

"Who was it, Eddie?" called a hoarse female voice from the back of the house. "More flowers?"

"Someone from the governor's office," he called. He fingered his cross, then turned to Mary. "Please have a seat. That was my wife, Carrie. I'm Edward."

They shook hands. Mary sat down on the sofa just as a woman dressed in torn jeans and a dirty sweatshirt entered the room. Her blond hair curled in greasy strands around her neck and dark circles underscored her eyes. Had she been clean and healthy-looking, she would have been considered pretty; now she looked like someone in the last stages of a disease. *Such is grief*, Mary thought as she gave the woman a sad smile.

"She's from the governor?" The woman stared at Mary, then turned to her husband as if he were making a joke.

"I'm Mary Crow, the governor's special prosecutor," Mary explained. "Governor Chandler is very concerned about anti-gay sentiment in this area. She sent me to investigate your son's death."

"My son's murder," Mrs. Taylor corrected, her eyes blazing. "At least get it right. Somebody beat his brains out. He didn't just die."

"Yes ma'am. I'm sorry."

"Do you have any new leads in the case?" Reverend Taylor tried to redirect his wife's close-to-the-surface rage.

"Not as yet," replied Mary. "But your police force is excellent and they are determined to find his killer."

"If they're so great, then why are you here?" asked Mrs. Taylor. "Why does Ann Chandler suddenly give a shit about my boy?"

Mary didn't quite know how to answer. She couldn't tell this woman that it was basically all about bringing jobs to an out-of-work county and getting Ann Chandler reelected. Instead, she decided to tell her the same thing she'd told the two DAs. "Your son is the second homosexual homicide in this area in the past eight months. Governor Chandler is determined to add sexual orientation to the hate crimes statute, and make sure that no more North Carolinians die because of whom they chose to love."

"Well isn't that just dandy!" Mrs. Taylor threw back her head and gave a bitter laugh. "I'm so glad my little boy's murder got Ann Chandler on the bandwagon."

"Carrie," Reverend Taylor said gently, long fingers again going around his cross. "Ms. Crow's here to help—"

"Ms. Crow's too late, Eddie. Maybe if Ms. Crow and Ann Chandler had come here a year ago—or even two months ago—they could have done something—but it's too late now. All those posturing fools in Raleigh can shove their statutes up their asses—nothing will bring my boy back." She walked over and picked up a small photo from the end table beside the sofa. She traced the outline of a young man's face—then she started to sob. Clutching the photograph, she ran out of the room crying.

"I'm sorry." Reverend Taylor stood there looking confused, as if he didn't whether to go after his wife or remain in the living room, talking with Mary. "It's been hard on Carrie... Bryan was her baby."

"I understand," said Mary. "I've spoken with grieving parents before—losing a child is the worst kind of pain. If you'd like to talk some other time, I could come back later."

"No." He held up his hand, as if that could stop the sound of his wife's tears. "Let's talk now... it might help Carrie handle this a little better if she knows the governor's involved. She thinks the police aren't interested in finding who did this to Bryan."

"I can assure you that good people are working on it, Reverend. I've talked to them myself."

"I suppose." The man sighed. "But I also know cops don't go overboard protecting gays. Bryan told me that years ago."

"Well, you've got the governor's full attention now, so that should help. Can you tell me a little bit about Bryan?"

The priest shrugged. "He was the third of our three boys. He was a good kid, made good grades, played shortstop on the high school baseball team. He came out to us after his freshman year in college."

"And were you surprised?"

"A little. He wasn't an effeminate boy. He dated in high school, had friends of both genders."

"Did he have any same-sex relationships in high school?" Mary wondered if this wasn't some secret, long-term gay relationship gone sour. An old love upset that Bryan had married someone else.

"Not that I know of." Taylor shook his head. "Being gay at Campbell County High is the last thing a kid would admit to. I think going away to a more liberal college gave Bryan the courage to be honest about what he'd apparently known for a long time. He said as much, when he told us."

"So he knew Campbell County was not safe for gay people?"

"Apparently." Sudden tears came to the man's eyes. "We never talked about homosexuality when he was growing up. But I should have…I should have addressed it from the pulpit and told all my parishioners that God doesn't care who you love…God only cares that you love."

Mary could tell that Bryan's father was grieving just as deeply as his mother was—he'd just turned his anger inward on himself. "*Should* is an awfully burdensome word, Reverend Taylor," she said softly.

"I know." Embarrassed, he wiped his eyes. "I just should have listened more. I didn't worry about him at all until he came out; then I worried about him all the time. I remember one time he told me to relax, that they'd never 74 him here."

Mary shook her head. "I'm sorry—I'm not familiar with the term."

The priest shrugged. "Nor am I. I started to ask him about it, but he was on his way back to school, in Winston-Salem. In a hurry, as usual."

Mary made a note on the little pad she carried. "Was he happy in his personal life?"

"He graduated from North Carolina School of the Arts and went to New York after graduation. He was a cinematographer. He'd just married his partner, Leo, and was filming documentaries." He walked over to a bookcase, returning with a photograph of a group of young men in tuxedos, all gripping Oscars. He pointed to a muscular young man with blond hair. "That's Bryan."

Mary frowned at the picture, astonished. "He won an Academy Award?"

"For *Orange Julius*. A documentary about slave labor in the Florida agricultural industry."

"You must be very proud," said Mary.

"He put his gifts to good use." For the first time, his father's voice cracked. "He couldn't stand unfairness—people taking advantage of others."

"And what is his partner doing now?"

"Leo's in Brooklyn, trying to put his life back together. He was devastated, just like the rest of us."

Reverend Taylor gazed at the floor, his fingers twisting the cross around his neck. "You know what's ironic about all this?"

"What?"

"Bryan had no intention of playing baseball that night. He was really excited about a new film and wanted to get started on it here, but the team captain called—they were one player short. Bryan didn't want them to forfeit."

"Did any of his teammates report any strange behavior after the game that night?"

"No. They all went to Clancy's Grill. Bryan had a hamburger and a beer. He told everybody good-bye—he was leaving for New York the next day."

"Yet they found his car at a truck stop on I-85," said Mary.

"I know the police think he drove there for sex, but I think someone moved his car there after he died. He wasn't looking to hook up with anybody—he loved Leo, they were newlyweds."

Mary sighed. There was a lot about this case that didn't make any sense. "What was his new film about?" she finally asked.

Taylor shrugged. "He said it was about lizards."

"Lizards," Mary repeated. "Like reptiles? Skinks?"

"I guess so. He was really pumped up about it. I can't help but think that he'd still be alive if he'd just stayed home and worked on that movie."

Mary cautioned the heart-broken father. "That kind of thinking is right up there with the word *should*, Reverend."

"You're right, of course. Some questions are not answerable. Our friends and neighbors and the community of faith have certainly shown us the love of God in all this."

"Really?"

"The local churches have all helped out. The Presbyterian ladies bring over casseroles every day, two Methodist ministers have taken over some of my pastoral duties." He gave a sad smile. "It's the grace of God in action."

Mary had to ask the question. "Have you had any help from the One Way Church?"

"From the infamous Brother Trull?"

Mary nodded.

"They've come by," he replied. "Offered to cut our grass, water our flowers." His voice dropped to just above a whisper. "Carrie has a hard time with them—"

"Tell her the truth, Eddie," Carrie Taylor's harsh voice came from behind them. "Tell her that Reverend Trull and his sanctimonious little band of Christians are scared to come over here."

Mary turned to find Carrie Taylor standing there, her eyes on fire, still holding the photo of her son. "Why is that, Mrs. Taylor?"

"Because they know I hate their fucking guts. They know the minute they stepped on the porch, I'd grab a knife from the kitchen and hack them to pieces. Then they could all see what hell is like first-hand."

FOURTEEN

MARY DROVE AWAY FROM the Taylor home sad. It was always diffi-
cult to talk to people who were in mid-grief—that awful time when
the anesthetic shock of a sudden death had worn off, leaving the raw,
throbbing memories of love and the endless questions of *why* and *if
only*. Reverend Taylor, she figured, would ultimately be okay. He was
relying upon his faith; you could tell by the way he constantly fingered
the cross around his neck. Mrs. Taylor might not fare so well. The
anger in her eyes burned endlessly, seeking not comfort but revenge.
Reverend Trull's congregation would be wise to leave their prayers for
that poor woman on the altar of their own church.

Still, she'd learned a little about their son. Bryan Taylor had been
successful, talented, and married. Excited about a new film, eager to
get back to New York. So why was his car found in a truck stop twenty
miles from the ditch where he'd been dumped? What was so intriguing about making a movie about lizards? And what did getting 74'ed
mean? She drove back to Galloway's office. Maybe he could shed
some light on everything. She found him at his desk, holding an ice
pack to his right elbow.

"What's the matter?" She dropped Bryan Taylor's case file back on his desk. "Did you bend your elbow too much at the bar last night?"

"No, I did something to it in my one and only throw from right field. It hurt a little last night, but a lot more this morning." He frowned at his elbow, concerned.

"I'm so sorry," said Mary. "You had such a promising career in church league baseball."

"I know." Galloway stuck his lower lip out, as if she wasn't taking his injury seriously enough. "I'm Derek Jeter and you're Nancy Drew. Did you find anything in that case file?"

"No, but I went to see Bryan Taylor's parents this morning."

He lowered his elbow and looked at her sharply. "And?"

"Did you know the kid had won an Oscar?"

"I knew he was a filmmaker."

"He did a documentary on slave labor in Florida that won an Academy Award. He was starting a new project, about lizards."

"Lizards?" Galloway reapplied the ice pack to his elbow. "Wow."

"Have you ever heard the term '74'ed'?"

He looked at her, his eyes again serious. "74'ed? Like deep-six'ed?"

Mary shrugged. "I don't know. Edward Taylor said Bryan once told him not to worry, that he'd never get 74'ed here."

Galloway thought a moment. "Maybe it's a gay sex thing—you know—like 69?"

"69 isn't necessarily a gay position. And anyway, it makes physiological sense. I can't come up with any sexual position for 74."

He gave a quick, appreciative glance at her chest. "Maybe we should go check out the Kama Sutra."

"You can go check out the Kama Sutra. I'm going back to Asheville. If getting 74'ed means something, somebody there will know."

"Why there?"

"It's a rainbow town. If 74 is truly gay slang, somebody will know about it."

Galloway frowned. "You're coming back, though, aren't you?"

"If I find out anything." Mary turned to leave, then stopped. "If you can manage it with that elbow, give me a call if anybody figures out why they found Bryan Taylor's car twenty miles away from his body."

"Don't worry, Ms. Crow. I'll call you even if I have to punch in the number with my teeth."

———

She headed out of town, then remembered that she still hadn't talked to Chase, her little hitchhiker. Again she punched in his number; again she got no answer. She called Galloway, hoping he hadn't left his office.

"Hey, give me that guy Gudger's address," she said. "I want to stop by and tell my little buddy that his sister called from Charlotte and is probably with her boyfriend."

"I don't know if I can." Galloway moaned. "My elbow . . . just won't bend in that direction."

"Come on, Galloway. Give me the address."

"Oh, all right. Hang on." Papers rustled, then he said, "514 Kedron Road."

"Thanks."

She entered the address into her smart phone. As the directions came on the screen, she remembered the boy's terror at being seen with her. How would the stepfather react if she, a total stranger, knocked on the door with news of the missing sister? *Be careful*, she told herself. *This kid might be a nut case, but the fear on his face was real when he saw his stepfather out by their mailbox.*

She followed the directions down the same road she'd driven the boy, turning to drive up a long gravel driveway to a neat brick house. A split rail fence surrounded a modest front yard, leaving the rest of the five or so acres to roll out like a golf course, grass no doubt clipped short by the stepfather's brand-new tractor. She saw no cars in the driveway, nor did any barking dog rush out to greet her as she got out of her car. There was such a stillness about the house that she wondered if they all hadn't taken off on a vacation. Nonetheless, she'd come all the way out here—she may as well see if someone was at home. She walked to the front porch, knocked on the door. She heard nothing but the chirp of a robin, hopping in the grass. She knocked again, louder. Still nothing—no footsteps approaching the other side of the door, no distant TV playing. Hoping that the little boy was on some pleasant outing with his stepfather, she'd just turned to leave when a small face appeared in the window next to the door. It was Chase, peeking out from behind a curtain. Smiling, she waved. A moment later she heard locks turning. The door opened. She looked at the child and gasped. His face was a doughy mass of red pustules that covered him from his hairline to his collarbones.

"Honey, what happened to you?" cried Mary.

"Poison ivy," he croaked, his voice hoarse.

"Did you roll in the stuff?" An equally angry rash covered the boy's arms and legs.

"Gudger made me clear off the back fence yesterday. I got some on me." He looked up at her with puffy eyes. "Did you find out anything about Sam?"

"I did." Mary peered behind the child, wondering what sort of household he lived in. "May I come in?"

"Better not," the boy said, quickly stepping out on the porch. "Gudger would kill me if I let a stranger inside."

"Is Gudger here?"

He shook his head. "That's why I could answer the door."

"Okay. Well, I told my friend Victor, who's a detective on your police force, what you told me. He looked up Gudger's phone records, and someone did call you yesterday. They called from a cell phone with a Charlotte exchange."

Chase's eyes brightened. "I knew it was Sam!"

"Well she called on someone named Arthur Howard's phone," said Mary. "Is he a friend of hers?"

The boy shook his head. "Not that I know of."

"Well, it's a pre-paid phone, so it could be stolen. Are you sure your sister didn't have a boyfriend? Somebody she was keeping secret from you and your mom?"

"No," he began shaking his head. "She didn't. I know she didn't. She wouldn't run off with a boy without telling me."

Mary wanted to put her arm around him, but there was not a spot on him that wasn't red and swollen. Instead, she brushed his hair back from his forehead. "Chase, sometimes teenaged girls do crazy things. They aren't happy at home, then they meet a boy who promises them a better life, and off they go. Maybe Sam met somebody on the Internet, somebody who seemed like a knight in shining armor. When she went with him, she just wasn't thinking about who she might be hurting here."

"No." He shook his head, tears welling in his swollen eyes. "She wouldn't do that ... not without telling me."

"I know she's hurt you," Mary went on. "But you've got to believe that she's okay ... and that she'll come back." Her heart aching for the child, she dug in her purse, looking for some shred of hope to offer him. She pulled Galloway's card from her wallet. "Here, this is Detective Victor Galloway's card. He's a good guy. You can trust him. If Sam calls again, you call him."

Chase took the card, but his tears did not stop. "But I heard Gudger on the phone, laughing about how she'd gone! Three days after she leaves, he shows up with a motorcycle. Right now he's out looking at a boat. I'm telling you—he sold her to somebody!"

"People don't just sell people, Chase. He'd probably been wanting a motorcycle for a long time. Maybe now he thinks a boat would get your mother's mind off your sister— "

The boy started to protest, then his face suddenly went white beneath his rash. "Oh no!" he breathed. "Here comes Gudger!"

Mary turned to see a black Ford pickup come rolling up the drive. Chase jumped in front of her, tugging on the sleeve of her blouse.

"Please!" he whispered, breathless. "Please don't tell him you know anything about Sam. If he finds out I've said anything, he'll kill me!"

"Don't worry," said Mary. "I promise I won't tell."

The two stood there watching. Gudger got out of the truck carrying a paper sack, eyeing them both with a cold cop stare. Mary could see why the boy might fear the man—he walked with military stiffness, his movements quick and decisive.

"Good afternoon." He gave Mary a brisk nod as he drew near, not once looking at Chase. "Can I help you?"

"I'm sorry to intrude, but I was looking for an address and got lost. I pulled in to ask directions. Your son was trying to help me."

"Well, I doubt he was much help," said Gudger. "He hasn't lived here long himself."

"He's got quite a case of poison ivy." Mary turned to Chase and gave him a quick wink.

"I know. Yesterday he got mixed up what was poison ivy and what was blackberry bushes." He handed the paper sack to Chase. "Here, buddy. I got you some medicine." He pulled out a bottle of pills and a tube of cream. "You're supposed to take one of these pills and put that ointment on the worst places."

"Yes sir." Chase took the sack of medicine but did not move.

"Go on now and take your pills. I'll help this lady get where she needs to go."

Chase shot a furtive, pleading look at Mary, then slowly went back inside the house.

"Kids." Gudger shook his head, his rigid demeanor softening.

"They can get banged up pretty fast," said Mary.

"Oh, that was more my fault than his. I sent him to grub out the back fence, thinking he'd know poison ivy when he saw it. He's my wife's child—a little bookworm of a boy. This is his first summer here."

Mary nodded. "So you and his mother are recently married?"

"Eleven months of wedded bliss on the twentieth." Smiling, Gudger lifted his left hand to display a silver ring on one finger.

"Congratulations." Mary smiled. "How do you like stepparenting?"

He sighed. "I don't have any kids of my own, so I'm just winging it. Seeing what works and what doesn't, you know?"

"All too well," said Mary. With a pang she thought of Lily Walking-stick, and the disaster that had become.

"I'm an old army non-com, so all this sensitivity stuff's a little new to me." He shrugged. "Bought him a big-screen TV and a motorcycle he can ride in a couple years, but it's been rough. A month ago his sister ran off with some boy."

"That is rough," Mary agreed. "Especially on a new family."

"I know. My wife's just going through the motions of living, and the boy sneaks around like a little detective. I keep telling both of 'em that the girl will wise up and come home, but they're both convinced she's gone for good." Gudger stared at the ground for a moment, then returned his gaze to Mary. "But none of that is your concern. Who is it you're trying to find out here?"

117

For an instant Mary panicked, unable to think of anybody. "Jonathan Walkingstick," she finally blurted, going to the default name that haunted her dreams. "He's supposed to live at 2112 Kedron Road."

"Then he lives a couple of miles up the road, honey." Gudger laughed. "This here's 514."

"It is?" Mary feigned surprise. "Gosh—I guess my GPS is really off. I'd better get going. Tell your son I hope he feels better soon … he seems like a nice little boy."

"Thanks," Gudger said, following her out to her car. "Probably did him some good, getting up and out into the fresh air for a few minutes. Otherwise, he'd just lie in bed and read Sherlock Holmes all day."

"Well, thanks," Mary said as the man held the door of her car open. "Again, I'm sorry to disturb you."

"Not a problem." Gudger stepped back and pointed down the driveway. "Just go back to the road and take a left. 2112 should be on the east side of the road."

Mary turned around and drove as Gudger directed. As she headed down the driveway, she noticed in her rearview mirror that he made no effort to go inside the house and see about his stepson; instead he just stood in the driveway, his eyes hard on her until she disappeared from view.

FIFTEEN

INSTEAD OF DRIVING TO the home of the mythic Jonathan Walking-stick, Mary retraced her route and headed back to Jackson Highway. As she drove, she thought about the little boy and his obsession with his sister. The stepfather had not seemed like a monster—a little stiff, but not uncaring. Certainly he'd made an effort to get poison ivy medicine for the child. Yet Chase had gone white with fear when he saw the man's truck pulling in the driveway. Did this Gudger turn into a fiend behind closed doors? Or was Chase, as the cops had said, simply an unhappy little boy with an overactive imagination? She couldn't say— all she knew was that Chase and his family seemed more like a case for social services than law enforcement. With a reluctant sigh, she turned her attention back to Bryan Taylor. There, she at least had a clue.

———

Compared to the grim little town of Manley, Asheville felt like a different universe. As she walked from her condo to her office, she watched street musicians busking in front of the bookstore, while businessmen in suits relaxed in the little park that hosted a drum circle every Friday night. A beautiful old basilica overlooked it all, its rose gardens resplendent in the warm afternoon sun.

"And it works," Mary said aloud, hoofing it up the hill to the Flat Iron building. Though Asheville had its share of conservative Christians, she sensed no underlying hatred for any group—gays or Hispanics or even the Ukrainians, who were settling in impressive numbers. The city simply put its important signage out in three languages—English, Spanish, and Russian. She guessed Asheville was like Britain in its acceptance—people didn't much care what you did as long as you didn't scare the horses.

She entered her building and pressed the button for the elevator. Franklin must have been on a ganja break—the needle indicating where the machine was never budged from the seventh floor. Giving up, she walked up the stairs to her office. She unlocked the door to find five messages on her answering machine. The smallest hope that they might be from Jonathan flickered and then died—all were from Jake McKenna, asking with growing impatience that she call him immediately—the governor needed to know how her investigation was going. Mary shook her head, knowing this was all about the paranoid McKenna trying to stay in the loop. She would have much preferred to just call Ann Chandler and talk to her, but Jake was the one leaving messages on her machine. She picked up the phone and called him; he answered on the first ring, his voice warm, enthusiastic, and totally political.

"Mary!" he said. "The governor was just asking about you. How are things going?"

"Pretty good." She sat down and put her feet up on her desk, telling him that she'd visited Trull's church, the family of the murdered boy, the DA, and the ADA who prosecuted the case in neighboring Sligo County.

"The laws are being enforced, but since there's no statute addressing sexual orientation, the charges have to reflect that," she said. "In fact, this Sligo defense attorney used homosexuality as part of his defense."

"And how does that work?" asked McKenna.

"It's pretty clever. He claimed his client was defending himself against a sexual advance from a gay man. He thought touching a gay man would send him to hell and he suffered a bout of gay panic."

Jake laughed. "Gay panic?"

"That's an actual defense in Queensland, Australia," said Mary. "I looked it up."

"But this is North Carolina, Mary. Not Australia."

"Well, they bought it in Sligo County. A lot of folks there think homosexuality is a sin."

"What about this Reverend Trull character?"

"That's where it gets interesting. The guy who got off in Sligo County is now playing on Reverend Trull's baseball team. I was going to check into that, but Campbell County's got a cop undercover at the church and I figured too many new people sitting in a small rural church might blow his cover."

"You're a fast worker, Mary." For once, Jake's admiration sounded genuine.

"I try to be," said Mary. "I know the governor's got a deadline. I'm back in Asheville, checking out a few more leads."

"In Asheville?" Jake sounded surprised.

"Yeah. I heard some gay slang down there that might have a bearing on the Campbell County case. I can find out about it here a lot faster than down there."

"Okay, Mary," he said. "You're doing a great job. I'll give the governor your report."

Mary hung up the phone, disgusted. "I just bet you will, Jake," she whispered. "Wonder if it will bear the slightest resemblance to our phone conversation."

She sat down at her desk. Since she'd given the case file back to Galloway, she didn't really have much in the way of notes. Still, she remembered the haunting words of Reverend Taylor's murdered son: *Don't worry, Dad, I won't get 74'ed here.* They made no more sense here, at her desk, than they had in the Taylor living room. She needed to talk to someone in the gay community—maybe they would have a clue. The trouble was, she didn't know any gay people here. She doubted that her neighbor, Mr. Kuntz, had had sex with anybody since 1952, and the people she'd chatted with in her karate class were either living with or married to partners of the opposite gender. Suddenly, she heard the ding of the elevator, arriving on the fifth floor.

"Franklin!" she cried aloud. He seemed to know everything that was going on Asheville. Directing her to some gay folks shouldn't be a problem. Leaping from her chair, she hurried out into the hall, catching Franklin as he was beginning to close the elevator door.

"Franklin, wait!"

He stopped, poked his head through the little brass grille. "I'm going up," he said, as if warning her that he wasn't in the mood for any riders.

"I don't want a ride," she said. "I need to ask you a question."

"What?"

"Do you know any gay men in Asheville?"

He gave her a dark look. "Not in the Biblical sense."

"No, no. That's not what I mean. I'm working on a murder case...I need to talk to somebody who's you know, in the life."

"Walkin' the walk, talkin' the talk," he chanted, his eyelids again drooping at half-mast.

She fought an urge to shake him—this man was so stoned she wondered how he could stand up, much less run an elevator car up and down a building. "You know anybody like that?"

"Pharisee."

"Pharisee?" She frowned. "As in Jesus and the Pharisees?"

Franklin pointed at the ceiling. "No, as in Pharisee the bartender at the Sky Bar, up on seven. He's gay *and* black. Come on and I'll give you a lift."

"Can you wait till I lock up my office?"

Giggling, he nodded his head. "The only bells I hear ringing are the ones in my head."

———

That afternoon, Mary was the Sky Bar's first customer. A tiny place, most of its tables were located outside, on the fire escape of the building. With an amazing view of the city and the western mountains, it was a great place to have a drink and watch the sun go down. Accommodations had been made for those with acrophobia or vertigo—a dark little bar was tucked into a room not much bigger than a closet. Behind that bar stood a handsome young man who had the face of a dark angel and the body of a football linebacker.

"Yes ma'am," he said, smiling. "What can I do for you tonight?"

"Are you Pharisee?" asked Mary.

The young man's gaze grew cautious. "Depends on who wants to know."

"I'm Mary Crow," she explained. "I have an office on the fifth floor—I'm a special prosecutor for the governor. Franklin sent me up here."

Pharisee held up his hands. "I don't know what Franklin told you, but I gave up smoking years ago."

"No, no." Mary had to laugh. "This isn't about smoking. I'm investigating crimes against gay people."

Pharisee's gaze softened. "You mean hate crimes? Beating people up?"

"Beating people to death, actually."

"Whoa, sister." He frowned. "That happen here? In Asheville?"

"No. Campbell County. A young man used an odd term before he was killed . . . have you ever heard the term '74'ed'? As in 'I'll never get 74'ed'?"

Pharisee looked at her as if she'd just been resurrected from a time capsule. "Honey, down here gettin' 74'ed means somebody's vanished on you."

Mary frowned. "I'm not sure I understand."

"Means out of here. Out of town, out of a relationship, out of someone's life. You don't have the guts to tell someone it's over, you 74 'em. You get 74'ed, then somebody's dumped you."

Mary thought of Bryan Taylor's body, crumpled by the side of the road. Somebody had certainly 74'ed him. "Is it a common expression? I mean, do they 74 people in Georgia, or New York?"

He shook his head "I'm from DC—I never heard it until I came here. Since I started working here, I hear it all the time." He turned and pulled a highball glass from the shelf. "You want to try my 74 Special?"

Mary blinked, astonished. "There's a drink named for it?"

Pharisee nodded. "Invented myself. Five years ago, when I first came to town, seemed like every gay guy in town was coming up here drinking away a broken heart."

"Only gay guys?" asked Mary. "No gay girls?"

"Not so much," said Pharisee. "Girls go crying to their friends. Guys don't do that." He grabbed a bottle of bourbon and poured a shot of it in the glass. "They'd come in here all down in the mouth, saying they just got 74'ed. I got so tired of pouring Jack Daniels and Johnny Red that I invented this drink, just to keep things interesting."

Mary leaned forward. "But why 74? It doesn't make any sense."

"It don't." Pharisee poured in a splash of some dark liquid, squeezed in some lime. "But it still means you're hurting so bad you might not recover."

Again Mary thought of Bryan Taylor.

He gave her a sly look as he started shaking the concoction up in a cocktail shaker. "You sure you're really an investigator? You sure you're not nursing a broken heart?"

Mary smiled. Like any good bartender, Pharisee tried to read his clientele. But in this case, he'd guessed wrong. She'd given up nursing the heart Walkingstick had broken—nothing she tried ever seemed to fix it. "Why does my heart matter?"

"Cause if you ain't about to cry, I'll give you the G-rated version of this drink. If you want to hide your tears, I'll give you the X-rated version."

"What's the difference?"

"The heat index. You can sit up here and get warm and fuzzy, or you can cry your eyes out and everybody'll think you just crunched a pepper."

"Oh, lay it on me, Pharisee. I want the total experience."

He poured some ginger beer in the cocktail shaker, threw in a dash of something else, then poured it in the highball glass with a long spear of cucumber. He served it to Mary with a smile. "Drink it and weep, girl."

She took a sip. It was delicious—fruity, but not sweet, the flavors complex. It wasn't until her second sip that the heat began. It seemed to build from behind her eyes, enveloping her mouth. Her tongue tingled, sweat broke out on her forehead. As she looked at Pharisee, involuntary tears began streaming down her cheeks.

"Bite the cuke," he advised.

She did, and just as suddenly, the heat was gone.

"Wow," she gasped. "That's a really good drink."

"I'm the man, sugar," said Pharisee. "Next time somebody 74 you, come see me. Pharisee'll fix you up."

"How much do I owe you?" asked Mary, her eyes beginning to stream again as a new wave of heat kicked in.

"On the house, baby. You fighting for us gay dudes, you okay."

SIXTEEN

BY THREE FIFTEEN GUDGER had learned that the black Miata pulled up in his driveway was registered to one Mary Crow, address Asheville, North Carolina. Her driving record was clean; she had no prior judgments, no outstanding warrants. The person she claimed to be looking for, Jonathan Walkingstick, did not live anywhere on Kedron Road. In fact, no Jonathan Walkingstick lived anywhere in Campbell County. "What the fuck?" he'd asked his old buddy Crump, who'd called in the plate numbers for him. "Why would some woman from Asheville be on my property, asking directions for somebody who doesn't exist?"

"What'd she look like?" asked Crump.

"Medium tall. Slender, short dark hair. Wore tan pants, turquoise earrings. Looked kind of Indian. Gave off a funny vibe—almost like a cop." Gudger strode into his bathroom and closed the door. He didn't want that idiot kid to hear any of this.

"Some dark-haired girl cop was here, Gudge," Crump said. "I talked with her the other day. She's the governor's super cop, come to light a fire under Drake about that gay kid's case."

"But why would she come out here? And talk to Shithead?"

Crump cleared his throat. "Uh, I think Shithead might have been talking to her."

Gudger went cold inside. "What?"

"She was at the station, talking to the new hire. Then she started asking about your stepdaughter's case. The new guy called me in, 'cause he knew I'd worked the case. The woman claimed that Shithead had come to see her about it, in Asheville."

"Asheville? How did Shithead get up there? He's afraid to step off the front porch."

"I don't know, but she knew all about Sam. I told her your kid was a head case and you were a stand-up guy."

"What did she say then?" Gudger was grasping his cell phone so hard his fingers had gone numb.

"Nothing—we talked about families for a minute, then she said that stepparenting was dicey work. I don't think she's here about you, man," Crump assured him. "She's all about hanging that queer's murder on Trull. She probably drove out to your place to tell Shithead he was crazy."

"I still can't believe that little asshole went all the way to Asheville to talk to some girl cop about Sam."

"I don't know, buddy. You'll have to ask him."

"Yeah," said Gudger. "That's exactly what I'm going to do. Thanks for running that plate for me, Crump. See you next week at poker."

Gudger clicked off the phone, then jerked the door open, expecting to see Chase standing there, eavesdropping. The room, however, was empty. All he saw was his bedspread smooth on his mattress, his dresser clean and uncluttered. Amy's side of the room was considerably messier, but he couldn't deal with Amy's slovenliness now. Now he needed to deal with Amy's son. With his heart beating like something trying to claw its way out of his chest, he pocketed his cell phone and headed for the den. He had to find out how bad this was, how deep this went.

Shithead was sitting on the couch, watching some TV show about the Lewis and Clark expedition. He walked over, grabbed a handful of the boy's hair, and lifted him to his feet. Chase's face contorted in pain.

"Ow!" he cried, trying to squirm away. "That hurts!"

"You might be hurting a lot more in a few minutes. Turn off that TV, boy. You and I are gonna have a little talk."

He released the boy's hair. Sniffling back tears, the kid grabbed the remote. The TV screen went black.

"What's the matter?" Chase asked. "I was just watching the History Channel."

Gudger stood there, legs spread, arms akimbo, glaring at the child. Though the medicine he'd brought the boy had turned his red blisters into a sick shade of pink, the kid still looked like his face had been cooked in a microwave. Gudger let him stand there for a long moment, then he spoke.

"How the hell did you hook up with Mary Crow?"

The boy paled beneath his welts. "I-I don't know what you're talking about."

"You don't know the pretty gal you were talking to when I came home?"

"I-don't know …"

"What do you mean you don't know? I know." Gudger grinned. He'd caught the boy, dead to rights. "Mary Crow works for the governor. She came down here to poke around that gay murder case."

The boy had no answer. He just stood there, his eyes wide with fear.

Gudger knelt down, nose to nose with Chase. "What I really wonder is why that particular woman, who works ninety miles away in Asheville, was on my front porch, asking directions to someone who doesn't exist?"

The boy's chin began to quiver, but then he set his jaw and lowered his head, focusing his gaze on the floor.

"You know what I think?" Gudger continued as the boy stared at his shoelaces. "I don't think you've told me the truth all week. I don't think you've told me the truth since the day I tore down that stupid pool."

He made no response, so Gudger kept on.

"You said you spent the day playing in the creek and just lost track of the time. But I think maybe you were doing something else. Something you had no business doing. Am I right or am I wrong?"

The boy stood silent.

"You know, Chase, real men tell the truth. I bet if your daddy were here, he'd look me in the eye and tell me exactly what had happened that day."

The boy lifted his head, his eyes suddenly dark with hatred. "If my daddy were here, he'd break your jaw."

A rage went through Gudger—there seemed no way he could escape the ghost of John Buchanan. He felt him in his wife's embrace, had seen him in the disgusted curl of Samantha's lip—now he was here, in the person of his sniveling, knock-kneed son, threatening to break his jaw. This was it; he would hear from John Buchanan's ghost no longer.

"Oh, yeah?" he said, rising to his feet. "We'll just see about that, boy."

He stalked into the kitchen, grabbed a bottle of hot sauce from the kitchen cabinet, then returned. "I'll give you one more chance . . . why were you talking to Mary Crow?"

Chase looked at him, his mouth shut, but his eyes defiant.

"Okay, buddy," said Gudger. "Don't say I didn't warn you." He uncapped the bottle of red-orange liquid and started sprinkling it all over the boy's poison ivy welts. Seconds later tears came to the boy's eyes, then he started twisting and squirming as if fire ants were attacking him. He turned to run to the bathroom, but Gudger grabbed his hair and held him in place.

"You answer my question, you can wash that stuff off. Until then, you're staying right here."

———

Chase held out through two more applications of hot sauce, then as Gudger uncorked the bottle for the third time, he started to cry.

"I went to see her about Sam," he confessed, gasping as snot began to drip from his nose.

"How'd you get up there?" cried Gudger. "Asheville's a long way away."

"I hitched a ride on a peach truck."

Gudger looked at the boy, stunned. The fact that Shithead had hitched a ride to anywhere seemed as unlikely as his going out for the football team. "What did you tell her about Samantha?"

Twitching, the boy furiously scratched the welts on his arms. "I told her I didn't think the cops here had done enough about her."

"What did she say?"

"She said she'd look into it." He wiped his nose. "Then she brought me home."

Gudger glared at him, hot sauce in hand. "What else?"

"Nothing," the boy said, miserable. "There wasn't nothing else to tell."

"Why was she up here on the porch?"

"She said nobody ever answers our phone, so she came by. She said Sam probably ran off with some boy, just like everybody else thinks."

Gudger looked at the kid. He doubted he was telling the whole story, but between the poison ivy and the hot sauce and the dripping snot, he was a mess. It was going on five o'clock; Amy would be home soon. Though Amy was as flat a doormat as you'd find, she would not be pleased if she came home and found her precious son looking like this. "I'm not done with you, but for now, go get that stuff washed off."

Weeping, the little boy ran to the bathroom.

"Just remember I gave you the chance to act like a man, Chase," Gudger yelled through the door. "So don't you go whining to your mama when she comes home."

———

While the boy went to clean himself off, Gudger retreated to the garage. He closed and locked the door behind him, then he reached behind the paint cans on one high shelf and pulled out a bottle of Wild Turkey. He took a long pull, trying to slow the edgy thrumming that echoed in his head. He needed to calm down, think about the best thing to do. Had Shithead actually put everything together? All the stupid kid did was read books and watch the History Channel. Yet he'd connected the dots better than every cop in the county and then blabbed his stupid, crackpot theory to the governor's girl in Asheville.

"Damn!" he whispered, taking another swallow of whiskey. "Who knew the little fuck was so smart?"

Now the question was, how much had Shithead figured out? And what had he told this Mary Crow? She'd seemed friendly enough when they talked, going on about being a stepparent. Still, there was something about her—behind the mascara and the pretty smile, her eyes were bright as a hawk's, watching him in a way that made him nervous inside.

Suddenly, he heard a car coming up the driveway. For an instant he panicked, thinking it was Mary Crow coming back, this time bringing real cops with her. But when he looked out the window—he saw only Amy's Dodge. *Damn*, he thought. *I need to get back inside before Shithead rats me out.* But before that, he needed to call Smiley. Whatever trouble Shithead might cause would be a picnic in the park compared to what Smiley could do. Taking a steadying slug of whiskey, he pulled out his cell phone and punched in the first number on speed dial. Smiley answered immediately, his voice a growl.

"Smiley, this is Gudger."

"Yeah?"

Gudger swallowed hard, the Wild Turkey threatening to fly back up his throat. "We may have a problem."

"So talk to me." Smiley's accent was Eastern—New York, New Jersey—it all sounded the same to Gudger.

"It's my wife's kid," explained Gudger. "He's cooked up some crazy theory about his sister—you know, the girl. A couple of days ago he hitched a ride up to Asheville and got the governor's cop in on it."

"Are you fucking kidding me?"

"No. I just found out a few minutes ago."

"How much does he know for real?"

"I don't know. I couldn't get it out of him."

"How much does the cop know?"

"Don't know that either," said Gudger. "But today I came home and she was on my front porch, talking to the kid."

"The cop's a she?"

"Yeah."

"Jesus, Gudger. Your stepkid rats you out to the governor's cop? What the hell kind of family are you running over there?"

"I don't know," Gudger said miserably. "I had no idea the boy was this smart."

"Yeah? Well, I had no idea you were this stupid." Smiley's voice could have etched glass.

Again, the sour taste of whiskey roiled in the back of Gudger's throat. He stood there, watching out the window for Amy, suddenly as twitchy as Chase covered in hot sauce. Finally, Smiley spoke.

"This cop got a name?"

"Crow. Mary Crow," Gudger answered quickly, a small tendril of relief inching toward him. Smiley was now focusing on Mary Crow instead of him.

"Mary Crow." Smiley repeated the name, as if he were making notes on something. Gudger waited, tapping his foot, eager to offer up what other information Smiley wanted. After several moments, he spoke again.

"I gotta tell you, Gudger. This is way off my grid. I gotta call my boss."

Gudger felt a great rippling in his bowels. Smiley was bad enough; he didn't even want to think about his boss. He clutched the phone harder. "Who's that?"

"Doesn't matter, but he'll probably send somebody to see you. And sooner than later, probably."

"But when? Tonight? Tomorrow? What are they going to do?"

Smiley growled. "I don't know, you stupid jackass. But odds are real good you aren't gonna like it."

SEVENTEEN

SAM AWOKE WITH A start. She'd been in a terrifying, coma-like sleep, aware of only a thick darkness that pressed down upon her like a coffin. *This is what death must be like*, a voice told her. No angels, no tunnel of light, nothing but an impenetrable emptiness that went on forever. It would just be her, all alone with no light and no sound—only her own consciousness, screaming for release, until eons hence, it, too, would flicker and die, joining the black void that surrounded it. The notion terrified her so that she screamed and pulled herself back from some unseen precipice. She sat up in bed, gasping and dizzy, grateful for the anemic fluorescent light that buzzed from the ceiling.

"I'm alive," she whispered, trembling—amazed that her lungs were still pulling in air, that her mouth still formed words. She wondered, for a moment, how her mind could have concocted a dream of such horror, then she remembered the Turk and his tea. He must have put something in it, to make her dream such a thing, she decided. A drug to subdue her, or maybe just frighten her into submission. Whatever it was, she wasn't drinking it again. She didn't care if he pinched her shoulder until she died. She'd swallowed her last cup of Yusuf's tea.

She looked around the room. She was still in the second one—the silent one without Ivan's bloodstains on the wall. A tray of food sat on the bureau, next to her bed. A cheese sandwich, covered in plastic wrap, an apple. As she stared at it, her stomach gave a loud growl; she realized she had no idea how long she'd been asleep. Hours? Days? She couldn't tell—no light seeped from around the window, and the florescent flickered all the time.

She reached for the tray and unwrapped the sandwich. Though the bread was stale and the cheese gummy, it still tasted wonderful. She wolfed it down, wishing she had another. She ate the apple, then suddenly, her stomach began to cramp. Throwing off her blanket, she hurried to the bathroom. As she sat down on the toilet, she saw that someone had left a cardboard box on the back of the toilet. Inside, she found a toothbrush and toothpaste, a small bar of soap, and a box of sanitary napkins.

"Are you kidding me?" She opened the box and pulled out one of the thick, cumbersome pads. She'd used them only once, for her first period, when she was twelve years old. Every month since she'd inserted tampons, preferring them to the bulky alternative.

Suddenly, she started to laugh. "They must want to keep my vagina clean of foreign objects." Disgusted, she stuffed the pad back in the box. How strange to be in a place where being a virgin made you special. At school, it made you the butt of jokes, put you on the Loser List of girls who never got asked out. But how could she have helped it? She was new at her school, and her mother made her come straight home every day and keep Chase safe from the crackheads next door. She barely got a chance to glance at a boy, much less have sex with one.

As her gut gave an ominous rumble, she put her head in her hands and sighed. She'd had no idea how good she'd had it, back then. Right now she would give anything to be at that crappy little duplex, playing

Clue with Chase, trying to convince him that their drugged-out neighbors were too stoned to break down their door.

"But that was then," she told herself sternly, wiping her eyes. "This is now." She flushed the toilet, then unwrapped the red toothbrush that lay in the box. As she brushed her teeth, she gazed in the mirror. Was this the same shattered glass she'd looked at earlier and decided she would kill herself with if things became unbearable?

Yes, she decided, staring at her kaleidoscopic reflection. *It was. And I will. And I'll take as many of these bastards with me as I can.*

She finished cleaning her teeth and rinsed her mouth in the yellowish water. After that she returned to her room to see if she could get anything beyond a shopping channel on that dopey-looking TV. If she could get a weather report, she might be able to figure out where she was and how long she'd been here. She'd just clicked the set on when the pipes in the bathroom started banging.

Ignoring the noise, she twisted the dial of the ancient TV. Through a screen of thick snow, she heard only Spanish programming—an overheated soap opera, then a woman chattering on what sounded like a talk show. She twisted the dial around three times, then turned the set off. Silence resumed, broken only by the banging pipes. Sinking to the floor, she buried her head in hands. In the first room she'd at least been connected with people—the girls going back and forth, Ivan bringing her food and tales of his Russian boyfriends. Here she had nothing but horrific dreams and crappy plumbing.

As she sat there, longing to hear someone speak a language she understood, she grew angry at the noisy pipes. "Shut up!" she finally cried, getting to her feet and hurrying into the bathroom. Maybe if she flushed the toilet again it would be quiet. She reached over to pull the lever on the thing, when she realized that the clanging wasn't coming from the toilet at all—it was coming from the pipe beneath the sink.

She knelt down, wondering if the U-trap was loose. Suddenly, the tapping grew much louder, taking on a new rhythm. Three taps, followed by a brief silence, followed by three more taps, followed by another silence. She sat back on her heels, her heart pounding. Was someone in the next bathroom? Were they trying to send her a message?

She reached for her toothbrush. Crouching beneath the sink again, she started tapping on the pipes herself—three shorts, three longs, then three short taps again. SOS in Morse code, a silly thing Chase had once taught her from one of his detective novels, in case they were ever on a sinking ship. She finished tapping her message, then listened. She heard nothing for so long that she decided she must have dreamed the whole thing, but then, just as she was getting to her feet, she heard her message coming back through the pipes—three shorts, three longs, then three shorts again.

Oh my God! she thought. *There's someone on the other side of that wall!*

She tapped back, this time just three short ones. The tapper answered in kind, then Sam saw the U-trap beneath her sink begin to wiggle. She realized that her sink and the one next door must drain into a single pipe—if she could remove the collar that covered the hole where the pipe entered the wall, then she might be able to talk to whoever was tapping. Sam crawled beneath the sink, wiped some mildew away from the sink baffle, and pressed her mouth close to the wall. "Can you hear me?" she whispered, praying that she wasn't blundering into a trap set by the Turk, or worse, that guy Boris.

At first she heard nothing. For a moment she thought it was a trap and the Turk would come barreling through the door to pour more tea down her throat. But then the tapping began again, this time rapid and urgent. When it stopped, Sam spoke again.

"Try to take off the collar that covers your sink pipe," she whispered to whomever it was. "I'll do the same."

She got to her feet, desperate to find something to loosen the collar with. The medicine cabinet was empty; the shards of the broken mirror would only break further in attempting to loosen a screw. Beyond that, the bathroom offered only a toothbrush and the box of sanitary napkins. She hurried to the bedroom, checking the drawers of the bureau. They held nothing beyond sci-fi paperbacks, printed in an alphabet she couldn't read. She looked under the bed, in the closet, but found nothing. She tried to pry off the TV's antenna, but it was attached firmly to the back of the set. Desperate, she lifted her mattress and looked at the box springs that supported it. Though they were old and squeaked every time she turned over in bed, they were far too strong for her to break off.

"Damn!" she whispered. "There's got to be something!"

She circled the room like a caged animal, searching for something she could make into a tool. There was nothing—the room had only a bed, a TV, and a single piece of furniture. Frustrated, she began to rub the place on her shoulder where the Turk had squeezed. As she moved her bra strap out of the way, she suddenly realized she'd had a tool all along! Quickly, she lifted her T-shirt and took off her bra. The little metal hooks that fastened the thing around her just might also loosen those screws!

Pulling her T-shirt back on, she ran to the bathroom, bra in hand. She ducked under the sink and listened for any sounds from the other side of the wall. No more tapping, but a scraping sound reached her ears, as if her companion was mirroring her efforts in the other bathroom.

She looked at the hooks of her bra—two, both tiny, both bent from many trips through the washing machine. She took the least bent one and began to work with it. At first the thing slipped off the screw every time she tried to turn it, but she figured out that if she leaned forward and applied pressure as she turned it, it would at least stay in place. With sweat trickling into her eyes, she kept pushing and trying to turn the stubborn screw. As the ends of her fingers grew numb with the effort, she decided it was hopeless, that she and whoever-it-was next door would never be able to see each other. Then, as she gave a final try, she felt the screw turn a fraction of an inch. She changed hands and worked on, pressing the bra hook into the screw until it slipped out, then beginning all over again. As her legs began to cramp, the first screw loosened to the point that she could grab it in her fingers. She unscrewed the first one. It dropped to the floor with a *ping*. She was halfway home.

Wiping the sweat from her forehead, she put the bra hook to work on the second. This one was rusted, even harder to turn than the first.

"No!" she whispered. "You aren't stopping me now!" She took the other, more bent bra hook and scraped the rust from the base of the screw. When she had a small pile of brown filings on the bathroom floor, she started in on the screw. At first, she couldn't budge it, then all at once, as if something had given way, the thing began to move. Desperately, she turned it, faster and faster. Then the second screw was falling to the floor, the collar of the sink pipe spinning away from the wall.

With a fervent prayer that she wasn't going to find the Turk or that creep Boris leering at her from the other side of the wall, she crouched down and peered through the hole. At first she saw only the dark backside of more plumbing, but then she saw cracks of light as another fixture loosened. She heard a scrape, then the sharp *ding* of metal against metal, then she saw the person who'd done all the tapping—a pretty blond girl whose tear-streaked face reminded her of her own.

EIGHTEEN

It took her an hour of slow sipping, but Mary finally finished her 74 Special. With her head spinning, she slid off her bar stool and stuffed a ten-dollar bill in Pharisee's tip jar.

"You okay, sweetheart?" he asked, grinning.

"Uh-huh," she said, her mouth still tingling from the spicy drink. "But I'm glad I didn't sit on the fire escape."

"Fire escape's only for the wine and beer crowd." Pharisee laughed. "All the 74 Special folks have to stay in here. We don't want nobody splatted down on the sidewalk."

"I guess not." Mary wobbled slightly on her feet. "I'm going back to my office."

"Come see me anytime. I know how hard lawyering can get."

Mary laughed, thinking of her mission to enforce a law that wasn't even on the books. "Pharisee, you have no idea."

Holding on to the bannister of the staircase, she made her way down to her office and flopped down on the small sofa that sat beneath her west-facing windows. As she looked out at the mountains, Pharisee's cocktail continued to soften the orange and fuchsia sunset, putting the troubles of her day far away. The drink really did dull the sharp edges of a broken heart, she decided. The danger was growing to like it too much—lingering in a 74 Special–induced haze when the next lover appeared on the horizon. With the sun casting the room in a rosy glow, her gaze wandered to the huge wall map of North Carolina, compliments of Ann Chandler. Three hundred miles to the east, Chandler was sitting in the statehouse, in Raleigh. Fifty miles west, in Hartsville, her friends Jerry and Ginger Cochran were expecting their first child. Somewhere, on a map much vaster than North Carolina, the lines of latitude and longitude would converge on the exact spot that Jonathan and Lily occupied. She'd always pictured them in South America, speaking Spanish, losing themselves in thick jungles where parrots squawked in the trees. But she had no real reason to think that—they could be anywhere—Canada, Europe, even Asia. They had steep mountains in Thailand and the natives were friendly enough not to turn Jonathan over to the cops.

"You bastard," she whispered, Pharisee's concoction loosening the tight lock she kept on her anger. "You could at least send me a message. You could at least let me know you're all right." All of a sudden little Chase Buchanan flashed across her mind and she thought that she and the boy were much alike—they'd both awakened one day to find the people they loved gone without a clue.

She stared at the map until her eyelids grew heavy. Lying back on the sofa, she was no longer in her office, but walking down a long highway that stretched through flat acres planted in corn and soybeans. Two figures plodded along ahead of her—one tall and angular, the other short, struggling to keep up the pace. At first she paid them no mind, then she realized that it was Jonathan and Lily. *Jonathan!* she called. *Wait for me!* They turned and stopped. She raced to catch up, but when she got within a few feet of them, Jonathan lifted his hand. *Don't come down this road*, he warned her. *You might get 74'ed.*

Mary sat upright on the couch, her heart thudding. She looked around the room, fully expecting to see Jonathan. But instead she saw only her desk, a bicycle she'd bought but seldom rode, and the map of North Carolina. She licked her lips, her mouth dry and wanting water. The dream had seemed so real—Jonathan standing there, Lily beside him. She'd better start watching what she drank and not make it a habit of visiting the Sky Bar when Pharisee was on duty.

Trying to shake off her fuzziness, she got up from the sofa and headed for the bathroom. As she passed by the big state map, she paused, wondering if Jonathan had fooled everybody and was living somewhere in Carolina, deep in the mountains, or even on one of the islands that dotted the Atlantic coast. Starting at Currituck Sound, she slowly traced the coastline of the state—the outer banks that curved south to Beaufort, then narrowed to the tiny thread of land that was part national seashore, part small beach towns that hovered on the edge of the ocean—Surf City, Ocean City, Topsail Beach. She'd traced down to the city of Wilmington, when her heart stopped. Running directly through the middle of the town was State Route 74.

"It's a road," she whispered. "74's a highway!"

She grabbed a red marker from her desk and began tracing the highway's route. It crossed the entire southern part of the state, traversing both Campbell and Sligo Counties, going from the Atlantic coast to the Georgia Mountains, Wilmington to Murphy. Though it was one of those older highways eclipsed by the interstate system, if you lived in certain counties, 74 would be the fastest way out of town, if you wanted to escape a relationship.

"No wonder I didn't put it together," she said. "I always drive I-40."

Suddenly, she started to laugh. What a fool she'd been! She'd been trying to make 74 a gay sex position when, all along, it had been a road. She stared at the map, stunned. But why had she, tipsy and dreaming from a drink, come up with this while Reverend Taylor had not?

"Because in Campbell County, 74 is Jackson Highway," she whispered.

She sat down at her desk, her hands shaking. Her first impulse was to call Galloway, but it was late and she still wasn't totally sober. She didn't want to call him up slurring her words as she explained her theory about what getting 74'ed really meant. But first thing tomorrow morning she would go back and tell him all about it. Then they could look at Bryan Taylor's murder with new eyes.

———

At nine the next morning, aided by three aspirin and a mega-cup of coffee, she stood in Galloway's cubicle, her map of North Carolina rolled out across his desk.

"You're telling me getting 74'ed is not a gay sex thing?" he asked, staring at her bloodshot eyes.

"No, it's not. I went back to Asheville, talked to a gay bartender. It's slang for getting ditched. If you get 74'ed, it means your lover has left you. They even have a drink for it."

He chuckled. "Like 'Fifty Ways to Leave Your Lover'?"

"Yeah. Except here in Campbell County, there might be a more sinister connotation to it." She pointed to the ribbon of Jackson Highway that traversed the county. "This is Highway 74."

He squinted at the map. "*La carretera del dolor*?"

"What does that mean?" asked Mary.

"Road of Sorrows," he explained. "The Latinos say it carries them far from home to a lot of hard work and pain."

"Well, the Latinos are on to something. It *is* the road of sorrows. Look at poor dead Bryan Taylor and Alan Bratcher."

"They were both dumped within two miles of Clancy's bar," Galloway admitted. "But this highway runs the length of the state. Probably half a dozen bodies are found along it every year."

"Okay," said Mary. "I'll give you that. But just for argument's sake, look back through your case files and see if you've got any other Campbell County deaths along 74."

He leaned back in his chair, dark brows drawn over those startling blue eyes. He started to say something, then stopped. "Okay," he finally said, turning to his computer. "But only because you're the governor's super cop. How far back do you want to go?"

"Three years," said Mary.

"Just as long as your boss has been in office?"

"Yeah. Everything on her watch."

His fingers flew over the computer keys. Mary watched as the computer churned, the official county seal spinning like a golden disk. A few moments later, the records appeared—all Campbell County investigated deaths in the past three years. Galloway scrolled through them, gleaning the particulars of the cases.

"Okay," he finally said. "Excluding Alan Bratcher, who's Sligo County's problem, in the three years of Ann Chandler's administration, three Campbell County residents have been found dead along Highway 74. Other than Bryan Taylor, a sixteen-year-old white female was found murdered three years ago east of the Poplar Springs Road intersection, six months later another female was found dead of undetermined causes a mile west of the Gaston County line." Galloway frowned at the screen. "Here's something interesting. Your little hitchhiking buddy? His sister's car was found empty a month ago, again near Poplar Springs Road."

Mary leaned over the desk, peering at the computer screen. "You found Samantha Buchanan's car on 74?"

"I didn't, but Crump did." Galloway read more of the case file. "Lights on and motor running, purse untouched inside the car."

Mary felt a thrum of excitement. "What about the other two girls?"

Galloway gave her an odd look. "What about them? I thought you were researching gay conspiracies."

"Indulge me," Mary said, trying to tamp down her enthusiasm over the two cold cases. "I used to be a prosecutor. Murder still gets my juices flowing."

With a snort, Galloway turned back to the computer. "Tiffani Wallace had a pretty thick jacket, but all petty stuff—shoplifting, D&D. She was found beaten and strangled to death. Maria Gomez was a Latina who'd worked on a sweet potato farm. Her injuries were consistent with a hit-and-run—the only thing odd about her was she had defensive wounds on her hands and arms."

Mary turned her attention away from the computer and back to the map still spread across Galloway's desk. "Can you show me exactly where these people were found?"

"Not on that map." Galloway grabbed a handful of push pins and walked over to the huge map of Campbell County that was tacked to the wall.

"Bryan Taylor was here, just inside the county line," he said, placing a red pin close to the western edge of the county. "Maria Gomez was here." He stuck a blue pin near the right border of the map. "And Tiffani was here." A yellow pin went in the western edge of the county. "Samantha Buchanan's abandoned car was about half a mile from where they found Tiffani's body." He stuck a green pin close to the yellow one.

Mary frowned at the map. "Do you know which side of the road everybody was found on?"

Galloway walked back to his desk to recheck his files. "Bryan Taylor was found by the side of the eastbound lane, within a mile of Clancy's bar," said Galloway. "The women were both found on the westbound side of the road, as was Samantha Buchanan's car."

"So whoever dumped them was going west. Presumably coming from the east." Mary stared at her state map on Galloway's desk. "So the killer or killers might have been coming from Charlotte or Hickory or even Gastonia."

Galloway shrugged. "They could have been coming from any-where. I-77 and I-85 go through Charlotte—not that far away."

"And the South Carolina line is about ten miles away?" Mary traced the road that ran due south, between Tiffani Wallace and Samantha Buchanan's pins.

"Yeah," said Galloway. "What are you getting at?"

"I don't know." Mary shook her head. "Maybe nothing. Is there somewhere I can set my computer up here? Or do I have to go back to the Gastonia Holiday Inn?"

"Nobody's using the cubicle next to mine," he said. "The sheriff probably won't like it, but I won't tell if you won't."

"What about Crump and all the other guys who wander through here?"

"They won't care. I'll only be here a few more minutes. I'm inter-viewing some people about our boy Honeycutt."

"Your teammate?" asked Mary.

"Yeah." Galloway stuffed his badge and ID in the pocket of his shirt. "Seems the stud muffin has an ex-girlfriend who does not hold such a high opinion of his batting ability."

"Is she a member of Trull's church?"

"She used to be," replied Galloway. "But she quit."

"Wow," said Mary. "That could be interesting."

"I'll let you know if I find out anything the governor might like to know."

"Thanks," said Mary.

Galloway lifted a hand in farewell. "Enjoy your time in the office."

"Enjoy your time with the fuming ex." Mary took a step toward the empty cubicle, then stopped. "And be careful, Galloway."

"I'm always careful," Galloway called over his shoulder as he walked out the door.

NINETEEN

WHILE MARY CROW WAS setting up next to Victor Galloway's office, Ralph Gudger was making another patrol of his house—marching through the kitchen, then the den, then onto the front porch where he would, sentry-like, reconnoiter his property. He'd kept watch throughout the night, as Amy and Shithead slept in their beds, listening for a twig to snap beneath his den window, a muffled footstep on his front porch.

"This is how they fuck with you," he whispered, holding his big Glock 17 close as he remembered what the old Nam vets had told him, back at Fort Bragg. *When you thought the gooks were coming at you, they didn't. You'd wait for hours, sweat dripping, hearing nothing but your heart beating. Then, when the Sarge called a stand-down, they'd open up on you. Just as you relaxed they'd come out of the jungle, screaming like demons from hell. It wasn't the shooting that drove you crazy... it was the waiting.*

He watched the sun come up, fixed a pot of coffee, then, after Amy left for work, he decided to call Smiley again. He was too old for this shit—his knees were stiff and his eyelids felt like sandpaper. He could volunteer to meet Smiley's people, to explain things to them in a logical way. He'd just started to punch in the number when he felt an ominous rumbling in his gut. Forgetting about the phone, he raced to the bathroom, reaching the toilet just in time.

"That goddamned Olive Oyl," he moaned as a wave of fiery diarrhea gripped him. "All this is his fault."

He leaned over and cradled his head on his knees. As much as he wanted to blame the boy, at heart he knew it wasn't Chase's fault. The true blame belonged to a younger, dumber version of himself, fifteen years ago. 1999, or maybe 2000. He'd finished his shift, gone to the Am Vet club in Gastonia, and put a five-dollar bet on the Braves. Though he'd always thought gambling was a fool's game with odds never in your favor, for some reason he'd placed a bet. Chipper Jones had driven in the winning run in the bottom of the ninth, and he'd walked away with two hundred bucks. From then on he was hooked—playing the slots at Cherokee, the poker machines at the 7-Eleven, putting bets on whatever sport was in season. Three years later he owed so much money he couldn't sleep at night. Then his bookie sent a barrel-shaped man named Smiley to see him. Though he was a pudgy five feet of gold jewelry and polyester pants, something about Smiley terrified him.

"You send us some lot lizards, we'll forgive the debt," the man's accent was so thick Gudger felt like he'd been dropped into a *Sopranos* rerun.

"Lot lizards?" he'd asked. "What the hell's a lot lizard?"

"Girls, mostly." Smiley reached across the bar for some peanuts, gold necklaces glinting through a dark forest of chest hair. "But sometimes boys, too. We'll let you know."

"For what?" he asked, still not understanding.

"For sex, you idiot." Smiley frowned. "Don't you-all fuck down here in Nawth Car-o-line-a?"

"Yeah, we fuck."

"Well, that's what you'd be supplying. Fresh fuck meat, for us."

Gudger laughed—he'd never been asked such a thing. "So where do I get this meat? The mall?"

"No, asshole. They're the kids you're collaring anyway. The druggies and the drifters—instead of taking them to jail, you just give 'em to us." Smiley tossed a peanut and caught it in his mouth, like a bass snapping a dragonfly. "It's a win-win. They stay out of the pokey, you get 'em out of your hair. Street crime goes way down, police department's bottom line improves. Your captain gives you a fucking medal for being such a good cop."

"Where do you take them?" Gudger asked.

Smiley gave a low chuckle. "Everywhere."

He couldn't, at first, believe what he was hearing. "But some aren't bad kids … some have families looking for them."

"So?" said Smiley. "Most wind up doing this anyway. We do 'em a favor—make sure they have a place to stay, bail money if they get caught. It beats hooking up with street pimps."

"But what if they come back? And finger me?"

Suddenly Smiley's eyes seemed like pools of darkness. "They don't come back, Gudger. Not ever." He slid a twenty to the bartender and stood up. "Don't wait too long on this," he warned. "I got another cop on the line in Gaston County, but they told me to give you first dibs. You owe us some big bucks. You don't pay up, some guys not as nice as me are gonna come looking for you. And they already know where you live."

The next day, Gudger made the deal. Twelve lizards, girls unless they let him know otherwise. They couldn't be so strung out that they couldn't move. Other than that, it didn't matter—black or white, fat or thin, blonde or dark—the clients didn't care.

"These truckers ain't lookin' for love," said Smiley. "Just a little pussy while they gas up their tanks."

Relegating that conversation back to memory, Gudger wiped his bottom and flushed the john. But as he pulled up his trousers, his first lizard came to mind. Lucinda, a sixteen-year-old crack addict he'd arrested many times for shoplifting and petty theft. She was weaving down Main Street when he picked her up. Pretty, in the hard way of street girls, she assumed he was taking her to jail. Told him she was grateful to have a warm bed and a couple of good meals. But he didn't take her to jail that night; he took her far out into the country, to a deserted road where a white panel van waited. His palms had grown sweaty as Smiley got out of the van and walked up to peer into the back of his cruiser. For a long moment he just watched as the terrified girl cried, shrinking back from the door, then he gave Gudger a thumbs up. "You got a keeper there, Gudger."

They'd had to wrangle her out of the car. She started shrieking, kicking and clawing like a little bobcat. When one of her feet connected with Smiley's jaw, he took a syringe out of his pocket and plunged it into her butt. She looked pleadingly at Gudger for one awful moment, then she went limp. They shoved her in the back of the van and closed the door. "One down." Smiley lifted a finger as he climbed back in the driver's seat. "Eleven more to go."

He'd gone home and gotten drunk that night, trying to erase the memory of the look in Lucinda's eyes. For months she haunted him, railing at him in dreams, appearing over his shoulder as he shaved. Then her image began to fade as he brought Smiley more girls. Though his first dozen girls ultimately grew to a dozen dozen, Lucinda's look of terror never left him.

"Let go of it!" he said as he gazed at himself in the mirror. "All that was years ago. You did what you had to do. Those kids had no future, anyway."

He left the bathroom and walked into the den. Shithead was sitting in a little puddle of sunlight, eating a bowl of cereal, staring at the TV. The sight of the little pock-marked weasel made him angry all over again. He ought to take off his belt and give the kid a taste of what his father used to do to him. But that would leave bruises— marks that Amy would take exception to. Right now, he needed peace inside his home. Better to put Mr. Charles Oliver Buchanan on the right path in less visible ways. "What are you watching, Olive Oyl?"

"The History Channel," the boy muttered, slurping Cheerios. "About the Mafia."

He looked at the screen. Men who closely resembled Smiley sat at a restaurant, shoveling spaghetti in their mouths, then a row of bloody corpses came on, all victims of the St. Valentine's Day massacre. Once again, his bowels clenched, but this time he made no move toward the bathroom. He had nothing left to donate to the toilet. Instead he left Shithead to his TV show and went back to the kitchen to get his phone. He was about to punch in Smiley's number when he wondered if he ought not to just go about his business, like normal. Forget about calling and making any plans to meet. Just go out to his garage, start the new tractor, get some mowing done. He had a frigging Glock 17—at ten rounds a second he could have his own little St. Valentine's Day massacre right here in the front yard. And it wouldn't be much of a stretch to convince his own police force that he'd acted in self-defense. Deciding that was a much healthier way to deal with everything, he opened the refrigerator and grabbed his fresh carton of Jo-Jo chocolate milk. He'd just taken two long swallows when he heard a car in the driveway. He put the chocolate milk down and hurried into the living room. A black

Mercedes sedan with smoked windows was bearing down upon the house, its wheels raising a cloud of white dust.

"Oh shit," Gudger whispered. He hadn't expected anything like this. He'd imagined thugs in pickups, or a rogue cop on the take, like him. This looked serious—*professional* was the word that came to mind. He realized he would have to approach things differently. Checking the safety of his Glock, he stuck the gun in the waistband of his pants, just beneath the small of his back. With its barrel pointing at his ass, he pulled his baggy gray sweatshirt over it and hurried out to the driveway. The car, a long, evil slug of a thing, pulled up to a stop ten feet in front of him. While the driver stayed in place, the front seat passenger emerged—a tall, beefy guy whose long black hair and beard gave him the look of a bear dressed in a shirt that strained to close around his neck. Without a word, he walked over and opened the back door behind the driver's seat.

"Are you Gudger?" came a voice from inside the car.

Gudger stepped closer to the car. A bald man in a white suit sat on the edge of the seat. His eyes were nearly colorless and his high cheekbones gave him a feline look—as if he might grow fangs and claws and leopard spots at the smallest provocation.

Gudger nodded, his heart beating like a drum.

"I am Boyko." The man patted the seat beside him. "We need to talk."

Before he could move or speak or even breathe, the bear-man who held the door open pulled his sweatshirt up over his head, taking his Glock and thrusting it so hard between his legs that his knees gave way. He fell to the driveway, paralyzed with pain as big hands pawed him, checking for more weapons. When no more were found, the goon lifted him up and threw him in the backseat as if he were a bag of dog chow.

Spots glittered on the backsides of his eyes as the man called Boyko started to laugh. "Never is it polite to greet people with hidden guns," he said, speaking in odd, accented English. "I expected better of you. Maybe is time you learn some manners."

By the time he could breathe again, they were heading back down the driveway. He turned in the seat, tried to grab for the door handle, only to find there was no door handle on his side of the car. He banged on the car window, but it was hopeless. All he could do was cast a long look at his house, where Shithead's pale, terrified face stared at him from the living room window.

TWENTY

MARY WORKED IN THE empty police cubicle for most of the day. At Galloway's suggestion, she requested Campbell County State Police records for the past three years. While those wheels turned, she ran the SBI database on the two new Highway 74 deaths. Tiffani Wallace had multiple arrests for silly stuff—shoplifting a CD, disturbing the peace, drunk and disorderly. Despite her penchant for petty crime, she had a pretty face that belied her sketchy lifestyle. Given different circumstances, Mary could envision her graduating from college, working at a job, going home to a husband and family. The second girl, Maria Perez, was even sadder. She had nothing beyond an autopsy photo—eyes shut, her complexion dark with lividity. She'd been identified by an empty pay envelope from a sweet potato farm in South Carolina. The post-mortem found defensive wounds—scratches on her arms, a broken nail. She had skin fragments beneath the nails of her right hand, but they didn't match anybody in the system. The skin of her own fingers was stained orange from her work picking sweet potatoes, and a small religious medal hung around her neck. Mary sighed. Latinos worked hard, usually sent most of their paychecks back home. What had this girl's mother thought when her money had quit coming? Did she think Maria had forgotten about them to run away with some man? Or did she know, in her heart, grieve with the sense that Maria had made her last contribution—that this little chick would not be returning to their nest?

"And what do you do then?" Mary whispered. "How can you stand the not knowing?" She knew not knowing well; there wasn't a day that passed where she didn't turn her head at some red pickup truck or scroll through her email, looking for a message from jwalkingstick. Beyond a single birthday gift, silently left two Januarys ago, she'd heard nothing.

Shaking her head, she turned back to Tiffani Wallace. At least she had a last name, a next of kin—Eddie, a brother who lived in Campbell County. Mary punched in the number and got a voicemail message. She hung up, knowing she'd have to call back later. You didn't leave questions about a dead family member on a recording device.

Mary stood up, stretched, looked at the papers strewn across the desk. Ann Chandler's anti-gay conspiracy theory was getting muddied by the other suspicious deaths along Highway 74. Of the four people she'd found dead along that road, only two had been gay white males. The other two were females, their sexual orientation undetermined. Yet "getting 74'd" was well known in the local vernacular; the Latinos called the road "the highway of sorrows;" and even Pharisee, in Asheville, had concocted a drink in its dubious honor. It made no sense.

Fighting a mid-afternoon droop, she walked out into the hall and bought a cup of coffee from the vending machine. When she returned to the cubicle, she considered calling Eddie Wallace again, but instead decided to check her email, on the outside chance the state police had responded to her request in a timely manner. Usually requests for old records took hours, if not days. But she'd tried using her governor's staff email address, mcrowgubstaff. When she opened her account, the report was waiting.

"Wow," she said. "Guess it pays to have friends in high places."

She opened the attached file and started to laugh. Though they'd sent her both Sligo and Campbell County complaint data, they'd covered the past thirteen years, rather than just the past three. What a difference a digit can make.

"Oh well," said Mary. "At least they got some of it right." Taking a sip of coffee, she started looking through the data. Slowly, she pieced together the statistics. In the past three years, both counties had similar numbers: six homicides in Campbell County, seven in Sligo. Of the murders in Campbell County, three had a Highway 74 connection. In Sligo County, only one body, Alan Bratcher, had been found on 74.

"So half the homicides in Campbell County wind up on 74, but only one in Sligo," she whispered. "But the highway bisects both counties, straight as a ruler." She sat back and frowned at the computer screen. Was something cooking here, or was it just random?

"Since you've got thirteen years here, just expand the data pool," she told herself. "See if there's a pattern."

Thankful that she'd paid attention during her statistics course in Raleigh, she pulled up the two counties side by side. For the past thirteen years, Sligo's numbers had remained constant—roughly the same numbers of burglaries, assaults, D&Ds, homicides, soliciting, controlled substance violations. Campbell County, though, looked very different. In 2001 and 2002, the numbers were similar to Sligo. Then, in 2003, things began to change. Each year the crime statistics fell. By 2009, the crime rate was half of Sligo's; then in 2011, the numbers began to inch up. By the end of last year, they once again matched Sligo's.

"Maybe *that's* why they hired Galloway," she whispered. "Maybe it was less about speaking Spanish and more about getting their crime rate under control." She was sitting there, frowning at the screen, when her cell phone rang. She picked up to find Galloway himself on the line.

"Hey, how are you doing?" he asked, his voice bright.

"I'm okay," she said. "How are you doing?"

"Are you still at the office?"

"I'm doing a little statistical comparison. Your county's crime rate sucks."

"That's because I haven't worked there long enough to change it. Come back in a year. You'll see vast improvements."

"I bet." She laughed. "Did you find out anything about Honey-cutt?"

"Nothing actionable. The old girlfriend said he was a bully, showed me the scars to prove it."

"So he's not homophobic?"

"He's poly-phobic. Hates gays, hates blacks, hates Muslims, hates Jews. And don't even get him started on Congress."

"Women, puppies, and Christmas, too?" asked Mary.

"Wouldn't surprise me," said Galloway. "But he's not stupid and he learns fast. Hey—would you like to go out to dinner with me tonight?"

"Not if it involves a sermon or a baseball game."

"No. Just you and me. Two old cops, swapping war stories."

"I'm not a cop, Galloway. Nor am I old."

"Okay, one old cop and a cute young lawyer, swapping war stories."

"Then sure." She smiled. Dinner with Galloway would be a nice break from her statistical straw grasping, plus she could get his take on Campbell County's growing crime rate. "When and where?"

"How close are you to finishing?" he asked.

"I've got another phone call to make, then I'm done."

"There's a little Italian restaurant in town—Angelo's. Good food and the beer's cold. Should I come pick you up in an hour?"

"No, I'll meet you there. I'd kind of like to get out of here for a bit—put the top down and feel the wind in my hair."

"Okay, then. Angelo's is on the corner of Main and Georgia. I'll be waiting for you and your wind-blown hair."

She hung up, cheered by the thought of dinner with Galloway as opposed to another meal at the Gastonia Holiday Inn. Turning back to the computer, she highlighted the graphs she'd generated and punched the print button. As the printer began to crank out the pages, she tried Eddie Wallace's number again. This time the line was busy. Mary waited, then tried the number again. Still busy. After the third busy signal, she wrote his address down on a note pad and got up from her desk. She wanted to get out of the office for a bit anyway—might as well drive over to Wallace's house and ask him about his sister in person.

———

Mary put the top down on her car and keyed the address into her smart phone, wondering if the GPS would think "County Road 218" was a real street or some typographical error. Apparently, she hadn't been the first to key the location in—a little blue dot blinked 14.72 miles northwest of her current location.

"Okay, buddy," she whispered as she backed the car out of the parking lot. "Let's see where you're taking me."

The GPS took her first through town, then through a residential area, and then out into the country, following a meandering creek that traversed acres of green pastureland dotted with grazing cows. Small trailer parks hugged the road, each unit with a dish antenna pointed to the southwest quadrant of the sky. After ten miles, the road intersected with County Road 218. She turned right, as the GPS indicated; a half-mile later she turned into the long driveway of number 320. It led to a white doublewide trailer surrounded by American muscle cars in varying states of repair. She saw a little Chevy Impala with no wheels, a Chrysler with the stuffing coming out of its upholstery, and an old Dodge Charger that had, in a former life, apparently been a race car. A tall man wearing jeans and a dark scruff of a beard stood by the Dodge, arms folded, eyes hard.

"Hi," Mary called as she got out of her car, suddenly wishing she'd told Galloway where she was going.

"I don't work on nothin' foreign," the man said, spitting in the direction of Mary's Miata.

"I'm not here for a car repair." Mary pulled her ID from her purse. "I work for the governor—we're looking into some cold homicide cases here in Campbell County. Are you Eddie Wallace? Tiffani Wallace's brother?"

He hesitated a moment, then nodded as he spat another bullet of tobacco juice.

"I'm just trying to connect some dots here," she explained, wanting to assure Eddie that she had no law enforcement interest in him. "Were you close to your sister?"

"Close enough."

"Did you know who her friends were? Who she hung out with?"

"Scumbags, mostly."

"Was she seeing anyone? Have any special boyfriend?"

"I didn't keep up with her like that."

Mary nodded. "Do you know what your sister's sexual orientation was?"

He frowned. "Her sexual what?"

"Orientation. Did she like to have sex with men or women?"

"You mean was she queer?"

"Yes. Was she queer?"

"Good God, no." Wallace spat again. "Queers made her want to puke. Me too, as far as that goes."

"I see," said Mary.

Wallace picked up a tire iron that rested against the Dodge's front fender. "Are you saying some queer killed her?"

"No, I'm just trying to see if there's any connection between her death and another man's murder."

"Tiffani may have run with some real losers," he said, "but never with faggots or homos." Wallace slapped one end of the wrench against his palm. "You wouldn't be putting it out that she was a dyke, would you?"

"No, Mr. Wallace. That's not the way the law works."

"Good," he said, slapping the wrench against his hand again. "Me and mine would take a dim view of that."

Though Wallace's threat was implicit, Mary did not back up an inch. "Is there anything else you'd like to add to this investigation? Anything you don't feel the local cops looked into closely enough?"

He gave a bitter laugh. "The local cops are probably missing Tiffani pretty bad, right now."

"How so?" asked Mary.

"Any little piece-of-shit charge they could come up with, they'd hang on Tiff. Off she'd go to jail, then to court. What with all the fines she had to fork over, she probably made Campbell County more money than a damn speed trap."

"I see. Well, every little piece of information helps. Thanks for your time." Mary pulled a business card from her pocket and laid it on the fender of the Chevy. "If you remember anything else, call me. I'm sorry about your sister. She was a pretty girl."

She turned and got back in her car, knowing that Eddie Wallace would probably throw her card away the minute she pulled out of the drive. Though his attitude toward gays was harsh, it fit in with the rest of Campbell County's. What was interesting was his take that the police department had turned Tiffani into their own little cash cow. It was ridiculous, of course, but Eddie Wallace was one of millions who believed that the judicial deck had been stacked against them since birth. Never was any arrest their fault; always it was the cops who were acting on some personal, undeserved vendetta against them.

TWENTY-ONE

CHASE STOOD BY THE window terrified, the taste of fear sour in the back of his throat. He'd left his television show when he heard the car coming up the driveway. He knew something odd was going on—in all the months he'd lived here, only two people had ever come to call—the UPS man, delivering Gudger some new tool for his workshop, and Mary Crow. When he first peeked out the window, Chase thought one of Gudger's cop friends had come to visit, but he realized the car was all wrong. All the ex-cops he'd met drove big-ass pickup trucks or gas-guzzling monsters like Suzie Q. This car had the sleek lines of a limo. Even stranger was the guy who'd gotten out of it—he was as big as a gorilla, with massive shoulders straining against a light-blue dress shirt. The gorilla kept watch as Gudger leaned over to talk to someone in the backseat. Then, in one slick move, he came up behind Gudger and pulled his sweatshirt over his head. Gudger's pale belly jiggled as he tried to squirm away, but the gorilla was too fast. He found a gun Gudger had apparently hidden in his pants and plastered Gudger between the legs with it.

Chase unconsciously grabbed his own crotch as Gudger crumpled to the ground, his legs twitching uncontrollably. He thought for a moment that Gudger was dead, but then the gorilla lifted him up, and tossed him into the backseat. After that, the gorilla returned to the passenger seat and the car oozed back down the driveway. Not hurrying, not spraying the gravel—just driving off, as if throwing people in the backseat was something they did every day.

For a long time Chase stood staring out the window, stunned, waiting for the car to come back and let Gudger out. But that did not happen. The dust slowly resettled in the driveway, birds flitted back to the bird feeder, and the humming quietness of a June afternoon returned. It occurred to Chase that he ought to be happy, dancing with joy. Gudger was gone! He'd watched a big goon kick his ass! He'd gotten to watch somebody else do what he'd longed to do for months.

But for some reason, he didn't feel like dancing. For some reason, he felt more like he wanted to vomit.

His first instinct was to call the police, just as he once did with the crackheads at their old duplex. But then he remembered how Gudger had leaned over and whispered to him the day they'd all moved in here: *You ever call the police to this house and I'll kill you, boy.*

Though Chase had taken his threat seriously, this was different. This wasn't one of his crackpot theories about Sam or even his suspicions about the drug dealers who used to live next door. A black car had rolled up in his driveway; a thug had beaten up and then kidnapped his stepfather. And he'd seen it all—he could give descriptions, of both the goon and the car.

"It's okay," he told himself. "Gudger would probably want me to call the cops now."

He hurried to the den and Gudger's precious landline. But the old black phone was missing from the table beside the Barcalounger. He searched the kitchen, Gudger's bedroom, then he ran out to the garage. He found Gudger's whiskey, Gudger's *Playboy* collection, even Gudger's stash of ammo, but not Gudger's phone. He'd either hidden the thing or thrown it away. Chase had no way to call anyone.

Not knowing where else to look, he went back in the house. The History Channel had become a din of noise, now showing some documentary about the D-Day invasion. He turned it off. The house settled into an expectant silence, as if it too were holding its breath, waiting to see if Gudger would return. Chase went back to the living room. Perching on the edge of the sofa, he tried to keep watch on the driveway, but all his poison ivy itchiness seemed to have gone deep inside him. He couldn't keep his legs still and he felt as if worms were crawling beneath his skin. Finally, he stood up and walked over to the window.

"It was probably nothing," he said, scanning the driveway for an approaching car. "Probably some dumb joke Gudger dreamed up with his old cop friends. *Hey, let's have some fun. I'll hide the phone, then you guys drive up and pretend to kidnap me. Shithead will piss his pants he'll be so scared!*"

That notion calmed him for a moment—he could just hear Gudger saying something like that. But then he remembered the look in Gudger's eyes when that car had rolled back down the driveway.

"It was real," Chase whispered, his itchiness returning. "You couldn't fake looking that scared."

———

Chase went to the kitchen and poured a glass of water. As he drank it, he glanced at the clock above the stove. He couldn't believe it was nearly four o'clock! Though he'd planned to make himself a peanut butter sandwich back when the D-Day show was on, Gudger and the gorilla had made him forget all about his empty stomach. Now it was late afternoon—Gudger had easily been gone three hours. Was the gorilla going to bring him back? Or would that sick expression on Gudger's face be the last he'd see of him? As much as hated Gudger, he hoped not. Nobody deserved to die that scared.

He went back to the living room. As he looked at the window for the hundredth time, two black shapes swooped down from the oak tree. He jumped at the sudden movement, then he realized they were crows, coming to scavenge beneath his mother's bird feeder. While he watched the sleek black birds peck in the grass, he thought of Mary Crow and how she'd stood right on the porch and talked with Gudger without once letting on how much she knew about him.

"Wish she were here now," he whispered. Mary Crow would know what to do about all this. She was really smart, and she was friends with the governor. Then a thought occurred to him. Gudger had started acting strange right after Mary Crow left. He'd been furious at her visit, but then he'd started pacing around the house, muttering to himself under his breath. He'd stomped out to the garage and stayed there for a long time. When he finally came back, he'd seemed calmer, but he smelled of whiskey. All at once Chase felt a tightness in his chest. Was there some kind of connection between the men in the black car and Mary Crow? Would the gorilla now be out to get her, just like he'd gotten Gudger?

"No," he said, trying to put the brakes on his rising panic. "She's the governor's cop. They wouldn't mess with anybody like her." But what if they weren't afraid of the governor? They sure hadn't been afraid of Gudger.

He turned away from the window and hurried to his bedroom. He had to get to a phone and warn Mary Crow. If he ran through the back yard and along the creek, maybe he could persuade Mrs. Carver to let him use her telephone. Gudger was the one she hated, not him. He pulled on jeans, his sneakers, a long-sleeved shirt. Stuffing Sam's little change purse in his back pocket, he was heading for a final pit stop in the bathroom when he heard footsteps on the front porch. He froze. Was Gudger back? Or had the gorilla in that black car now returned for him?

His knees quivering, he stood in silence. He heard the squeak of the screen door, the door knob jiggling. He held his breath as the front door opened, praying to hear his mother call his name or even Gudger bellowing out *Shithead*. But he heard only silence, as if someone were just standing inside the door. His stomach clenched. Maybe it was the gorilla; maybe he was out there sniffing the air, trying to smell where he was. For an instant he considered diving under his bed and hiding, but that was crazy. The gorilla would find him in a heartbeat and probably be mad at having to look for him. Better just sneak out the back door, he decided. And run like hell to Mrs. Carver's house.

Trembling, he held on to the doorjamb and peeked around the corner. Down the hall he could see a man in a gray sweatshirt and khaki pants, leaning against the front door, head down, holding one hand under his armpit. A wave of relief washed over him. It was Gudger. Still alive, still in one piece.

Yet something wasn't right. Gudger usually roared into the house, slamming doors, calling names, hurling curses. That he was standing in silence with his head bowed could not be good. Walking on tiptoes, Chase inched down the hall to get a closer look.

Gudger looked like a department store dummy. His bald spot was the color of pale wax and the three long locks that comprised his combover hung limply behind his ears. As Chase watched, Gudger pulled the door shut and locked it. As he withdrew his right hand from under his arm, Chase fought back a gasp. Gudger's hand looked as if it had been cooked in a microwave. The skin was red to the point of blistering, his fingers were swollen like sausages. Gudger gazed at his disfigured self for a long moment, then he started to cry.

Chase gulped, his terror now a living thing. Gudger in good health was bad enough—he couldn't imagine what Gudger might do wounded and in pain. He eased back into the shadows of the hall. If he could get back to his room and push his dresser in front of the door, he could barricade himself in there until his mother got home. That way, he would at least be safe for a little while. Turning, he started to tiptoe back down the hall. He hadn't taken three steps when he felt something grab the back of his neck. Gudger whipped him around with his good hand, slamming him against the wall. Wasps started buzzing inside Chase's head.

"You little smart-assed bastard," Gudger whispered, his face dark with rage. "Did you actually think you could mess with me?"

Chase tried to shake his head, but Gudger was gripping him too tightly.

Gudger held up his ruined hand. "You know what this is? This is what happens when little boys go poking their noses into business that doesn't concern them."

"Wh-what happened?" Chase asked, unable to take his eyes off Gudger's raw-looking flesh.

"Two Russian bastards thought it would be fun to hold my hand down in a tub of battery acid," said Gudger. "They had a great time, too. Me, not so much."

Chase kept staring at the scalded fingers, his heart racing. He was too scared to think, to speak.

"But don't you worry, Olive Oyl," Gudger growled. "I've still got one hand that works just fine. And that's more than enough to take care of you."

He shoved Chase into his bedroom. "Here are two things you can think about for a while," he said, as he pulled a door key from his pocket. "The first is that your pal Mary Crow won't be stopping by here ever again. The second is that real bad things happen to little boys who fuck with me."

168

TWENTY-TWO

HER NAME WAS ALICE; she was from South Carolina. She was more cute than pretty—brown eyes, blond hair, freckles across her nose. Sam could tell by the way she talked that she would have been one of the popular girls at Sam's school—a cheerleader, or a band majorette. Now, as they both lay beneath their bathroom sinks, whispering to each other through a hole in the wall, the cheerleader looked like a little rat in a cage, just as terrified as Sam. She'd been here for two months.

"How do you know that for sure?" asked Sam. "There aren't any clocks, and I can't get anything but Spanish channels on the TV."

"I've gone through two boxes of Kotex," Alice replied. She gave a sardonic laugh. "Yusuf gets real excited when he finds dirty pads in my trash. It's like he's relieved I haven't gotten pregnant on his watch. Like I could in this room, all by myself."

"I haven't had a period since I've been here," said Sam.

"Well, you'd better have one soon," Alice warned. "If you don't, they'll call a doctor."

"That gross old man?" Sam shuddered at the memory of her last pelvic exam—the man's dirty lab coat and rimless glasses, and the way he'd stripped off her clothes while those other men watched.

"No, not the Meat Inspector," said Alice. "If you start bleeding, or if you never bleed, they call in somebody else. A woman doctor who looks and sounds like a man."

"How do you know?" asked Sam, rubbing her arms against a sudden chill.

"Because they called that doctor in for Michaela. She was in that room before you came." Alice closed her eyes. "I listened to the whole thing through this pipe. It was horrible..."

"What happened?"

"Michaela did something to herself, you know, to make herself not a virgin anymore. She started bleeding, really bad."

"Did the doctor take care of her?" asked Sam.

"I don't think so. Everybody—Yusuf, the doctor, that guy Boyko—they were all in the room. Michaela was crying, screaming that she didn't want to die. It was so scary I had to put the sink back together and go to bed. I put my pillow over my head and cried. The next morning, Michaela was gone."

"When did all this happen?" asked Sam.

"Two weeks ago. I didn't think they were going to put anybody back in that room, then you came along."

Sam sank back on the floor. She could still see the words *this place is a hell hole* scratched on the wall in front of the toilet. She pictured Michaela scratching those words into the wall, then plunging the same implement into her vagina. The image made her sick inside.

"You know what's funny?" whispered Alice. "Not funny ha-ha, but funny peculiar?"

"No." Sam rose up on her elbows. Through the hole she could see half of her new friend's face. "What?"

"Bobby—that's my boyfriend—Bobby and I were going to do it the night they grabbed me."

"Do what?"

"Have sex. End my virginity. We crashed a frat party at Clemson. I was a little nervous, since it was my first time, so Bobby thought I'd be more relaxed if I had a drink or two. There were some guys sitting around a picnic table in the back yard of the Chi Nu house. I didn't think they looked like frat guys, but Bobby said they were okay. They'd mixed up a big bowl of Purple Jesus and gave us a couple. I took a sip and it was really good. Bobby and I both got pretty relaxed," she whispered. "So we went back to Bobby's car. We were in the backseat, kissing, about to take off our clothes when I got so sleepy I couldn't keep my eyes open. When I woke up, I was here."

"What happened to Bobby?" asked Sam.

"I don't know. They won't tell me."

"I thought somebody had left a baby by the side of the road," whispered Sam. "I went to see, and somebody grabbed me from behind."

"They got Michaela that way, too," said Alice. "Somehow they figure out the ones they want to take."

Sam shifted on the cold tile floor. "Do you know where we are?"

"Somewhere near an interstate. There's a place where the boards don't meet, up high in my window. If I stand on my tiptoes, I can watch them take the lot lizards out every night."

"The lot lizards?"

"You know … the girls who have to work the truck stops."

Sam knew exactly who she was talking about—the girls who'd trudged down the other hall every night and come back every morning.

"Those girls get twenty bucks for ten minutes in the back of a cab," said Alice. "And they have to do whatever the driver wants. If they don't, they get punished."

Sam thought about the parade that had passed by her door—the black girls who'd made fun of the white men, Dusty's loud boasting about how much money she could make in a night. She'd thought it awful back then; now she thought those girls were lucky. At least they had each other. At least they got to go outside and breathe fresh air. At least they got to stay where everybody spoke English and could pronounce your name. "You know," she whispered to Alice, trying not to cry. "I used to feel sorry for those girls. Now I think they're lucky."

Alice wiped away her own tears. "I do, too."

They were silent for a moment, then Sam spoke. "Do you know what's going to happen to us?"

"Is Yusuf bringing you weird food? Like olives and goat cheese?"

"He is."

"Then you're going overseas, just like me."

Sam couldn't believe what she'd heard. Though Ivan had told her virtually the same thing, she thought it was one of his crazy exaggerations, like how he said Moscow was the most beautiful city in the world, and all Russian men were hung like horses. She'd thought they might shuffle her off *somewhere*, but overseas? To some country she's never heard of? She'd never see her mother again!

"They're going to sell us," Alice went on. "To rich men who hate America."

"But why?" cried Sam, her heart beating a thousand miles an hour. "If they hate America, why would they want an American girl?"

"Because getting one of us is like giving America the finger. They get to be even badder asses in their own country."

"How do you know this?"

"There are ways of finding stuff out here."

A hard look came in her pretty brown eyes. "There are ways of finding stuff out here."

"Yusuf?" asked Sam, remembering the way the man's gaze roved over her body.

Alice's lower lip began to quiver. "He kept asking me to suck him off. For a long time I refused, then I decided it might be a way to get some information." She wiped a tear from the corner of one eye. "I've probably done that guy off fifty times. The info comes right out with the kum."

"Do you think he's telling the truth?"

Alice gave a loud sniff. "I'd like to think he's lying, but something tells me he's not."

For a while neither of them spoke, lost in the looming terror of their futures, drawn closer with every drip of the faucet in Alice's sink. Then, suddenly, the pretty blond cheerleader stuck one nail-bitten finger through the hole in the wall.

"Touch me," she whispered.

Sam reached out, twined her finger around Alice's.

"You know before," said Alice, "I hated my mother. Hated the way she dressed, hated the perfume she dabbed behind her ears, hated her stupid little checklist of things that would help me get into college. *Keep my grades up, take charge of the cheerleaders' service project, try out for the senior play.*"

Sam fought back an ironic smile. Though her mother's checklist had not included cheerleading projects or senior plays, she'd had an agenda for Sam as well. *Don't talk to those men in the duplex. Stop Chase from calling the cops.* And later, *Don't get on Gudger's nerves.*

"Now," Alice continued, "I would give anything to see my mom in her stupid jeans or get a whiff of her Obsession. Just for a minute, you know? Just to tell her that I love her."

"I know what you mean." Sam squeezed Alice's finger.

For a moment they remained silent, touching. Then suddenly, Alice jerked her finger back through the hole. "Quick! Put your sink back together! Yusuf's coming. Don't drink the tea if you want to keep your head on straight. That's where he puts the drugs!"

173

Before Sam could say another word, the little hole between their shared wall shut. She heard a door open, then Yusuf said, "Why you down there? You sick?"

"Yeah," Alice replied, her voice now muffled. "I'm real sick."

Sam heard footsteps, movement in Alice's bathroom. She knew she'd better reseal her part of the hole fast. She crouched beneath the sink and tried to screw the flange back in place with her home-made bra-hook screwdriver. But her fingers were shaking so that the little hooks continued to slip out of the proper slots. Clumsily, she dropped one screw. She tried to catch it as it bounced across the old tile floor but instead managed to knock the flange to the bottom of the U-trap. It made a loud ping that sounded like a bell ringing. She held her breath as Alice's bathroom grew ominously quiet.

Don't let him look under the sink, she prayed, not daring to move for fear of making more noise. She sat there, holding her breath, listening to the pounding of her own heart, then all at once, Alice's flange fell away. The little hole reopened, only this time not a pretty young face peered through it, but an olive-skinned man whose thick brows made a dark, angry V above his nose.

"You two have been talking!" he cried, incredulous.

Sam didn't know what to say—to deny it seemed bad, but to admit the truth seemed worse. She settled on staying mute, hoping that Alice would know what to do.

"You little bitches!" Yusuf thundered. "You little whores!"

"We are not!" cried Alice, starting to slap Yusuf on his head and shoulders. "We just want to go home!"

Yusuf gave Sam a final, furious glare, then he turned away from the drain pipe, slamming Alice's flange shut. Sam knew it would never be opened again—they would close it with nails, plaster it over before they would let her talk with Alice again. Still, she put her ear to the wall and tried to hear what was going on next door. She heard Yusuf's

174

yelling in Turkish, Alice crying, then the sound of glass breaking. After that, she heard nothing but silence.

She waited, crouched on the bathroom floor, for what seemed like hours, hoping to hear something from Alice's room. When she didn't, she kissed the finger she'd intertwined with Alice's. For a few minutes, she'd had a friend—a pretty girl who'd spoken English with a Southern accent and who, like her, had never had sex. If everything Alice had told her was true, they would soon be sold to people who would treat them like slaves. After that, who knew? After that, who cared? She patted the old tile wall softly, as if that might give comfort to her friend next door. She knew she would never see Alice again. She also knew that the next time she saw Yusuf's face, he would likely be coming for her.

TWENTY-THREE

MARY LEFT EDDIE WALLACE's house/stock car garage quickly, eager to get away from the self-pitying homophobia of clan Wallace. She took a circuitous route to Angelo's restaurant, driving along roads that bisected corn fields, enjoying the warm summer wind that whipped through her hair. As she drove, she composed her report to Ann Chandler.

"The demographic of Campbell County is largely Christian and extremely conservative," she said. "The majority of those Christians believe that being gay is not only a choice, but a sin that will send a homosexual person to hell."

Here she stopped, unsure of her conclusion. Unless Galloway had come up with some new bit of incriminating evidence, she'd found nothing at Trull's church to indicate that his parishioners wanted to do anything beyond turn gay people straight and save their souls. Though Trull's sermons were fiery and hugely offensive, the man had not advocated violence to anyone, beyond parents spanking their children. Nonetheless, two gay men had been murdered within ten miles of each other. Somebody either living in or passing through Campbell County had a hatred of gays that ran deep and occasionally lethal.

"If I were the governor, I'd just offer Ecotron a sweet deal in a more progressive county," she said. "Any gay person who moves *here* will have to keep looking over their shoulder, 24/7."

She sighed. She knew that wouldn't be what Ann Chandler wanted to hear, but she couldn't help it. In Campbell County, homophobia was an acceptable, Bible-endorsed prejudice. There was little the governor could do to change that. Certainly not with people like Reverend Trull in the pulpit.

As the western sky grew pink with the setting sun, she headed toward Angelo's. She pulled into a moderately full parking lot and walked into a restaurant decorated in an old-fashioned way, with red-checked tablecloths and candles stuck in empty Chianti bottles. Galloway lifted a half-filled wine glass at her from a small table in one corner, tucked in beneath a big poster of Venetian gondoliers.

"I was beginning to think you'd stood me up," he said as he rose from his chair.

Mary smiled. "I took a little detour on my tour of the county."

She sat down. Immediately, a little old man in a black tuxedo jacket appeared with a basket of warm bread and two menus.

"This joint's a real trip, isn't it?" Galloway filled her wine glass from his bottle of Valpolicella.

"I haven't seen candles in Chianti bottles in years," Mary admitted. "Or formally dressed waiters."

"Angelo is definitely old-school Italian. If the food weren't so good, I'd think he was some wise guy, hiding out from the mob."

Mary took a sip of wine. "This county is just full of surprises."

He gave her a half-smile, revealing a dimple in his left cheek. "Oh, yeah? What surprises did you uncover, holed up in your little cubicle?"

"You really want to know?"

"I never ask questions I don't want the answer to."

She closed her menu. "Well, after I found out your police department has a funny little bubble in its statistics, I went to see Tiffani Wallace's brother. He spit tobacco juice at me, then started whacking his hand with a tire iron."

Galloway's eyes narrowed. "He what?"

"Oh, I'm exaggerating. He didn't do anything, but he let me know that police investigations were an unwelcome intrusion on his car-repair business. I'm sure you've run into the same behavior a thousand times."

"Why did you pay him a visit?" Galloway pressed, angry.

"I wanted to find out if Tiffani might have been gay."

"And?"

"And if she was, she wisely kept it to herself. Otherwise, I think her brother would have taken that tire iron to her head and buried her behind his grease pit."

"Not an evolved family, I take it." Galloway was simmering down, though slowly.

Mary shook her head. "You'll never see the rainbow flag waving in their front yard."

Galloway took a sip of wine. "So tell me about this bubble in our statistics."

"Somebody at the SBI punched the wrong computer key and sent me the crime stats for the past thirteen years, instead of the past three. Crime in Sligo County has remained fairly constant throughout that time. Campbell County started off almost identical to Sligo; then in 2003, things started to change."

"What do you mean?"

"From 2003 until 2010, your numbers dropped to half of Sligo's rates."

"What happened after 2010?"

"In 2011, the numbers began to inch up. By the end of 2013, they matched Sligo again."

Galloway shrugged. "Maybe we had some super cop on the payroll."

"That's what I thought, too. But here's where it gets even weirder ... the domestic assaults and armed robbery numbers remain constant. But prostitution, soliciting, D&D, larceny, and shoplifting literally drop to zero."

"Kiddie crimes, for the most part."

"Right." Mary looked up to see the waiter reappear, order pad in hand. She ordered the chicken cacciatore while Galloway opted for spaghetti.

"Anyway, had Sligo's petty crime rate risen while Campbell's fell, then I would say kids were just heading over to the next county for their mischief. But Sligo's figures never change."

"It might be Reverend Trull," said Galloway. "He does have an unbelievable youth outreach program. His kids play every sport on the planet, plus they camp and hike and run after-school programs at the high school and the grammar school. Campbell County kids might be too tired to get into trouble."

Mary shrugged. "Possibly. Something sure got the marginal ones off the streets." She took another sip of wine—it was perfect for a summer evening, mellow and fruity. "Did you find out anything about Honeycutt and the Taylor case?"

"Only that he didn't do Bryan Taylor."

"Seriously?"

Galloway nodded. "He wasn't even in town when Taylor got it."

"Where was he?"

"Just this side of Raleigh. The landscaping company he works for was doing a new golf course. Honeycutt stayed in the Motel 6 for two weeks."

"You know this for sure?"

"I've got copies of his phone records and his credit card receipts. I talked to the desk clerk who checked him in and out."

Mary sighed. During her drive she'd fantasized that she might be able to call Ann Chandler tonight and tell her that even though her conspiracy theory was dead, they'd found a single serial killer with a hard-on for homosexuals. That they were, at that moment, gathering evidence to indict him. With Honeycutt's alibi this tight, that conversation with the governor would probably not occur.

She started to ask Galloway if he had any more suspects up his sleeve when the waiter appeared, placing a steaming dish of chicken cacciatore down in front of her.

"Thank you." She smiled up at the silent little man. "This looks wonderful."

Nodding, he left Mary to her chicken and Galloway to his plate of spaghetti.

"So how does my Honeycutt news stack up for you?" asked Galloway, twirling pasta around his fork.

"Not so hot. Since I haven't found a conspiracy, I was hoping to give Chandler a single homophobic serial killer. Looks like she's not getting either."

"And her big company will go somewhere else. No new jobs or tax revenues for North Carolina. No new Campbell County votes for Ann come the next election."

Mary nodded. "That's right. She loses the county, the state loses jobs. But by God, you guys won't have any homosexuals to deal with."

Wiping his mouth with a red-checkered napkin, Galloway leaned back in his chair. "Can I ask you a personal question?"

"You can ask," said Mary. "I might not answer."

"How do you come down on this, personally?"

"On what, personally?"

"You know—being gay."

Mary looked at him. "You mean did the governor send me here because I'm a lesbian?"

His face flushed, but he nodded.

"No, I'm not, and no, she didn't."

"Then how do you feel about Trull and gay rights?"

"I'm an attorney. I'm sworn to enforce the law. As near as I can figure, Reverend Trull hasn't broken any."

"You're dodging my question."

"Gay people are citizens. They pay the same taxes, so they are entitled to the same rights and protections as anybody else."

"So you're okay with gay marriage?"

She gazed into her glass of wine and thought of Jonathan. Somewhere, far away, was the man she wanted, the man she should be married to. She thought of his smile, the way he made her laugh, how good she always felt with him. If she'd found that in a woman instead of Jonathan, would she want it any less? She looked up at Galloway and tried to smile. "I think if you're lucky enough to find someone to love, then you ought to get them to a church or a judge and marry them as fast as you can. And then work like hell to make it last."

"Sounds like you're speaking from experience," he said softly.

"Yeah," she said. "I guess it does."

After that they moved on to broader subjects—the traffic in Atlanta, Galloway's efforts to teach Crump a little Spanish, how he'd like to visit Asheville if he ever got the time. They ended their dinner with a glass of brandy, then walked out into the parking lot together. As Mary unlocked her car, Galloway touched her arm. "I know you've just pretended to be my girlfriend," he said, a sheepish look on his face. "But do you think we might take a step in that direction for real?"

She considered his question. Years ago she'd resolved never to date cops, but something about Victor Galloway was different. He was funny and smart and wasn't caught up in interdepartmental pissing contests the way most cops were. She smiled. "I'd be willing to consider it."

He took her in his arms and kissed her. His shoulders were broad, his back muscular. His smelled of shaving cream and laundry starch— oddly sexy aromas she had not known in months. He finally broke their kissing with another question. "Would you like to have dinner again tomorrow night?"

Mary laughed. "Don't you have to go to church?"

"Wow, I guess I do. I'd forgotten all about that. How about I call you tomorrow? We can meet after church."

"You've got my number. I'll be in Gastonia all day, writing my report to the governor." He held the door open as she got in her car. "Thanks, Galloway. I had fun."

He leaned down and kissed her once more. "You do realize you're going to drive down *la carretera del dolor* tonight, don't you?"

"Doesn't scare me," she replied. "I'm not gay and I never stop for strangers."

"Then watch out for the cops. I hear Gaston County speed traps are cash cows."

"Funny you should say that," Mary replied. "That's exactly what Eddie Wallace said about his sister and the Campbell County cops."

———

She headed back to Gaston County, the little town of Manley dribbling away in a small flurry of gas stations and convenience stores, a roller skating rink that had pink flamingos skating on a neon sign. The four lanes narrowed to two, with a wide gravel shoulder on each side of the road. She came up fast on a kid doing thirty on a liquorcycle; he wisely pulled to the shoulder of the road as she passed him.

"Must be hurrying to get into trouble in Gaston County," she whispered, now wishing she had the crime stats for it as well. She drove on, the tiny scooter vanishing behind her. The houses that sat back from the road disappeared altogether, replaced by the tall pine forests that covered this part of North Carolina. The air smelled faintly of turpentine, and above her she could see the twinkling of stars. As her thoughts returned to Galloway, she shifted into Overdrive, lowering the pitch of the engine, cruising along at seventy—too fast, really, but the road was mostly straight, and if she ran into a cop she would flash her governor's staff ID card. Surely that would get her out of a Gaston County speeding ticket. She flew by a sign advertising some kind of creek chapel church, then she saw an odd-looking shape by the side of the road. Squinting as she passed it, it appeared to be a plastic box of some kind, then seconds later she realized it wasn't a box at all. It looked exactly like a child's car seat, upright, as if someone had dropped a baby off on the side of the road. "Oh, come on," she said, checking her rearview mirror. "Nobody would do that."

But what if it somebody had? This was *la carretera del dolor*. What if some desperate Latina had abandoned her child? Given her up to the kindness of passing strangers? Mary put on her brakes and screeched to a stop. Though she knew it was crazy, she also knew she'd spend one long, sleepless night if she didn't go back. She made a U-turn in the middle of the road and roared back in the opposite direction. When her headlights flashed across the car seat, she pulled to the shoulder of the road. She blinked, unbelieving. The car seat was wiggling slightly—somebody had actually left a child in the dark, on a highway with traffic flying by at seventy miles an hour! She pulled up her handbrake, then ran across the road. She could see something squirming in the car seat, heard whimpering, as if some child cried in a blanket.

"Honey?" she said. "Sweetheart?"

She pulled the blanket back. In the darkness she saw a chubby leg, a head with only peach fuzz for hair. She reached to touch the child's arm, but instead of feeling tender flesh, she grasped some kind of cold plastic thing.

"Ugh!" she cried, recoiling from the strange, alien appendage. She didn't want to touch the repulsive thing again, but she was curious about how it worked and why someone had put it out here. Steeling herself, she again stepped forward, this time digging deeper into the blanket. Ignoring the creepy feel of the ersatz flesh, she pulled out an incredibly realistic-looking doll wired up to a small battery. When Mary held the thing by its neck, its legs twitched in a bizarre imitation of human movement while making an odd kind of mewing squeak.

"Whoa," whispered Mary. "This is way too weird. I'm going to call Galloway."

She dropped the doll back in its car seat. She turned to hurry back across the road to her car when she felt a hot stab of pain in the back of her right thigh. She gasped, wondering if she'd gotten a sudden cramp, but the strange heat spread up and down her leg, crumpling her knee, turning her hip to jelly. She tried to walk, but her leg was useless, unable to support her. As she spread her arms to catch her balance, she felt rough hands grabbing her, forcing her to the ground. Suddenly she was staring up into an obsidian sky, listening to that strange, manufactured baby crying its mechanical plaint to anyone foolish enough to listen.

TWENTY-FOUR

CHASE LAY ON THE floor of his room, his ear pressed against his locked door. He'd lain there for hours, listening to the drama transpiring outside his room. For a long time he'd heard only Gudger, talking on a phone. His first call had been pleading—he'd walked up and down the hall, asking some medical person what to do for his hand. For the second call he'd stationed himself right outside Chase's door, speaking loudly to someone named Smiley about "some boy meat that would make a sweet little piece of ass for the right person." They'd gone back and forth, then there was a long beat of silence, after which Gudger said that tomorrow would work just fine. "And tell them not to worry," Gudger added. "The kid's too scrawny to put up much of a fight." At first Chase couldn't believe what he'd heard, but then Gudger rapped hard on his door. "You hear that, you little sneak? They're coming for you tomorrow, just like they came for your sister. Your poor mama's heart will be broken all over again."

A numbing frost went through Chase as Gudger's laughter echoed down the hall. Was Gudger serious? Was *he* the boy meat they'd talked about? Had Gudger just set up a deal for him? His mother had warned him to be careful in restrooms, that there were men who liked little boys in the way that most men liked women. Was he now going to be sold to one of them? The cold inside him turned into a hot panic. He needed to get out of here, and get out fast. He leapt to his feet and hurried over to the window beside his bed. Gudger had nailed iron bars to the outside of the thing, but if he could pull the top part of the window down, maybe he could climb out over the iron grid. He pushed aside the plaid curtains his mother had made and raised the shade. His heart sank. Gudger's burglar-stopping grid went all the way to the top of the window frame. He could knock out every pane of glass and still not get through those iron bars.

Suddenly, he heard a new noise. The back door slammed—his mother was home! She would get him free! She would make Gudger let him out of his room, if only to eat supper. Then he could sneak out the back door and run, for as long and as fast as he could. He'd go to Mrs. Carver's house and beg her to let him use his phone. Then he could call the cops and tell them what Gudger was planning to do. He listened as his mother came in the house.

"Gudge?" she called. "Chase?" Her voice always carried a small note of hope, as if Sam might be back, just waiting to pop out and surprise her.

Gudger yelled something from the den, over the blare of the TV news. Chase heard her muffled reply, then the TV went off as Gudger started to yell. A moment later, Chase heard urgent footsteps coming down the hall, stopping just outside his room.

"Chase?" His mother pounded on the door. "Are you in there? Are you all right?"

He raced to the door. This was his chance to get out, to tell her what was really going on. "He locked me in here, Mama! Tomorrow they're coming for me, just like they came for Sam!"

186

"See?" came Gudger's voice. "I told you he's gone crazy. He came at me with a knife, then he poured drain cleaner all over my hand. Look at my fingers!"

"That's not true, Mama!" Chase cried. "I didn't do anything to him. Two Russian guys came up in a big car and took him away!"

"Listen to that nonsense!" said Gudger. "Russians on Kedron Road! Next he's going to say there are aliens in my tomato patch!"

His mother said something he couldn't understand, then he heard their footsteps going away, both voices growing louder in the den, then faster, urgent footsteps returning to his door.

"Mama?" he cried. "Is that you?"

Someone rattled his doorknob, then he heard the metallic sound of a key shoved into the deadbolt that locked his door. He stepped back, praying that his mother could get the door open before Gudger came back. But heavy, urgent footsteps came down the hall. He heard a bumping sound, then his mother cried out.

"Stop it, Gudger!" she said. "He's my son! You can't lock him up like an animal!"

"He's crazy as a shit house rat!" Gudger yelled back. "He thinks I sold Sam and now I'm going to sell him. If you let him out, he'll probably kill us both in our sleep!"

"That's not true!" Chase pounded on the door with his fists, tearing a big hole his poster of Peyton Manning as a Denver Bronco. "Mama, he's lying!"

"See what I mean?" said Gudger. "He's about to break down the door, calling me a liar! You've got one sick little ticket on your hands, Amy."

"I don't care," said his mother. "I'm going to let him out!"

He heard more fumbling with the key, then a thud, as if one of them had pushed the other against the wall. After that, slaps—hard ones—one, two, three. Then his mother began to cry. He leapt forward, screaming through the door. "Leave her alone, Gudger! I'll kill you if you hit her again!"

But their battle did not stop. It gathered heat like a hurricane and whirled past his room, moving down the hall and into the kitchen. He heard a pots-and-pan clattering that sounded like the refrigerator toppling over, then a scream. For a long moment he heard nothing, then the baseball game came on, turned up so loud he thought the windows would break.

"Mama?" he called. "Mama? Are you out there?'

This time, no one answered. Sinking down against the door, he started to cry. What had Gudger done to his mother? Was she lying in the kitchen, unconscious, while Gudger watched a stupid baseball game? Hot tears stung his eyes as his throat grew thick. If Gudger had touched a hair of his mother's head, he would kill him. Even if he got sold to those men tomorrow, he would come back someday and throw Gudger in a whole pit of acid, all by himself.

He took several deep breaths. As scared as he was, now was not the time to act like a baby. Now was the time to get out of here and get them both away from Gudger. He looked around the room— the window was hopeless—the only other way out was the door.

Getting to his feet, he took down his torn poster of Peyton Manning and studied the door. It was nothing special, just an ordinary door with three barrel hinges, to which Gudger had, of course, added a deadbolt lock. He realized that made it more of a jail cell than a bedroom, but he'd once watched a YouTube video where someone picked a deadbolt lock with two hairpins, so he knew it could be done. If he could just figure out how to do it himself, he could escape while Gudger watched the ball game. Then, he could at least find out what had happened to his mother.

Hurrying over to his dresser, he retrieved the Swiss Army knife that had been his father's. He turned his overhead light on and pulled the bedspread from his bed, stuffing it under the door in case Gudger walked by. After that, he started to work. He tried to thread the smallest of the knife blades into the lock, but he couldn't catch the mechanism that turned it. Frustrated, he tried a different blade. He had no luck with that either, so he pulled out the little plastic toothpick that came with the knife. That seemed to catch the mechanism better, but every time he almost got the thing to turn, the toothpick would slide out of the notch. He worked doggedly, his neck muscles burning with fatigue as tears of frustration rimmed his eyes. Finally, when he heard a screech owl's quivery call outside his window, he sat back on his heels. He knew then that he could work this toothpick until the sun came up—it was never going to open this lock.

He slumped to the floor, his stomach growling, eyes grainy with exhaustion. It had been dark for hours and he hadn't eaten since early morning. Maybe if he slept a few minutes, he might wake up less hungry, with a new idea about how to open the door. He reached up to turn off the overhead light and wrapped himself up in the bedspread. Cool wisps of air-conditioning came under the door, and he heard the refrigerator shudder as it came on. He realized then that he hadn't noticed when Gudger turned off the baseball game, had been unaware of the silence that had fallen on the house. *Wonder where Mama is*, Chase thought, his eyelids drooping. *Gone to bed with Gudger? Or stretched out on the kitchen floor, dead?*

He pushed the image out of his mind, replacing it with a happier one, back when he and Sam would both run and jump in their parents' bed on Christmas morning. His mother would get up to make coffee, but his father would scoop them both up at the same time and carry them into the living room, plunking them down beneath the Christmas tree. "Can you believe all these presents Santa Claus left?" he would say. "You two must have been awfully good this year!"

He nestled down into the warmth of the dream, remembering how strong his father's arms were, how his mother smiled at his father in a way she never smiled at Gudger. He was remembering that smile when, suddenly, he heard his mother's voice, just outside the door.

"Chase, I know you're probably asleep..." she whispered.

He bolted upright. "Mama?" he cried, pressing his mouth close to the door, praying he wasn't still dreaming. "Are you okay?"

"But I'm going on in to work," she said. "I'm going to give Dr. Knox my notice and come home early. When I do, we're leaving. Gudger got real mad last night. He did something to my ear..." Her voice dissolved in sobs.

A wave of sweet relief washed over him—Mama wasn't dead—Gudger hadn't killed her. "Oh, Mama, please don't leave," he begged. "Stay here and call the police! Gudger's gonna sell me to the same people he sold Samantha to!"

"Anyway, I'll see you soon, sweetheart."

"Mama! Wait!" he pleaded. "Don't you hear me?"

Apparently she didn't, because all he heard next was her footsteps padding softly to the back door. He held his breath, listening, wondering if Gudger was going to wake up and storm after her. For a long moment the world seemed suspended in silence. He heard the engine of her old Dodge catch, then diminish as she drove down the driveway.

He sat on his haunches, wondering if his mother had really said those things and then left for work, or if he'd just dreamed she had. It seemed odd that she hadn't heard him, but she said Gudger had hurt her ear. He would, he decided, accept it as real—that she was alive and coming home from work early to leave. He only hoped he would still be here when she came.

He got to his feet, feeling a sudden need to urinate. Hopping on one foot, he went to the window and raised it as far as it would go.

Then he unzipped his pants and let fly a stream of urine that arced out into Gudger's yard, splatting against the big oak tree outside his window. Somehow the act of pissing cleared his head, gave him fresh energy. When he turned away from the window, he looked at his bedroom with new eyes. He remembered that his mother had hung their winter coats in his closet—maybe he could make some kind of lock-picking tool from one of her coat hangers!

He hurried to open the closet door. He turned on the single light bulb that dangled from the ceiling. The pale light illuminated their cold weather wear—jackets and sweaters, Sam's blue parka, a frayed black coat his mother brought from West Virginia. He pushed the clothes along the rack, looking for the thinnest coat hanger. He found it at the end of the closet—a slender white wire that held the near-weightless lining to a raincoat. He shoved the other clothes down the rod, then his gaze fell on a tattered cardboard box lying in the far back corner of the closet. He blinked, wondering if he were hallucinating. That box looked exactly like the one that held Cousin Petey's gun!

"Oh my gosh!" he whispered. Forgetting about the coat hanger, he pulled it out of the closet. It was heavy, the twine wrapped diagonally in the same odd way his mother tied up their Christmas presents.

"But Mama was supposed to get rid of the gun!" he whispered, still unwilling to believe his good luck. "Gudger made her promise!"

Clutching the box to his chest as if it were some rare and precious jewel, he took it to the middle of his bed. He cut the twine with his father's little knife and opened the lid. Inside, nestled in some old quilt batting and smelling sharply of oil, lay the Army Colt Cousin Petey's father carried in Cuba, during the Spanish-American War. The barrel was dark blue while the handle was satiny brown wood that felt as smooth as silk. Gudger had taken it away from him, back when they were living in the duplex and Gudger still wore a uniform.

You don't need to be playing with guns, son, he'd warned, holding out his hand for the gun. *Your mama needs to get rid of that thing before you blow your own foot off.*

Though he'd begged her not to do it, his mother had said Gudger was right—he probably would blow his own foot off. *Dr. Knox, at work, collects old guns,* she'd told him. *Maybe he would like to buy it. Anyway, Chase, we can use the extra money.*

That had been the last he'd seen of the gun. He assumed she'd sold it to Dr. Knox—he'd never mentioned it again, and she'd never brought it up. But apparently she had, for once, not done what Gudger told her to do. Here was the gun, ready to do the bidding of anyone who could load it with bullets and pull the trigger. At that moment, it felt like a gift from God.

Chase picked up the revolver—it was cool to his touch, but so heavy that he had to hold it with both hands. There was a graceful lethality about the old gun that made him tremble; he couldn't imagine the terror of having such a thing pointed at your heart. Cousin Petey had thoughtfully included a dozen bullets inside an empty cold cream jar. He smiled, remembering the day she gave it to him.

This is my varmint gun, she'd croaked, in her old-woman voice. *I've run many a fox out of my hen house with this. Since you're the man of your family now, you might someday need to do the same.*

"I think I do, Cousin Petey," he whispered, fitting six bullets from the jar into the empty chambers of the gun. "And I think today might be the day."

TWENTY-FIVE

SHORTLY AFTER 2 A.M., Boyko Zelinski's cell phone beeped on the bedside table. Though the naked woman who lay next to him only murmured in her sleep, Boyko sat up in bed immediately. The ring was "Borodin's Night on Bald Mountain," a piece that had denoted discordancy to him ever since his childhood in Kiev. He'd assigned the piece to emergency calls only; that there was an emergency while he was spending the night with a lingerie model troubled him.

"Boyko here," he answered in English. He frowned as the man Smiley began speaking.

"Sorry to wake you up, Boyko, but we got a situation here."

"Tell me."

"We did the baby trap tonight, to clean up a pal's mess. We got something we didn't expect."

"What?" Boyko looked over as his bed partner rolled over. Her sheet slipped down, revealing amazing breasts—natural breasts, not a trace of silicone in them.

"A girl cop."

"So?" said Boyko, slowly peeling the sheet down to the girl's navel. "Take care of her like the others."

"You don't understand. This one's special. She's the governor's cop."

Boyko frowned. American government confused him at times. He knew the president led the country and the Congress collected huge salaries for little work, but he was hazy on what governors did. Mostly, he just dealt with police chiefs and union bosses. "What's a governor's cop?"

"She works for the governor of North Carolina, Boyko. Aren't you in Charlotte now?"

"Yes."

"The governor runs the state, up in Raleigh. And she's not somebody we want to mess with, if you know what I mean."

Boyko sighed. Sadly, he knew what Smiley meant. It meant no more nibbling the model's rosebud nipples or having her wrap those long legs around his waist, at least for tonight. It meant getting up, putting on clothes, driving over to figure out what to do with this cop. Still, he knew he had no choice. His employers would not be pleased if he remained here and let that *durachit'* Smiley take care of things.

"I'm coming now," he said. He clicked off the phone, then after a long, regretful look at the girl's magnificent breasts, he pulled the sheet back up to her chin.

———

He dressed quickly, redonning the white linen suit he'd worn earlier. He decided against the less traveled highways and took I-85 west to Smiley's place. It would get him close enough, and he liked the way his white Mercedes ate up the straight superhighway. As the mile markers flew by, he wondered about the cop who'd fallen for Smiley's trick. Probably fat, he decided. Most American girls carried an extra ten kilos, the Southerners even more. Occasionally the weight was nicely proportioned—large breasts, round butts. More often it was pot bellies and lard-dimpled thighs. He pictured this cop as one of the *politsiya korov* in Moscow—fat, short-haired women with wide duck feet shod in black athletic shoes. He snorted with disgust at the thought. Until he'd removed them, his model had worn red spike heels with tiny little straps that crisscrossed her ankles.

He continued down I-85, exiting just shy of the South Carolina line. From there he drove northwest, to Smiley's dump. It was an old hunting camp that had expanded to a motel, then shriveled to extinction when the interstate opened some fifteen miles to the east. It backed up against a forest thick with dark pine trees, much like the Ural Mountain work camps his grandfather had described. He pulled up beside Smiley's Cadillac and walked into what had once been the lobby. Smiley sat behind a battered desk, his oily face shiny with sweat and concern.

"Thank God you're here," Smiley said, getting to his feet. "I was beginning to worry."

"Don't be such an old woman," Boyko snapped. "You only called two hours ago. Where's the cop?"

"Follow me."

Smiley locked the lobby door, then led him down a dark hall. He housed the girls awaiting transport here, far away from the ones who took their baggage to the street every night. He walked to the second room on the right and unlocked the door. On a single bed, away from the boarded-up window, a woman lay on her back, her legs spread, one arm dangling off the mattress. Boyko walked over to get a closer look.

"This is the governor's cop?"

Smiley shrugged. "According to Ralph Gudger. "

"You didn't take any IDs, did you?"

"No, we didn't touch nothin'. She came out of her car like they all do, all panicky over a kid being dumped by the side of the road. Her name's Mary Crow. Gudger says she's investigating gay hate crimes for the governor."

Boyko frowned. "Gay hate crimes?"

"Queers," explained Smiley. "Homos."

Boyko shrugged but leaned over the bed, moving the woman's head to get a full view of her face. She didn't look like any policewoman he'd ever seen—high cheekbones, straight nose, a lower lip that begged kissing. He straightened up and saw that though her breasts were not especially large, neither were her hips, and she wore leather sandals instead of the boxy black walkers he'd been expecting. He turned to Smiley. "You know, certain men would find this woman very attractive."

"She's better than most of girl cops we get." Smiley looked down at the drugged woman. "Personally, she don't do so much for me."

"That's because you like big tits and small brains," Boyko replied. "This woman goes far beyond that."

"What do you know about her brain? She's fucking out cold!"

"You look at the details—her clothes aren't cheap. Her hair's clean. No silly tattoos, nothing pierced except her ears. A beautiful mouth. I cannot imagine what she must look like with her clothes off and her eyes open."

"She's working on this gay thing," said Smiley. "She might be a dyke."

Boyko threw back his head and laughed. "Even better. I know fifty men who would pay a fortune to have a pretty *lesbiyanka* cop tied up in their bedroom."

Smiley gaped at him, wide-eyed. "You mean you don't want me to get rid of her?"

"Absolutely not!" said Boyko sharply. "Phone calls must be made quickly about this one."

"But this is a real woman—a policewoman—not some doped-up dropout teenager."

Boyko laughed. "The greater the risk, the greater the reward, Smiley. Isn't that what you Americans say?"

"But what do you want me to do with her?"

"Is that little blonde still here?"

Smiley nodded. "They're picking her up tomorrow."

"Then put this one down the hall."

"I don't know. I've never done a cop before."

Boyko looked at Smiley's anxious expression and slapped him on the back. "Calm down, my friend. This particular American cop will also be gone tomorrow. And she's going to make us a lot of money."

———

Some miles away, Victor Galloway rolled over in bed, knowing dreamily that his alarm would soon go off, sending Bon Jovi's "I'll Sleep When I'm Dead" through the room at full volume. He'd woken up to that song since he was in high school, and though it had been the anthem of his youth at Saint Pi High, at thirty-eight he felt more like the lyrics should go, *I'll sleep so I won't feel like I'm dead.* He nestled deeper under his covers, waiting subconsciously for the music to start, for the day to begin. He was thinking about yesterday, wondering what Mary Crow had done last night when his cell phone erupted with the Chipmunks singing "I'm Gonna Whip Somebody's Ass." He bolted upright and reached for the phone—that was the ringtone he assigned to Dispatch, for when shit was hitting the proverbial fan.

"Galloway here," he croaked, his voice grainy with sleep.

"Galloway, this is Pike."

Pike, Pike. He thought for a moment, then remembered Pike—a lanky patrol officer with buck teeth and acne scars on his cheeks. "Yeah, Pike. What's up?"

"We got a 10-53 here that Crump says you might know something about."

"A 10-53?" Abruptly, the Bon Jovi drums launched. Galloway swatted the alarm off. "Abandoned vehicle?"

"Yeah," said Pike. "A '99 black Miata, registered to a Mary Crow. Crump says you know her."

He sat up straighter in the bed. "Yeah, I know her. Where's the car?"

"Jackson Highway, about three miles this side of the Gaston County line."

He remembered they'd been drinking at the restaurant—wine during the meal, a brandy afterwards. Still, Mary had seemed okay to drive. "Does it look like she had an accident?"

"No, no accident. No nothin'. It's like that other girl—lights and engine left on, keys still the ignition. Purse is still in the passenger seat. Nothing—"

"I'm on my way," said Galloway before Pike could finish his sentence.

———

He dressed in two minutes, pulling on jeans as he called her cell phone, then grabbing his keys, weapon, and IDs as he tried the Holiday Inn in Gastonia. At one number he got her recorded greeting; at the other just a telephone that rang repeatedly, with no one ever picking up.

"I should have followed her home," he whispered as he bolted out the door of his apartment. It was late, they'd been drinking, she didn't know the roads that well. But she'd seemed fine when they'd walked to the parking lot. And when he kissed her ...

When I kissed her, she kissed back, he told himself. She'd looked at him with those incredible eyes and kissed him back. Now she'd vanished, just like Gudger's stepkid.

He raced down the stairs, through the parking lot, over to the green Mustang he'd babied for the past ten years. Tires squealing, he navigated the long driveway of his apartment building, then pulled out onto the highway. As he drove, he kept calling her cell phone, each time getting the same recorded greeting.

Ten minutes later, he turned on Jackson Highway; fifteen miles farther down the road he saw the lights flashing. Two squads were there, along with the unmarked speed trap car that usually worked the Sligo County line. Some inner part of him offered a tepid prayer of thanks; at least they hadn't put up crime scene tapes or called for a body bag yet.

He pulled in behind the nearest squad and hurried over to where Pike and two other uniforms stood staring at Mary's black Miata. No other detective was there, which meant he was officially in charge.

"Find anything?" he asked Pike.

"Nothing to find," the tall man replied. "Nothing's missing, except the driver."

Galloway scanned the woods that lined the road. "Where have you looked for her?"

"We fanned out and searched about fifty feet on both sides of her car. We didn't find anything."

"Nothing?"

"No broken twigs, no footprints. No nothing."

Galloway peered down into the little convertible. Mary's purse lay unopened on the passenger's seat. A half-empty bottle of water stood in the car's cup holders, a pair of Asics running shoes stashed in the well behind the driver's seat. The engine was still running, the radio still playing the NPR station out of Charlotte. The car reminded him of a loyal dog, told to stay until its mistress returned. Galloway reached in with a tissue and turned the ignition off, then lifted Mary's purse. He looked inside—everything of value was there—cell phone, checkbook, a wallet that still held her driver's license, two credit cards, and $34 in cash.

Pike frowned. "Aren't you polluting the evidence?"

"No point in wasting her gas," said Galloway.

Pike wrote something in his notebook. "Crump says you know the driver?"

"Mary Crow. Special envoy from the governor."

"This the gal tryin' to hang that preacher?"

"He may have been a part of her investigation."

Pike laughed. "Maybe she went up in the Rapture."

"Shut up," said Galloway.

Pike's eyes narrowed. "Something going on between you two?"

"No," said Galloway. "I just doubt that Chief Ramsey wants to call the governor and tell her we've lost her super cop."

Pike caught Galloway's drift. He gathered the two other uniforms and told them to go search deeper in the woods. While they did that, Galloway made a wide circle around Mary's car. He saw no skid marks, no footprints on the either side of the road, nothing to indicate anything out of the ordinary. As he walked, he went over the details of last night in his head. They'd finished dinner around 9:30, he'd kissed her around 10:15. He'd jokingly warned her about driving down *la carretera del dolor*, but she assured him she'd be okay, that they would talk tomorrow. Somewhere between then and now, Mary Crow pulled over to the side of the road and vanished.

He knelt down beside the driver's side of the little car, trying to imagine what Mary might have seen last. Pine trees. Darkness. A fifty-foot stretch of rural Carolina road no different from a thousand others. He stood up and reached to turn off her lights, when something on the other side of the road caught his eye. He walked over to find a large oil spot, shiny in the rising sun. He extended a finger, touched it. It was fresh, still viscous. A car had recently stopped directly across from Mary's, and had stayed long enough to drip a couple tablespoons of motor oil. It could have been somebody curious about why a sports car had been left running by the side of the road; it could have been something far worse.

He looked at the officers standing around the car. "Who called this in?"

"I did," said Pike. "Crump was going off shift and told me to call you."

"Where you pull up?"

Pike nodded at the shoulder of the road, twenty feet past Mary's car.

"Any of you guys pull up here?" Galloway pointed to the oil drip.

They all shook their head. He looked over at Pike. "Get on your radio," he told him. "Call the forensic people, then call the chief. This just went from a missing person to an abduction."

"On whose call?" asked Pike.

"Mine," replied Galloway. "Some kind of vehicle was parked close to her car, long enough to spill a fair amount of oil. Anybody who was just curious about an idling car wouldn't have stayed that long. Anybody who wanted to make off with her money and credit cards would have left fast." Again he looked at the shiny spot glistening in the sun. "Whoever left that oil spill knows what happened to Mary Crow."

TWENTY-SIX

CHASE SAT ON HIS bed, holding the big Army Colt, listening to the raspy gurgles of Gudger's snoring. For hours he'd gone over Cousin Petey's instructions on shooting the gun—aim down the barrel, squeeze the trigger instead of pulling it, and most important, try to avoid shooting yourself in the foot. In retrospect, he marveled at Cousin Petey's own ability with the weapon—the day she'd showed him how to shoot it, she was eighty-two, a dried little apple of a woman who wore a cotton housedress and old-fashioned tennis shoes. She'd held the gun as if were no heavier than a can of bug spray and demolished the empty Coke can she was using as a target. Tonight, resting in his lap, the gun seemed to weigh fifty pounds, at least. An impossible thing to point and fire at anything. Still, Cousin Petey had given it to him as the "man of his family." Probably she thought he'd protect Sam and his mother from foxes or rats. Never would she have dreamed that he was going to aim it at a man.

"But I am," he whispered. He stood up, practiced the motions again. Holding the barrel of the gun in his left hand, he had to use all the strength in his right to cock the hammer. With that in position, he braced himself against the bed and aimed at the door, his arms straight, like he'd seen cops do on TV shows. If he locked his elbows, he could hold the thing steady for fifteen seconds. Beyond that, his arms began to shake as the gun grew too heavy for him to hold.

"Maybe I won't have to shoot," he whispered, aiming at the spot his Peyton Manning poster used to occupy. "Maybe when I point it at Gudger he'll get so scared that he'll do what I want."

He knew most people would react that way, but most people didn't include Gudger. If anything, pointing a gun at him would be like swatting at a hornet with a broom—it would just make him madder. Nonetheless, Chase had to take his chances. The gun was the only thing standing between him and that gorilla in the black car. Uncocking the hammer, he hid the gun under his bed. "Whatever happens will be better than being boy meat," he said. "Even if I wind up dead."

He lay back on the bed. He tried to pass the time reading some of his Sherlock Holmes book, but he couldn't concentrate on the words and Gudger's snoring soon lulled him into a kind of waking dream. As the night outside his window lightened into day, the dead and the living all gathered around his bed—Sam, his father, Cousin Petey, even Mary Crow. They were all telling him things, warning him about what to do. Mary Crow was about to show him how to shoot her Glock, when suddenly, everyone disappeared. He opened his eyes, lifted his head. Something had changed. For an instant he couldn't figure out what, then he realized—Gudger's snoring had stopped.

He hurried over to the door, put his ear to the crack. Someone hacked up phlegm, then the toilet flushed in the bathroom. He went cold inside—Gudger was up!

Chase ran back to the bed and grabbed the Colt. With shaking hands, he held the old revolver by the barrel as he pulled back on the hammer. By the time the thing clicked into place, he was sweating.

"All you have to do now is point it," he whispered, trying to calm down, knowing that with one squeeze, he could blow Gudger to Kingdom Come.

Pointing the gun at the floor, he walked back to his door. He took a single deep breath, then he put his plan in motion. "Gudger!" he cried, banging hard on the door. "Gudger are you out there?"

"What?" Gudger mumbled from the hall, still sounding groggy with sleep.

"You gotta let me out of here!" Chase tried to sound desperate. "I need to go to the bathroom!"

"Piss in your pants, you little faggot!" said Gudger. "I've got to make some coffee."

"It's not piss," Chase cried. "It's the other. You know, diarrhea."

For a moment, he heard nothing. Then Gudger started cursing—something about goddamn kids. Footsteps thumped down the hall, a key started rattling in the deadbolt. Chase backed away from the door, holding the gun tight, his heart beating like some wild thing in his chest.

He stood there, waiting. Gudger was apparently having trouble with the lock. Chase heard him curse again—finally, just as his arms started to shake, the deadbolt slid back with a *snap*. The door opened. Gudger stumbled into the room, holding his scalded hand close to his chest, wearing jockey shorts and a T-shirt that rode up over his beer gut. He looked at Chase through squinted eyes, his mouth curved down in anger.

"You shit your britches in here and you'll be the one cleaning it . . ." The words died in his throat as he saw the Colt pointed at his chest. His eyes grew wide as his face turned the color of pie dough.

"What the fuck are you doing with that?" he whispered. "I told your mother to get rid of it."

Chase held the gun in a death grip, trying to keep his arms from trembling. "For once she didn't do what you told her," he said slowly, his voice taking on an unaccustomed deepness.

"So I see," said Gudger. "So what are you going to do with it, Olive Oyl? Shoot me?"

"Not before I find out what you did with my sister."

"Man, are we back to that again?" Gudger shook his head, disgusted. "Son, what will it take to convince you? I didn't do anything with your sister. She ran off with her boyfriend."

"Then why did you go crazy after Mary Crow came here? Why did you tell that man I was sweet boy meat? Why did you lock me in this room and then beat up my mom?" His voice cracked, soared back into soprano range. He willed away hot tears.

Gudger leaned against the doorjamb and chuckled, as if everything had been a joke. "Hey, I was just fooling around. Trying to see how tough you were, you know? My old man played the same kind of tricks on me. One time he told me he'd shot my dog when he really had the pup tied up in the barn. He got a good laugh out of that. That thing about you being boy meat wasn't true. I was just teasing you."

"It didn't sound like teasing to me." Chase raised the gun higher, pointing it at Gudger's heart. "Now tell me where Samantha is!"

"You need to calm down, son. You could go to jail for what you're doing now." Gudger backed up a step and held out his scalded hand, as if to ward off a bullet. "I've heard some rumors about your sister, but I'm not telling you anything with a gun pointed at me."

"You know a lot more than just rumors about my sister." Chase took a step forward. "And you're gonna tell me right now."

Gudger inched backward into the dark hall. As he did, the meanness returned to his eyes, and his lips drew back in a sneer. "Oh, yeah? You gotta catch me first, Olive Oyl."

Gudger turned and ran down the hall toward the living room, his bottom jiggling in his sagging jockey shorts. Chase ran after him, the gun feeling like a lead weight in his hands. Gudger banged into an end table and almost knocked over a lamp, but he made it to the front door faster than Chase thought possible.

"Stop, Gudger!" he cried, hurrying after him. "Turn around and talk to me!"

Gudger ignored him. Already he'd gotten the chain unhooked; five more seconds and he'd have the door open. With the big revolver shaking in his hand, Chase lifted the gun and took aim.

"I'm telling you to stop!" he screamed at Gudger. "Turn around!"

Gudger turned, long enough to lift his middle finger. "Fuck you, you little faggot!"

With a silent prayer to his dead father, to Cousin Petey, to all the people who'd ever held out the hope that he might be a person of worth someday, he squeezed the trigger. For a split second, nothing happened. Then came a roar so loud he thought the roof was caving in. The gun flipped back, hit him in the face. As one front tooth skittered across the floor, Chase fell on his back, blood spurting from his nose. Though his ears rang as if he were inside a bell, he could hear a scream of agony. He lifted his head to see Gudger lying across the front door, his right kneecap gleaming white as a new baseball against a field of red.

Chase looked around for the gun. Somehow it had fallen underneath the coffee table. Shaking the ringing from his head, he crawled over and grabbed it. The long barrel was still warm to his fingers. Flush with triumph, he got to his feet and walked over to Gudger, who lay writhing on the floor.

"I can't feel my leg!" he shrieked, spit flying from his mouth as he tried to scramble away from Chase. "I can't feel my goddamned leg!"

Now a strange new person spoke through Chase's voice, used Chase's arms to again point the revolver. "You tell me where Sam is, or you're not going to feel anything much longer."

Gudger rolled over on his back. The front of his jockey shorts were stained bright yellow. Sweat dotted his forehead and he gasped like someone who'd just sprinted up a mountain. "Get an ambulance. Then I'll tell you."

Chase shook his head. "You tell me first. Then I'll get an ambulance."

"Okay, okay." Gudger gasped, grimacing in pain. "There's an old motel near Hubbard Mountain. Last time I heard, she was there. Now call me an ambulance!"

Chase shrugged. "I don't know where the phone is."

Gudger looked at him. He opened his mouth, as if he wanted to speak, then his jaw went slack as his head hit the floor.

Just like that, the powerful stranger who'd inhabited Chase's body vanished. Once again it was just eleven-year-old Charles Oliver Buchanan who was standing over his stepfather's body, an Army Colt pointed at his heart.

"Oh no," he whispered. He knew if he didn't call an ambulance, Gudger would probably bleed to death or die of shock. If Gudger died, then Chase would spend the rest of his life in prison. He'd shot an unarmed man who was trying to get away. He'd read enough detective novels to know how bad that was.

He put the gun on the coffee table and ran through the house, desperate to find something to call an ambulance with. The phone jack in the den was empty, and the wall phone in the kitchen had long since been disconnected. He did a cursory search of all the bedrooms, then ran out to the garage. He looked through Gudger's tool bench and on the seat of his car, but again, he found nothing. Frantic, he returned to the house. There had to be a phone somewhere in here! He'd heard Gudger telling someone he was sweet boy meat just last night.

He ran down the hall and returned to Gudger's bedroom, rifling through his dresser. He found socks, T-shirts, even Gudger's Taser, but no phone. He ran over to the bedside table, pulled open that drawer. Gudger kept only a Bible and a tube of Mentholatum to see him through the nights. Chase collapsed on the bed, fighting back tears. "Where is your stupid phone, you idiot? Why do you have to hide it all the time?"

Frustrated, he hit Gudger's pillow with his fist. His knuckles grazed against something hard. He looked under the pillow. *There* was Gudger's cell phone! He grabbed it and punched in 911. The phone rang three times, then a girl with a thick mountain accent answered.

"911," she said. "What is your emergency?"

Chase gulped. "Someone's been shot. You need to send an ambulance to 514 Kedron Road, right now!"

TWENTY-SEVEN

GALLOWAY HELPED PIKE CORDON off a perimeter around Mary's car, then he told the tall uniform to stay put until the search team arrived.

"Where are you going?" asked Pike, surprised. "You're the detective."

"Gastonia. Mary Crow was staying at the Holiday Inn there. I'll check in with you later."

Pike watched as a car heading east slowed to gape at Mary's car, then sped on to its destination. "These morning commuters will shit if we block off the road."

"Let them through, but don't let anybody go in those woods."

Pike frowned but walked over to his cruiser. He kept the blue lights flashing and assumed a posture of command, glaring at the oncoming traffic, his arms folded across his chest.

Galloway hurried back to his Mustang. He headed east, toward Gastonia, the sun a distant orange ball rising on the horizon. The two-lane stretched through farmland and stands of scrub pine. No cross streets intersected it—only the long driveways of farm houses, set acres back from the highway. Highway 74 was, he'd learned, a quick and dirty way for locals with cars to avoid the interstate and get to Charlotte via the back roads. For the transient Hispanics who had no cars, it was a way to walk from farm to farm, crop to crop. Sweet potatoes and corn in the summer; Christmas trees in November. Galloway sped by a family of five as he drove—a man and a woman, three children trailing behind them like small brown ducks.

"*La carretera del dolor,*" he muttered. Maybe Mary was on to something—maybe the road was more than just a flat strip of pavement that Latinos walked to get to the hard, bone-wearying jobs America offered. Maybe it was a dumping ground for Campbell County's unwanted, where some people vanished and others turned up looking like Bryan Taylor.

"At least it's not that," he told himself, remembering the way Mary Crow had smiled at him last night. "At least not yet." He sped on, crossing the county line, coming to the town of Gastonia. The Holiday Inn was new, near I-85. He parked by the entrance and asked for the manager.

"I'm Victor Galloway, Campbell County Police," he explained, flashing his badge at a blond woman who'd apparently gotten up so early she'd pinned her name tag on upside down. "We have a problem with one of your guests. I need to check Mary Crow's room."

"Do you know the number?"

"No."

The woman's fingers flew over the computer keyboard. "212" she said, a moment later. "Let me get my master key and I'll take you up there."

She led him quickly through the lobby mostly, he thought, to get him and his gold badge out of view of the other guests who were trooping down for the free breakfast buffet. He followed her to the elevator, where they rode up to the second floor. Mary's room was at the end of the hall. The manager opened the door, turned on the light, then stepped aside. Galloway walked in. The room had apparently not been disturbed since housekeeping had cleaned it the day before. The bed was made, there was unopened soap in the bathroom, and the hand towels had been neatly folded into little fan shapes. A zipped-up make-up bag lay beside the sink, while an open suitcase lay on the dresser beside the flat-screen TV. Galloway walked over and looked through Mary's still packed clothes—underwear, two white blouses, a pair of jeans. He felt a lump under the jeans and lifted them to find a Glock 9 lying in an oiled shoulder holster, a box of ammo beside it.

Damn, he thought. *If she'd taken that, she might be here right now, asking me why in the hell I'm going through her underwear.* He turned away from the suitcase, looked in the closet. A single linen jacket and a navy skirt were hanging on a hanger; beyond that, nothing. The room looked as if she'd just stepped out of it, would be back any minute. Barring a miracle, that wasn't going to happen.

He checked to see if she'd made any notes on the pad beside the phone, checked to see if any of those small sheets had fallen underneath the bed or behind the desk, but he saw nothing. He turned to the manager. "Could I talk to the housekeepers who cleaned her room yesterday?"

"Certainly." The woman picked up the phone, murmured something into it. In a few minutes two wide-eyed Latinas pushed their cleaning cart to the door.

"*Buenas dias,*" he greeted them in Spanish. "*¿Visto a la dama en la habitación desde ayer?*"

They both shook their heads. The younger one said, "*No, señor. Nunca hemos visto en absoluto.*"

He asked when they'd last made up the bed.

This time, the younger one held up two fingers. "*Hace dos mañanas.*"

"*Gracias.*" He frowned. Neither housekeeper had seen Mary at all, but they'd made up her bed two mornings ago. He went back over to her suitcase, wondering if he'd gotten the right room, if she'd been here at all. He looked through her clothes for a cleaning ticket or a business card but found nothing. Closing the suitcase, he searched the side pockets for any identifying information. His finger curled around a piece of paper shoved into one. He pulled it out. It was an old plane ticket stub to Tulsa, Oklahoma. The passenger was one Mary Crow of Hartsville, North Carolina.

"Okay," he whispered. "She went back to Asheville the night before last, and had her 74 Special at that bar. She spent the night there at her home, then came back here yesterday morning." Her abandoned car was the only clue as to her whereabouts after she'd left him at Angelo's.

He gave the manager his card, telling her to call him immediately should Mary return.

The woman took his card hesitantly. "So should I assume this woman's coming back? Consider this room occupied?"

"Yes," Galloway told her with a confidence he did not feel. "You can absolutely assume she's coming back."

———

He drove back to her car. Pike was still there, watching as the forensic squad was pulling away.

"They find anything?" asked Galloway, hopeful.

Pike shook his head. "No bloodstains, no semen. They'll run the prints this afternoon."

Disappointed, Galloway thought back to Mary's conversation last night—she said she'd gone to see a man whose sister had been found murdered on 74; a man extremely hostile to the notion that his sister might be a lesbian. Was there some kind of connection here? Had the man been so upset that he'd killed the messenger to save his sister from the taint of homosexuality? It was possible—Mary said the guy kept slapping his palm with a tire iron. But what was his name? Williams? Watson? She'd told him, but he'd been watching her eyes, looking at her mouth like the lovesick fool he feared he was becoming.

He turned back to Pike. "I need to use your box a minute." He walked over to Pike's cruiser and logged on to his computer. He keyed in homicides, 2010–2013. The name popped up immediately—Wallace, Tiffani, white female, age 19. Next of kin, Eddie Wallace, 320 County Road 218. He got out of Pike's cruiser and headed toward his Mustang.

"I'm going to check out a guy named Wallace," he told Pike. "Get the wrecker out here and get this car into the police lot."

"Then we're done out here?" asked Pike, his tone hopeful.

"We are for now," said Galloway.

———

He drove fast, against the traffic, heading toward the South Carolina line. 320 County Road 218 was an old white doublewide trailer, set on blocks. A wrought-iron sculpture of a donkey sat in the front yard, next to a faded plastic candy cane from several Christmases ago. Galloway pulled around to the back of the place, where a skinny, barefoot man wearing cut-off jeans and a dirty T-shirt stood peering under the hood of an ancient Dodge Charger that had, in a former life, had the number 11 painted on its side. He looked up from the car and frowned as Galloway's black Mustang nosed up the driveway.

"Bway-nos dee-os, Pedro." The man flicked a cigarette out of his mouth as Galloway got out of the car. "Kay passa?"

"*Muy bien, pipucho*," Galloway replied, the Spanish rolling off his tongue. He lifted a friendly hand towards the man as he moved toward him; then he drew close, grabbed the man by his hair, and slammed his face down into the head gasket of the car.

"What the fuck?" the man cried. He squirmed, tried to get to his feet, but Galloway kicked the man's leg apart and shoved his knee firmly against his balls. His legs were pale, splotched with red-looking flea bites.

"This is what, dickhead." Galloway switched to perfect English as pulled out his badge for the second time that morning. "I'm Detective Victor Galloway." He dangled his badge in front of Wallace's face. "I used to play soccer in Argentina and my goal-kicking knee is aimed right at your nuts, so cut the Speedy Gonzalez crap."

"Okay," Wallace whimpered, breathing hard.

Galloway lifted the guy's head up and whopped his nose against the manifold, just for fun. "Are you Eddie Wallace?"

Wallace nodded as blood seeped from his nose.

"You speak Spanish. You know the word *ayer*?"

"No." Wallace sobbed, trying to breathe.

"It means *yesterday*, *pipucho*."

"So?"

Galloway tightened his grip on the man's hair. "Do you remember yesterday? Or are you too fucked up?"

Wallace nodded. "I remember," he said, his voice coming out strangely muffled.

"You remember a good-looking woman coming over here, asking about your little sister?"

"Yeah."

"You remember spitting tobacco juice at her? Threatening her with a lug wrench?"

"I didn't threaten her." Wallace gulped. "She pissed me off. She thought my sister was a dyke."

"Yeah, well that woman was a cop. She happened to go missing last night," said Galloway, pressing his knee harder into Wallace's scrotum.

"I don't know anything about that!" cried Wallace.

"Sorry, *pipucho*. You gotta convince me better than that."

"She came over, asking all these questions about Tiffani. Who she hung with, if she had a boyfriend. When I said I didn't know, she asked if I thought Tiffani was queer. She made me mad, saying those things about my sister. Plus she kept looking at me like I was a piece of shit. So I grabbed a tire iron. Big deal. I never hit her with it."

"You're a real *caballero*. What happened next?"

"Nothing! She was driving a black '99 Miata. She got in it and left."

"And what did you do?"

"I worked on this car till dark. Then I went to work."

"Where do you work?"

"Walmart, in Gastonia."

"Did you take Jackson Highway?"

"Yeah, I guess," replied Wallace.

"You drive this heap?"

Wallace shook his head. "No. I drove that truck over there."

Galloway looked across the weedy back yard, where a Dodge Ram was parked on a concrete slab, underneath an aluminum canopy. "You park it there all the time?"

"Every night," said Wallace.

"Where are the keys?"

"In my back pocket."

He loosened his grip on the man's hair but pulled out his service weapon. "Go back it up."

Wallace stood up and wiped the blood from his nose. He stared at Galloway as if he were crazy. "Back it up where?"

"Off that concrete slab, asshole." He took the safety off his weapon. "Go an inch in any other direction and I'll consider you avoiding arrest."

Wallace gulped, then walked over to the truck, his bare feet making little slaps on the ground. Galloway watched as he started the car, then backed it just out of its concrete parking space. When he'd cleared the canopy, Galloway told him to turn the motor off.

"Toss the keys out the window," he said, still holding his gun on Wallace. "And get out of the truck."

Wallace did as he was told, still wiping blood from his nose.

"Okay. Go over and lie face down in the driveway. Make one move and you will have changed your last spark plug."

Wallace glared at him, but he went over and lay face down in the drive. When Galloway saw that the stupid bastard was well away from anything he could use as a weapon, he walked over to the concrete slab where the truck had been parked. He bent down and studied the middle of the slab, where all the drips and oozings from an engine would splatter. Though Eddie Wallace's worth as a sensitive human being might be up for grabs, he was a damn good mechanic. Not a drop of oil stained the pavement where his truck had been parked— certainly not the big glob of stuff that gleamed from the pavement next to Mary's abandoned car. Whoever had been there last night hadn't been driving Eddie Wallace's truck.

"Okay." Galloway rose to his feet. "You can get up."

Wallace hauled himself up. His already-swelling nose looked like a turnip stuck in the middle of his face.

"Well?" he said. "What are the charges?"

"No charges," said Galloway, heading for his car.

"No charges? You come up here and break my nose just to get me to move my truck?"

"You got it, *pipucho*. But let me give you a piece of advice. Next time a cop asks questions about your dead sister, don't spit tobacco juice at them, and don't go near a tire iron. And if you want to be extra nice, don't call any Latino cops Pedro. It just makes us grumpy as hell."

TWENTY-EIGHT

CHASE DROPPED THE CELL phone and hurried back out to Gudger. He lay sprawled beside the front door, his knee a bloody red mess, his lower leg bent at an impossible angle to his thigh. His eyes were closed, but his mouth was sipping shallow little gasps of air, like a goldfish in a bowl of scummy water.

Chase grasped the doorjamb, dizzied by the odors of blood and urine. "Please be okay," he whispered, for the first time in his life praying for Gudger to live instead of die. As he stared at the wounded man, he fought back the urge to vomit. What should he do now? Stay here and wait for the ambulance? The cops would come, too. Should he tell them that Gudger knew where Sam was? That Gudger was planning to sell him to some people as boy meat? The cops already thought he was crazy; they would never believe that Gudger would do such terrible things. To them, ol' Gudge was a stand-up guy.

Run, some inner voice told him as he stared at Gudger's yellow-stained underwear. *Get out now while you can still save Sam.*

Leaving Gudger sipping air, he turned and headed for the kitchen door. He ran out into the back yard, figuring he'd slip under the fence and follow the creek down to the highway. He'd just passed the marigold patch when he heard a siren coming down Kedron Road. The sound grew louder, was soon joined by other sirens, wailing like coon dogs in full cry.

"Oh man!" he cried, tears coming to his eyes. "How did they get here so fast?"

Gudger's one of their own, the voice whispered again. *They're going to come fast, and come hard.*

He looked around. He didn't have time to get to the creek now—he would have to hide. But where? The cops would search the house and shed immediately. He turned around, desperate for a refuge, when his gaze fell on the maple tree in the side yard. For months he'd tried to climb it to hide from Gudger, but he'd always been too short to reach the branches. Was he tall enough to climb it now? He didn't know, but he had to try.

His heart thudding, he raced toward the tree. As the sirens split the stillness of the morning air, he ran to the tree, then leaped with all his strength. His fingers scraped along the bark, then caught. Tightening his hold, he swung himself forward. His legs wrapped around the next branch and he began to shimmy up into the thick green leaves. Branch after branch he climbed, twenty, then thirty feet into the air. He glanced down once, dizzyingly, to see the red lights of the ambulance turning into the driveway, followed by three sets of flashing blue lights. Then he kept his eyes on the tree, climbing until he reached a deep crotch that held him like a cradle. Ten feet higher and the limbs would be too slender to hold him, but here, it was perfect. Though it made him dizzy, he could stretch the length of one branch and get a clear view of the house, yet remain hidden by the foliage. Wrapping himself tight around the branches, he settled in and turned his attention to the house. Already the paramedics were heading inside, red backpacks in hand. Three cop cars had pulled up behind them, their radios blaring. While one cop hurried to the back of the house with his gun drawn, the others rushed the front porch and pounded on the door. When they got no answer, one of the beefier cops put his shoulder to the thing. It opened slowly. He heard one cop call, "Heads up! Somebody's lying against the front door!"

The others pulled their guns and crept inside. Chase started to tremble, his arms and legs quivering so badly he feared he might fall out of the tree. For a long time nothing happened, then the paramedics came out and retrieved a gurney from the back of their truck. They took it inside. Chase waited, his stomach prickling with fear. If they brought Gudger out in a black body bag, he would be arrested, convicted of murder, and would spend the rest of his life in a prison cell. Better to just let go of these branches and break his neck right now. He waited, hardly daring to breathe, when finally, the door opened again. A paramedic came out, slowly pulling the gurney. On it was not a black bag, but Gudger, wrapped in a red blanket, an oxygen mask over his nose. As the second paramedic eased the gurney off the porch, a cop walked beside them, holding an IV bag over Gudger's arm.

Chase felt weak with relief. Gudger wasn't dead. He wasn't guilty of murder—at least not yet. He watched as they loaded Gudger into the ambulance, then drove off, sirens blaring and lights flashing all over again. He figured the cops would soon follow—their precious Gudger had been taken care of. But that didn't happen. They all stayed—two searching the house, another doing a sweep of Gudger's property, his eyes on the ground, looking for clues.

Chase wanted to cry, wanted to wish himself as far away from here as he could. But all he could do was cling to the tree branches, being as still as he could, praying that nobody would think to look in the maple tree.

The cops seemed to stay for hours, wandering in and out of the house. One cop brought out Cousin Petey's gun. "Look at this," he cried. "Little fucker nailed him with one shot from this old Army Colt. Five bullets left in a six-bullet barrel."

"I'm surprised he had the strength to hold it up," said another cop Chase recognized from Gudger's bowling team. "Kid doesn't weigh eighty pounds, soaking wet."

"He weighs a little bit less than that now," the third cop announced as he came out of the house, tossing something in his hand. "I found his front tooth under the sofa."

With his tongue, Chase felt the empty space where his left front tooth had been. It was now just a jagged edge of bone, close to his gum. He hadn't even realized it was gone.

"Guess the recoil must have knocked it out of his mouth." The cop put the tooth in his pocket and shook his head. "We're done here, guys. The kid's taken off. We've got a good description—somebody will pick him up from the APB."

"Chief will be pissed," warned the bowling team cop. "He wanted that kid, bad."

"Then he'll just have to be satisfied with his front tooth," said the one who was apparently in charge. "The little bastard ain't anywhere around here."

"Goddamn!" The third one put his hands on his hips. "We got here seven minutes after the 911. How could a little kid vanish in seven minutes? On foot, too."

"Maybe he hitched a ride," said the bowling cop. "Crump was telling some crazy ass tale about how he'd thumbed up to Asheville on a peach truck."

Their radios started to crackle. Two leaned closer to hear the dispatch, but the third cop turned in a slow circle. Chase watched him look down the driveway, across the front yard, up the side yard, then he stopped and stared directly at the tree.

Chase gulped. His arms and legs turned to stone as the cop's gaze seemed to penetrate every leaf on the tree.

"Anybody check that big maple tree?" he finally asked.

The others turned to follow his gaze. "I didn't," said the bald-headed cop. "I was searching the shed."

"I was working inside," said the one who had his tooth.

"I'm gonna go have a look. Used to be a tree-climber myself, when I was a kid."

Chase watched as the cop started toward the tree. Fighting a real panic, he knew if he climbed higher, he would fall. If he climbed anywhere lower, the cop would see the branches moving. All he could do was lie still and hope the leaves hid him. He curled his arms and legs along the branch and held his breath, watching through slitted eyes as the cop drew closer. He was almost directly underneath him when one of the other cops called out.

"Hey, Brady! Fuck the tree! Chief wants us back now!"

"Thirty seconds," said Brady. "Just to be sure."

"Suit yourself. I'll tell him you were climbing a tree when he asks where you are."

Brady stopped. He peered up into the tree one more time. For an instant his eyes seemed to lock on Chase's, then they slid away, trying to penetrate the green leafiness. "Probably up there," he muttered to himself as he turned to rejoin the others. "Probably up there laughing his fucking little head off."

———

Barely daring to breathe, Chase clung to the branches as they got in their patrol cars and left. When the last light bar disappeared from view, he closed his eyes and started to sob. The world had gone crazy, out of control. All he'd ever wanted was to find his sister. How he'd wound up here with Gudger carried off in an ambulance, he didn't know.

He stayed in the tree until he was sure the cops weren't coming back. Then slowly, with stiff legs and numb arms, he began to inch his way downward. When his feet touched the ground, his legs felt wobbly, as if he'd been on a merry-go-round too long. Gudger's last words echoing in his head: *Last I heard, she was at an old motel near Hubbard Mountain.* Was Sam possibly still there? Still alive? All he had to do was figure out how to get to her. Call somebody, he supposed. But who? The cops hated him. His mother was probably weeping at Gudger's bedside. Mary Crow, according to Gudger, had been taken care of. That left him with no one.

"I'll just go myself," he said.

He walked, lurching, back to the house. Inside, blood was all over the living room floor. The paramedics had left empty plastic bags that held needles and IV solutions. Beyond that, everything seemed to have been demolished by some interior tornado—sofa cushions lay on the floor, the drawers of the end tables stuck out like open mouths. He made his way to his room, where the destruction was even worse. The cops had stripped and overturned his bed, pulled out his drawers, dumped his clothes on the floor. Even his books lay in a pile in one corner, his favorite picture of his father thrown on top of them.

"You didn't need to do that," he said, tears coming to his eyes as he grabbed the photograph. He looked at the picture a moment, then he carefully put it between the pages of the Sherlock Holmes volume Cousin Petey had given him. He could look at his dad later. Now, he had to get to Hubbard Mountain.

He took off his blood-spattered clothes and pulled a pair of jeans and a clean T-shirt from the pile on the floor. He looked for his one pair of sneakers that weren't held together with duct tape, but he couldn't find them.

He turned to the closet, where the cops had dumped all their winter coats on the floor. He found an old pair of his mother's sandals, the heels Sam wore for special occasions. Fumbling through the clothes, he looked for his shoes. He had a brief, horrible thought that the cops might have taken them, then, at the very back of the closet, beneath an old parka, he found them. He grabbed them, laced them up, got to his feet. He was halfway out the door when he remembered Sam's little purse with the money in it. He had no idea if Hubbard Mountain was near or far; certainly he would need money to get there.

He returned to the middle of his room and again started pawing through the mess the cops had left. He found underwear, pajamas, some marbles from Cousin Petey. Finally he saw the little purse, pushed back beneath the box springs of his mattress. Lying on his stomach, he stretched out on the floor until his fingers curled around it. He pulled to him, wondering if the cops had taken his $94.70 and just shoved the thing back under his bed. He unzipped the purse to check—much to his relief, the money looked undisturbed. Just the same, he decided to count it. If Gudger had taught him one thing, it was that not all cops could be trusted. He was counting the ones and fives, had gotten up to $67 when he found a business card nestled between the bills. He pulled it out. It read DETECTIVE VICTOR GALLO-WAY, CAMPBELL COUNTY POLICE DEPARTMENT.

"That's the guy Mary Crow told me about," he whispered. He'd hidden it while she and Gudger had talked on the porch; with everything that had happened since, he'd forgotten all about it. He was a good cop, according to Mary. Somebody he could trust. Chase leaned back against the overturned mattress and stared at the card. If he called this guy, he might be bringing the whole police department back down on his head—he'd heard one of the other cops say that the captain wanted him bad. But he also might be calling the one man who would take him seriously about Samantha. Someone who might be able to reach Hubbard Mountains a lot faster than he could. He ran his finger over the raised lettering of the card, then got to his feet.

"I just hope everything Mary Crow said about you is true," he whispered, running down the hall, hoping the cops hadn't taken Gudger's cell phone.

TWENTY-NINE

MARY WAS SWIMMING; GLIDING weightless through the sunlit waters of Atagahi, the secret Cherokee spring that was supposed to heal all your wounds. The light was green and shimmery around her and she seemed to be floating through her own memories—her mother laughing, then her father singing, as if on some distant radio. Another kick of her legs and she heard Jonathan calling her. *Where are you? Why can't I find you anymore? Why did you leave us alone?*

"I'm here!" she tried to call, but all the water vanished and she was no longer swimming. A great weight seemed to press down upon her, paralyzing her on her back as a strange voice talked over her.

"*Chudovvy,*" the voice says. "*Yaka znakhidka!*"

She felt someone brush her hair away from her forehead, gently trace the shape of her mouth. At first she thought it was Jonathan, but the voice wasn't right; the touch foreign. Whoever it was smelled of florid cologne, with underlying notes of body odor, as if they used fragrance as a substitute for soap and water. She lay still as they stroked her neck, then lifted the front of her blouse.

"*Chudovvy,*" the whisper came again.

She almost slapped the hand away, but something caught her attention. She'd heard that word before. Lying still, she tried to remember who had said it, why she would know it. *Chudovvy, chudovvy.* In a rush it came back—her old clients in Hartsville, the Kovalenkos had said that. She'd negotiated an excellent price on a small piece of land for them. Vadim had clapped his hands like a child, repeating the word *chudovvy.* Luda had laughed and said, "Forgive him. When he's excited, he goes back to Ukranian."

"What does *chudovvy* mean?" asked Mary.

"Beautiful. Splendid. Wonderful." Luda beamed, her fat cheeks rosy. "You have saved us lots of money."

So now why was she was lying here with another man saying *chudovvy* over her? She doubted that she'd saved him any money—what it all meant beyond that she had no idea. What she did know was that it might be better to keep feigning sleep, at least until she figured everything out. Trying to keep her eyelids from fluttering, she thought back. Her memories were random as clouds, forming and dissipating. She recalled a meal in a restaurant, a man kissing her, and her kissing him back. Then driving in her car, a baby's car seat by the side of the road. At that moment everything aligned, like cherries on a slot machine. She'd eaten dinner with Galloway, they'd kissed, she'd headed back to Gastonia and seen this car seat on the side of the road. Some sort of mechanical baby was inside. She'd just realized she'd been tricked when her lights had gone out.

But why? She wasn't working on any hot trail. She was just going back to her motel room to write a report for the governor. Her focus turned outwards as she heard the door open and someone else enter the room.

"Yusuf," said the first man. "*Dayte iy shcho nubed' poïsty.*"

"*Ben Rus anlammiyorum!*" replied Yusuf, his voice strident. "*No Rus. No Rus.*"

"Do you speak English, then?" asked the first one, growing impatient.

She heard a long pause, as if the man were trying to fit his mouth around unaccustomed words. "*A little.*"

"I'm going to Charlotte," the Russian spoke loudly and slowly, as if Yusuf were either deaf or mentally challenged. "You stay here, with Smiley. Feed this one, then the other. When I come back, we'll load them up." There was a long moment of silence, broken when the Russian said, "Understand?"

"*Olur!* Feed and guard. Then we take out."

She heard another silence, then the door opened. She looked through slitted eyes just in time to see two men going out the door. The first was just a shadow—the second was tall and rangy. His head was shaved and he wore a white suit that looked like rumpled linen.

That must be the Russian, she decided. What Yusuf looked like she had no idea. After they relocked the door, she was tempted to sit up and look around the room, but again she decided to lie still. They might have surveillance cameras. *If I'm going to get out of here, it's better that those bastards not know I'm awake.*

Still, she needed to know where she was, to see if there was anything here she could use as a weapon.

She tilted her head up slightly, looking through half-closed eyes. She saw an old-fashioned fluorescent light flickering from a concrete block ceiling. Wondering if they had her in some kind of prison cell, she pretended to yawn. While doing so, she turned her head to the left. On that side of the room she saw a boarded-up window and a television so old that it had a dial to change the channels. Yawning again, she turned her head to the other side. There, a battered door revealed a bathroom with a toilet as ancient as the television set. On the wall over the sink she could see where someone had written *I want to go home*—childish letters in a brownish ink that looked like dried blood. A chill went through her.

It's an old motel room, she decided. *But where? And who are these men? What do they want with me? And what happened to the person who wrote* I want to go home *in such clear and plaintive English that it could have been written on a blackboard?*

She turned back, flat on her back. Keeping a half-open eye on the door, she tried to clear the fuzziness from her head and remember what she'd learned from her captors' conversation. The man who'd fingered her face sounded Ukrainian and seemed to be in charge. He spoke English far better than his helper, Yusuf, whose vocabulary was mostly verbs. The Ukrainian had mentioned someone named Smiley, but made a point that he was coming back to help Yusuf load them up. She did not like the sound of that. *Loading up* implied cargo—cattle to market, sheep to shearing. And who was the other person the Ukrainian had told Yusuf to feed? Was there someone else locked up here besides her?

She opened her eyes wider and looked at the door, sorry that she hadn't gotten a glimpse of Yusuf. Was he big? Strong? Did he go around armed? If he did what the Ukrainian told him, then he would soon be coming with something for her to eat. And what then, she wondered? More drugs that would send her back to Atagahi? If that happened, then where would she wake up next? Russia?

"Not if I have anything to say about it," she whispered. She closed her eyes again and tried to calm herself by thinking of all the things Yamamoto had taught her in karate class: Release the tiger . . . come out fast, come out hard. Assume they have a weapon; assume they mean to kill you.

Okay, she thought, mentally preparing herself as she began tensing the muscles of her arms and legs. *Even if this Yusuf is big and armed, all you have to do is get through one guy. He'll probably be expecting a still-drugged woman, so you'll have the element of surprise. After you take him out, then get up and get yourself out.*

Trusting that her exact battle plan would come once she saw Yusuf, she lay there and waited, still pretending to be asleep. The minutes dragged on, dripping as slowly as the water that plunked from some faucet in her bathroom. Once she thought she heard the sound of cars starting; another time she could have sworn she heard the muffled sound of a girl crying.

The minutes dragged on, turning to ... hours? Days? She fell into a kind of waking dream about Jonathan and Lily the night they rescued the barn owl. Then she heard footsteps. Again, the sound was muffled—she couldn't tell if they were coming toward her room or away from it. She held her breath, listening; she heard a key turn in her door. Gulping, she lay back down on the pillow and watched through her eyelashes as a man came into her room. He was short but muscular. A tight white T-shirt covered olive skin and his jeans topped a pair of gray athletic socks. His hair was dark and curly and ended in a thick black beard cropped close to his chin. He was middle-aged, going to paunch but still handsome in the way of Persians. She knew her plan the moment she saw the way he looked around the room— his gaze darted from the bed to the TV to the bathroom as if he expected something to jump out at him. Yusuf was terrified. With a quick glance at the bed, he walked over to the bathroom door, where he put a tray of food silently on the floor.

Turning, he watched her for another moment, then slowly approached the bed. She lay still, concentrating on keeping her breathing even. As he drew closer, she caught the faint smell of grease and garlic.

"Girlie?" he said softly.

She could tell by his voice that he was too far away—she needed him to come closer. She lay motionless, waiting.

"Girlie?" He spoke a little louder, but made no move toward her. Again, she lay still.

"Hey, girlie," he said, now coming a step closer. "Time you eat."

She stirred, pretending to be on the edge of sleep. She wanted him to think she needed to be prodded awake. She turned her head and looked at him with hazy, unfocused eyes. "Hmmmm?" She gave a sleepy groan, soft as a kitten.

"Girlie!" he called. Newly emboldened by her lassitude, he stepped close to the bed, started tapping her on the shoulder. "Wake up. Time you eat."

She waited one more moment, then she opened her eyes and looked at him, fierce and full in the face. He jumped, startled by the intensity of her gaze, but before he could move farther she clenched her hands together and hit straight up, catching him squarely beneath his chin. His head snapped back as blood spurted from his lower lip. While he was still off-balanced and surprised, she took her shot.

She leapt off the bed and head-butted him in his gut. She heard the wind come out of him, in both a fart and in a great belch of air. He fell back and slid down the wall, struggling to breathe, limp for those precious few seconds his diaphragm would need to right itself. Mary did not waste those seconds. She grabbed the tray, dumped a plate of orange-looking stew and hot tea on his head. As he lifted his hands to cover his eyes, she leaned back and kicked him in his balls as hard as she could. He screamed in pain, but she kept kicking him—once, twice, three times, hard and fast. Weeping, he scrambled to his knees and finally started crawling, his fingers reaching for the tile floor of the bathroom. She let him go in, but only so far. He was just about to crawl beneath the sink when she picked up the food tray again and slammed it against the side of his head. He went down so quickly it surprised her—she figured his thick hair would cushion his skull well enough for him to last a few more licks.

Dropping the tray, she stretched him full length on the floor and unzipped his jeans. She pulled off all of his clothes from the waist down and then went through his pockets. He had a wallet but no driver's license, twenty-six American dollars, and a picture of a pretty girl who looked Indian, draped in a sari with a bindi dotting her forehead. Besides the wallet, she found a small knife and a ring of keys. She pocketed those items, then hid his jeans and underwear in the tank of the toilet. If Yusuf woke up and felt frisky enough to come after her, he'd have to find his wet clothes first or come in the nude.

"Okay, Yamamota-san," she whispered as she shut the bathroom door behind her. "I'm in touch with my tiger. One bad guy down. Probably considerably more to go."

THIRTY

For what seemed like hours, Chase frantically searched through the house for Gudger's cell phone. He'd almost decided the cops had confiscated the thing when he found it wedged behind the sofa in the living room. Either the cops had forgotten about it, or they hadn't wanted it to begin with. Weak with relief, Chase ran to the kitchen to call Galloway. He couldn't stand the bloody-pissy stink in the living room and the cops hadn't torn up the kitchen quite as badly as the rest of the house. With a silent prayer that he was doing the right thing, he hopped up on the cabinet next to the sink and punched in Galloway's number. The phone rang once, twice, three times, then a deep voice answered crisply, with a single word.

"Galloway."

"This is Charles Oliver Buchanan," Chase replied, his voice coming out in a squeak. "Mary Crow gave me your card. She said to call you if I ever found out anything about my sister, Samantha."

"Mary Crow?" Galloway now sounded even sterner, more serious. "What do you know about Mary Crow?"

"N-nothing," Chase answered. "But I think my stepfather might."

"Who's your stepfather?"

"Ralph Gudger." Chase tried to swallow. His throat felt like sandpaper. "I-I shot him this afternoon. But when the ambulance took him away, he was still alive."

For a moment, he heard nothing; then Galloway spoke. "Are you the peach truck kid?"

"Yes sir." Tears flooded his eyes. That seemed so long ago, he felt like some other boy had climbed in the back of that truck and ridden ninety miles, dizzy from the heady aroma of those ripe peaches. It couldn't have been him. "Mary Crow talked to Gudger on our front porch. Then Gudger got all weird. Then a big gorilla drove up in a black car, beat him up, and took him away. When he came back, he said they'd held his hand down in a pit of acid." He struggled to keep his voice level, to keep from crying like a baby. "That's when he told me Mary Crow wouldn't be bothering anybody anymore. The men in the black car were going to take care of her. Today they were supposed to come get me and sell me for boy meat..."

"What the hell are you talking about?"

"I just told you!" Chase cried. "Gudger knows where my sister—"

"I get that part," Galloway said. "But I also know you've got a bad rap in this department. If you're pulling my chain over something you've just dreamed up because you're scared, you need to get off my line now. I've got an officer missing."

"I'm telling the truth!" said Chase. "I shot Gudger to make him tell. But he told me about Mary Crow way before that—"

"Why didn't you call before now?"

"He locked me in my room!"

"Did he say where Mary Crow was?" Galloway interrupted.

"No!" Chase replied, desperate to make the man understand. "But I bet he knows where she is. He knows where my sister is. At a motel, near Hubb—"

Suddenly, he heard a noise outside the kitchen window. It sounded like gravel popping on the driveway. Was it the men in the black car? Had they now come for him? He hopped off the counter and peeked outside the back door. A police car had rolled up, lights off, no siren. Chase held his breath. Was it the cop who'd almost spotted him in the tree? Had he come back for a second, more thorough search? Chase watched, ready to run, as the car door opened. A tall figure emerged, then reached for something in front seat. As he did, Chase saw his face. It was Gudger's old partner, Crump. He didn't look particularly mad, just sad somehow, as if he had some very bad news to tell someone.

"I gotta go," Chase told the cop on the phone. "I think Gudger just died."

———

"Hello?" Galloway turned away from the black Miata and pressed the cell phone hard against his ear. "Hello, kid? Did I lose you?" He heard only the silence of a disconnected call. Immediately, he punched the call-back number. The phone rang several times, then a gruff male voice came on the line. "This is Gudger. Leave a message."

He didn't bother leaving a message. Instead he clicked off the phone and turned to Pike. "You hear anything from Dispatch about an officer getting shot?"

"There was some noise when you were in Gastonia, but it was some old cop. Retired guy."

"Was the name Gudger?"

"Yeah, it sounded something like that."

"Was he DOA?"

"Nah, I think they took him to the hospital. Domestic dispute."

He tossed his car keys to Pike, who was waiting for the wrecker that would tow Mary Crow's car to impound. "I need your cruiser," he told the officer.

"Where are you going now?" asked Pike

"County Hospital," Galloway replied.

He got in Pike's cruiser, first checking with Dispatch to make sure both the boy and Pike had gotten their facts straight; the operator confirmed a 10-54 earlier, at the residence of Ralph Gudger, retired CCPD.

"What's the condition of the officer now?" asked Galloway.

"He was in surgery," came the reply. "Don't know anything more."

"Shit," said Galloway. He turned on the siren and light bar, then hauled back to Manley, shrieking down the two-lane, passing cars on the left, the right, and once through somebody's front yard. All the while the boy's words kept going through his head. *Some men held Gudger's hand in a pit of acid … he said they were going to take care of Mary Crow. I bet Gudger knows where she is, too!*

"And if Gudger's still breathing, he's going to tell me exactly what he knows," Galloway muttered as he pulled off Jackson Highway and headed down County Hospital Road.

———

The surgical unit was on the fifth floor. "Ralph Gudger's just been moved to room 511," said a chubby blond nurse who wore a scrub outfit with Winnie the Poohs all over it. "He's just had some broth. He's doing well, but I'm afraid he can't have any visitors."

"I'm not a visitor." Galloway held up his badge. "I'm a cop."

The nurse started sputtering something about security, but Galloway walked on down the hall. In room 511 lay a dark-haired man with his left leg elevated in a kind of sling, IV drips going into both arms. Galloway walked into the room, locked the door, then strode over to the bed.

"Gudger?" he asked.

The man opened swollen eyes and nodded. "Are you Dr. Wheeler?"

Galloway shook his head as he flipped open his ID case again, showing Gudger his gold detective badge. "I'm one of your own."

"You arrest that little fuck who shot me?"

"Not yet," said Galloway. "That little fuck says you know what happened to Mary Crow."

Gudger licked dry, chapped lips. "He's a liar. Always has been. Now he's cost me my goddamn leg!"

"That's a shame." Galloway looked closely at the man's bandaged knee, then with two fingers, thumped the wounded knee like a ripe melon. "That hurt?" he asked, grinning.

"Owwwww!" cried Gudger. "Yeah, it hurts. What are you, crazy?"

"Maybe," said Galloway, easing up slightly on the pressure. "But for now, let's just say I'm a friend of Mary Crow."

"I don't know who the fuck you're talking about," said Gudger.

"Oh, I'm sure you remember." Galloway lifted his hand above the bed. "Pretty girl ... about this tall. Black hair, incredible smile. Special counsel for the governor."

"Never heard of her."

"Your stepson says otherwise." Galloway grabbed Gudger's scalded left hand and wrenched one the fingers, hard. "He says you two had a nice long chat, on your front porch. Then you got the jitters and made some calls. He says that the same guys who fucked up your hand have Mary Crow. And he says you told them where to get her."

Grimacing with pain, Gudger snatched his hand away. "He's a liar. I was changing a battery and dropped it. My fingers got burned trying to clean up the mess. It was an accident."

"That's funny," Galloway lied. "We've searched your house pretty good. Nobody saw any empty batteries lying on the garage floor. And nothing was etched with any acid."

Gudger stared at him, his eyes hard beneath heavy brows. "Get the fuck out of here or I'm calling security."

"No, you're not." Galloway grabbed the call button and moved it well out of Gudger's reach. "You're not calling anybody, Gudger. And even if you did, it wouldn't matter. I've locked the door. And since you're the only patient in here and the nurse knows we're talking about official police business, it's going to be just me and you for quite a little while."

Gudger tried to squirm away from Galloway, but the knee sling held him firm. "Look, asshole, you can't do this. I've got rights, you know."

"So does Mary Crow. So does your little stepson." Galloway leaned close, again squeezing the mushy spot that had once been Gudger's knee cap. "So did his sister, Samantha."

"I'm telling you I don't know anything!" Gudger cried, his face growing as white as his pillowcase.

"You sure about that?" Galloway gave the knee cap another long squeeze; blood began to ooze through the bandage. "Gee, I hate to tear out these sutures."

"Stop!" Gudger screamed, beads of sweat on his forehead. "I swear I never heard of the woman!"

"Okay." Galloway shrugged. "Then you're of no use to me whatsoever."

He removed his hand from Gudger's leg, then stepped over to the other side of the bed. He moved one of the IVs away from Gudger's grasp, then peered closely at the drip as he began to twist the valve on the intake line.

"What the fuck are you doing now?" Gudger wheezed, his eyes wide.

"I'm going to insert a bolus of air into this line," Galloway said breezily, as if he were going to fluff Gudger's pillow. "My mother's a nurse, so I know all about IVs. All I do is cut off the saline, then with a syringe, inject some air into the line that goes in your vein. It'll take me a couple of syringes' worth, but soon an air bubble will hit your heart, then your lungs, then who knows where. You could die immediately. Or you could have a stroke, which means you could be paralyzed from the neck down and have some grumpy, underpaid orderly wiping your ass for the rest of your life. Or you could be a vegetable and not know another fucking thing until the day they pull your plug." Galloway looked at Gudger's bandaged knee. "It's a shame, too. Somebody went to a lot of work saving that leg. Too bad you won't be needing it."

Gudger heaved his torso upright, tried to grab Galloway with both arms, but again, the knee sling held him back. Galloway simply stepped aside as the top half of Gudger's body dangled over the side of the bed.

"It's not totally uncommon for older people to stroke out after surgery, anyway. You'll have a seizure, I'll race to the door to call a nurse. They'll try to revive you, but it won't work. And they certainly won't blame anything on me, a fellow brother in blue."

Gudger managed to lift himself back on the pillow. "Who the fuck are you?" he whimpered, his eyes so wide Galloway could see the bloodshot sclera.

Galloway looked at him as he began to turn off the drip. "A friend of Mary Crow."

Gudger watched, chest heaving, as Galloway started twisting the little valve. He'd gotten it halfway closed when Gudger held up his hand. "Stop!" he gasped. "I'll tell you what I know."

"Like where she is?" asked Galloway, not removing his hands from the IV.

"I'm not sure where she is," Gudger gasped. "All I know is she sniffed around and got too close to an operation that runs out of the Tick Tock Motel. Near Hubbard Mountain Park."

"Where's that?"

"Close to Charlotte."

"What kind of operation is it?" asked Galloway.

"Part of it's prostitution," said Gudger. "Part of it's something else."

"Like what?"

Gudger swallowed, his Adam's apple coursing up and down his throat. "I don't know what you'd call it, but it's run by a bunch of Russians. They take the best girls—the pretty ones who haven't been fucked crazy—and sell them. You know, to one person, just for sex."

"Who do they sell them to?"

"I don't know. You'll have to ask them." He looked at Galloway and gave a soft, smirking chuckle. "But you'd better hurry. They turn their stock pretty fast, I understand."

"You'd better not be shitting me, you son of a bitch," whispered Galloway as he reopened the valve. "And Mary Crow had damn well better be there. 'Cause if she isn't, I'm coming back. And next time I'll make a bubble in your brain seem like a walk in the park."

THIRTY-ONE

CHASE WOULD HAVE RUN, except Crump knew he was inside. He'd seen him through the kitchen window, lifted his hand in greeting as he made his way to the back door. Chase had nowhere to go. He stood by the stove watching as the cop opened the door and stepped inside.

"Hey, boy." Crump never called him by his name—just *boy* or *kid*. His wide mouth stretched in a thin line—Chase couldn't tell if he was mad or sad or just disgusted at having to drive out here.

"Gudger's dead, isn't he?" Chase was almost too scared to ask the question. Ever since he'd fired Cousin Petey's gun, he'd seen his life spool out first in a courtroom, then in prison, being bullied by men like Gudger for the rest of his life.

"No, but he's hurt pretty bad," Crump replied, irritated.

Chase closed his eyes with relief. Again he'd been spared—he wasn't guilty of murder, at least not yet.

"Your mama sent me over here to get you," said Crump.

"She did?" His last memory of his mother was early this morning, when she'd told him they were leaving Gudger, that she would come pick him up that afternoon. "Where is she?"

"At the hospital. She's crying real hard." Crump put his hands on his equipment belt like an old-time gunslinger. "Shooting a cop's serious, kid."

"I know."

"You want to tell me why you did it?"

He stared at Crump's badge, wondering if he dared tell him the truth about Gudger and those men in the black car. It would be good to get it out that he hadn't just taken his gun and shot Gudger for the fun of it, but he doubted Crump would believe him. Crump had been Gudger's partner back during their duplex days, when Chase was calling 911 on the crackheads next door. He shook his head. "I'd rather tell my mother first."

"Then let's get going," Crump said, his gaze skittering around the kitchen, skipping from Chase to the bloody living room, then lingering on the clock over the stove, as if he were on some kind of time schedule. "She's been asking for you for a long time."

This isn't right, said a voice in Chase's head. *Mama wouldn't be crying over Gudger. She only cried over Daddy in her own bedroom, with the door shut. And she wouldn't be wanting me to come to the hospital—even when Daddy was dying she said hospitals were no place for children. And why wasn't Crump trying to arrest him, like those other cops?*

Something was going on here—he just had to stall long enough to figure it out.

"I need to change my clothes," said Chase. "Mama would be mad if I didn't wear nice clothes to the hospital."

"Your clothes don't matter, boy. She said to bring you now." He grabbed Chase's shoulder with a heavy hand and squeezed the same nerve that Gudger always squeezed. The calming claw, Gudger called it. "We need to get going."

Crump marched him out the door. Chase walked obediently, knowing that the slightest veer in a different direction would bring such pain that tears would come to his eyes. Still, as Crump moved him toward the police car, Chase kept wondering what was going on. Could this be some plan of his mother's? To keep him out of jail and away from those other cops? Did she think he'd be safe as long as he was with Crump? There was no real reason not to trust Crump—until he'd applied the claw on his shoulder, he'd never said or done anything mean to Chase.

They walked toward the cruiser. As they neared the front fender, Chase moved slightly to the left, assuming Crump would want him in the passenger's seat. Instead, Crump's grip on his shoulder tightened.

"I've got to drop something off before I take you to your mother," he said, opening the back door of the cruiser. "So I'm gonna let you ride in the meat locker."

Crump's thin lips stretched in a grin that made Chase go cold inside. As the lanky cop held the door open, everything crystallized into a sharp little diamond of revelation. His mother hadn't sent Crump to get him. Those men in the black car had. Crump and Gudger had been partners for years. If Gudger had promised them fresh boy meat, then Crump was bound to deliver it.

"Get on in there, boy," Crump said. "And don't look so scared ... it'll be fun. I'll put the siren on and drive fast. People will think you're some big bad criminal."

Crump's calming claw loosened on his shoulder as he put a practiced hand on the top of Chase's skull, pushing him head first into the back of the cruiser. When Chase got close enough to see the grid of the cage separating the front seat from the back, he made his move. He ducked down, put his arms on the backseat of the car, and kicked out backward with both feet. He connected with Crump's midsection—an instant later he heard a soft groan, as Crump's knees buckled. He thrust himself feet-first out of the car. His chin hit the lower edge of the door frame as he belly-flopped onto the driveway.

"You crazy little bastard!" Crump yelled.

He scrambled under the car, pressing himself into the gravel. Watching from beneath the passenger side, he saw Crump's feet, then Crump's knees, then finally Crump's red and raging face. Crump thrust a long arm under the car and made a grab for his leg, but Chase was ready. He scampered from beneath the passenger side of the car and leapt to his feet, running as fast as he could.

"What the fuck's the matter with you?" he heard Crump call. "I'm just taking you to your mother."

He wanted to call back over his shoulder and tell Crump he knew exactly where he was taking him, but he didn't dare waste the breath. Catching his jaw on the car frame had opened up a long gash beneath his chin. Blood gushed down his neck and onto his shirt with every stride he took.

He ran across the driveway, Crump's footsteps loud behind him. At first he headed back to the house, thinking he could grab Gudger's Taser, or even Gudger's gun. But the other cops had wrecked the house—it would take him hours to find any kind of weapon, and by then, Crump would most certainly be inside, breathing fire. *Forget the house,* he decided. *Just keep on running.* Crump was forty, maybe even fifty. Surely he could outrun an old man like that.

He took off across the side yard, heading for the maple tree. Maybe if he could gain some ground, he could climb up there again and wait Crump out in the highest branches. Risking a glance over his shoulder, his heart sank. For an old guy, Crump was fast. He was close and his long legs were getting him closer. Chase would never be able to jump to that first branch before Crump grabbed him.

Lowering his head, he pushed on past the tree, jumping over a little ditch in the yard that Gudger always had difficulty mowing. As he did so, the inside of his left arm brushed against something hard in the pocket of his jeans. He dropped his hand, dug down to figure out what it was. Gudger's cell phone! He must have stashed it there when Crump pulled up. If he could just get ahead of Crump long enough to call someone—but who would he call? Mary Crow was out, and he'd already hung up on that Galloway guy. That left either his mother or 911. 911, he decided quickly, blood still streaming from his chin. Better to be taken to jail by those three cops than be delivered as boy meat by Crump.

He ran for the shed. If he could beat Crump there in time to lock himself in, it might work. Crump might be able to run forever, but he couldn't; his breath was already coming in ragged gasps, and the front of his shirt was soaked with blood.

Clenching his fists, Chase dug his toes down into the earth and sprinted for the shed. He skidded through the still muddy ground around where the swimming pool had been and leapt over Gudger's pile of blue plastic shards. Twenty feet beyond that, he turned toward the shed. As he turned, he saw Crump slip in the same mud and fall forward, sliding into the stack of shards. His heart soared! Now was his chance!

He raced for the shed door and flung it open. Inside, Gudger's new tractor sat gleaming in the dim light, smelling of machine oil and gasoline. Chase dived inside, slamming the door behind him and jamming the key into the lock. His shaking fingers managed to turn it just as Crump flung himself against the other side of the door.

"What's the matter with you, you little idiot?" Crump wheezed, wrenching the door knob. "I'm supposed to take you to the hospital!"

"I know where exactly you want to take me," said Chase. "And it's no hospital!"

As Crump tried to force the door open, Chase hurried over and crouched down beneath the shelf where Gudger cleaned his guns. He pulled the cell phone from his pocket and with shaking fingers, punched in 911. He was waiting for the call to go through when the world exploded. He heard a great bang, then tiny bits of glass rained down like sleet on his head and shoulders. When he opened his eyes, he saw Crump standing in front of him, pointing his gun at his head. He took a step closer and kicked the phone from Chase's grasp, sending it clattering across the glass-strewn floor.

"What kind of bullshit call were you making this time, you little faggot?" Crump asked, his eyes burning with a dark fire. "Drug dealers on the front porch? Spacemen in the back yard? Or is it still how Gudger stole your sister?"

"It's still that." Chase swallowed hard, mustering his courage. "Only now it's you, too."

Crump shook his head. "You're dreaming, kid. I'm just here to take you to your mama."

"Then why'd you try to put me in the back of your car, in the *meat* locker? And what was the important stop you had to make before we went to the hospital?"

Crump said, "Why don't you tell me, since you're such a clever little shit?"

"Because Gudger freaked out when Mary Crow showed up. He called some men, to warn them. Only they came and took Gudger away and dumped his hand in acid. Gudger told those people they could have me. He called me fresh boy meat."

Crump sighted down the barrel of his gun. "So what do you reckon my part is in all this?"

"You're Gudger's partner," Chase said as his chin began to quiver. "And you know exactly what happened to Sam."

"How do you figure that?"

"Because why else would you be pointing a gun at me now?"

Crump studied him a moment, then he gave a mirthless smile. "I gotta hand it to you, boy. You're just too fucking smart for your own good."

His whole body shaking, Chase put his head down on his knees. He couldn't look into that gun barrel anymore. Nor could he get past Crump and run anywhere. He was going to die—right here in Gudger's garage, next to his new green tractor. Chase thought of his mother and started to cry.

"We can do this the easy way or the hard way, boy," Crump said. "The easy way is we just go back to my cruiser and you let me take you to the men who are waiting for you. The hard way is I put a bullet in your head and dump you in a place where nobody will ever find you."

A silence stretched between them. Chase wished he were brave, wished he knew how to respond to that—though he didn't know exactly what boy meat was, he knew dead. Dead was his father, stretched out in a pine box in their living room. Dead was Cousin Petey, stretched out in a fancier box at a funeral home. Dead could soon be him, a kid who'd just wanted to find his sister and wound up uncovering his stepfather's secret evil. Finally, he lifted his head and looked at Crump. "I don't know what to say."

"I do." A voice came from just inside the shed door. A woman's voice—high and delicate, but with steel in it, too. Crump turned. Chase peered around him to look—he gasped, amazed. His mother stood there, still in her work uniform, a shotgun pointed straight at Crump's heart. Behind her stood Dr. Knox, her boss from the nursing home.

"Drop the gun, Crump," his mother ordered.

"Hey, Amy, I was just kidding around," Crump began, his face suddenly the color of chalk.

"Do what she says, officer," Dr. Knox said, his own pistol at the ready. "You don't corner a little boy in a garden shed and point a gun at his head."

Crump just stood there, ashen-faced but still gripping his weapon. For an awful moment Chase thought he might shoot everybody, but finally, he lowered his gun, putting it gently on the hood of Gudger's tractor. His mother's eyes did not leave Crump's face once as Dr. Knox hurried forward to retrieve the weapon.

"Chase?" his mother said, her gaze still level on Crump. "Are you all right, sweetheart? That chin looks right bad."

"I'm okay," Chase croaked, relief coursing through his veins like warm honey. "It looks a lot worse than it is."

"Then you come over here by me and Dr. Knox," his mother said. "We heard everything Crump said. The police are on their way. Until they get here, we're going to find out exactly happened to your sister."

THIRTY-TWO

MARY OPENED THE DOOR of her room and slipped into a dimly lit hall. A threadbare carpet the color of dirt covered the floor, while dark spots of old knotty pine paneling seemed to crawl up the walls. Again, she looked around for surveillance cameras, but the only thing she saw near the ceiling were swollen lumps of drywall and wisps of rotting insulation. She fumbled with the dozen or so keys on Yusuf's key ring, looking for the one that would lock her door. She knew he would be out for a while, but eventually he would wake up, mad as hell and very sore. Better that a mad, sore Yusuf be locked in her old room than be coming after her with fire in those cold, dark eyes.

Hurriedly she tried the keys, finally finding the one that turned the lock of her door. If nothing else, it would buy her time. That room would be the first place the Russian would look for her; even a moment's delay would put her that much farther away.

She tested the door to make sure it was locked, then she stepped back into the middle of the hall. She seemed to be midway down a long, door-lined corridor. To her right she could hear the sound of a television—some kind of ball game—she guessed by the constant cheering. No sound came from rest of the hall—it stood empty—just door after door, all closed. Not wanting to surprise any sports fans, she turned left. There had to be an exit down here somewhere. Even old motels had doors to the outside. She was halfway down the hall when she remembered the Russian's parting instructions to Yusuf. *Feed this one, then the other. When I come back, we'll load them up.*

"Oh my God," she whispered, stopping in her tracks. "There must be somebody else in here." But where? Which room? Did she even have time to search before the Russian came back?

"Make time," she told herself, remembering the sad little *I want to go home* written on bathroom wall.

Hurrying, she tiptoed toward the sound of the television, trying the doors along the way. All opened easily, revealing rooms similar to hers—lumpy, stained mattresses on battered bed frames, fast food wrappers littering the floor. Some rooms had old TV sets, others had nothing but a bed. All were empty. She worked her way down the hall quickly. After she checked the last room, she was tempted to go and find out who was watching television. The noise was coming from what used to be the office—it was only a few feet away. Perhaps she could disarm the TV watcher as quickly as she had Yusuf. But just as she was starting to tiptoe forward, the TV program grew silent. She shrank back against the wall, her heart pounding. Through the open office door, she could see a shadow moving on the wall as a man began to speak.

"Everything's cool," he said in English, sounding as if he were from New York or New Jersey. "It's feeding time."

He's on the phone, Mary realized, watching the shadow move back and forth. Probably to the Russian.

"He knows what to do, Boyko."

Mary held her breath, listening.

"Fifteen minutes? No sweat. We'll be ready."

Then the shadow ceased its pacing. She heard what sounded like the squeak of a chair, and the television came on again. *Fifteen minutes*, she told herself. *Then the Russian will be here. To load us up.*

She crept back down the hall, trying to both hurry and remain silent. Fifteen minutes was not much time—she still had doors she needed to check and then she had to figure a way out of here for herself. When she reached her old room and pressed an ear to the door, she heard only silence. *Good*, she thought. *Yusuf must still be unconscious.*

She took a deep breath, then continued her search of the rooms. As she made her way to the end of the hall, she wondered if she hadn't just dreamed someone crying and misunderstood what the Russian had told Yusuf.

Lots of languages flying around, it would be an easy mistake to make. She reached for the last doorknob, grateful that this was the final one, but the thing didn't turn in her hand. She tried again, pushing and pulling against the door, but it was locked tight. She stepped back, wondering if this was just the storeroom at the end of the hall, or if somebody else was in there. With a glance toward the office, she risked a soft knock.

"Anyone there?" she whispered. She put her ear to the door. Nothing. "Hello?" she whispered again.

To her amazement, she heard the creak of bedsprings.

"I'm here," came a small, young voice.

Mary fumbled through her keys—going through each of them, quickly, always checking to make sure the TV watcher wasn't barreling down the hall. She'd just begun to think none of them fit this lock when one slid into place. She caught her breath as the cylinder clicked open. What or who was behind the door? The girl who'd written *I want to go home*? Or just some stupid thing with tapes and wires, like the fake baby in the car seat?

Readying her inner tiger again, she grasped the knob and opened the door slowly. She found a pretty blond girl standing there, clutching her bedpost. Somewhere in her mid-teens, she wore pink shorts and a dirty T-shirt, and she looked as if she might cry. Mary recognized the blond hair and wide blue eyes immediately—it was Chase Buchanan's sister.

"Who are you?" the girl asked, her voice thready.

"My name is Mary Crow," said Mary. "You're Samantha Buchanan, aren't you?"

"Yes!" The girl peered over Mary's shoulder. "Did Chase send you here? Are he and Mama outside?"

Mary closed her eyes, ashamed of her own stupidity. Why had she not listened to the little boy? Why had she been so quick to dismiss him? "Uh, not quite," she finally replied. "It's a long story that we'll have to discuss later. Right now, we need to get out of here fast. Do you know how many men they have here?"

"There's Boyko," said Samantha. "He's the boss. And Smiley and Yusuf, who brings the food. More men come, but not all the time."

"Well, we can count Yusuf out for now," said Mary. "He'll be on all fours for the next several days. But the Russian is on his way back to get us."

Samantha swallowed hard. "They're taking us away tonight?"

"Only if we're here when they get back," said Mary. "Come on, we need to hurry."

"Wait." Sam ran to the bathroom, extracted the long shard of glass she'd worked loose from the mirror. She held it up for Mary to see. "It isn't much, but it's my way out. I decided I'd kill myself before I'd go with those men."

"I don't blame you a bit." Mary smiled, thinking the girl had as much moxie as her little brother. "But use it on somebody else, okay?"

They crept out into the hall. It was still deserted, with only the sounds of the distant television wafting through. "Do you know of any other girls in these rooms?" asked Mary.

"Not that I've heard," said Samantha. "I guess American virgins are pretty hard to come by."

They padded toward the end of the long, shadowy hall, where a single exit door stood chained and padlocked. Halfway there, they heard a door open, far down the opposite end of the hall. Pressing themselves against a doorway, they listened. Soon laughter and the echo of foreign voices replaced the sound of the television.

"The Russian's back," whispered Mary. "Come on!"

They ran to the exit door. Mary knew that if none of Yusuf's keys worked, they would have to make a stand. The men would probably be armed now, even if they hadn't been before. Pretty, virginal Samantha was likely too valuable a commodity to kill; Mary was not. She might be able to take one down before he could fire his weapon, but that would be all. *On the other hand, if they think we're just too much damn trouble, then they might kill us both.*

"Keep watch," Mary told Sam as she started trying the keys in the lock. "If they start coming down the hall, then we'll have to go to plan B."

"What's that?" asked Sam.

"I'm not sure. But keep that shard of glass close."

Mary fumbled with the keys—the darkness that hid them from Boyko and company also hid the keys and the lock from her. She finally gave up on squinting at the thing and started trying the keys by feel alone. One key was a dud, then the next, then the one after that. She was about to curse all of them when Sam squeaked. "Oh God—here they come!"

Mary shrank back against the shadowy wall, pulling Sam with her. In the dimness she saw Boyko, in his white suit, unlock the door to her room. It would only be seconds until they found Yusuf stretched out in the bathroom with his pants in the toilet. Then everything will be over.

She returned to the lock, frantically searching for the right key, knowing that Boyko and Smiley and whatever other scumbags were around would soon come screaming out of that room.

She tried another key—no good—then another, still no good. Then one more. This one felt different, caught differently. It was tight, but she gritted her teeth and turned it with all her strength. With a rusty squeak, the padlock opened. She flung it from the chain, then as quietly as she could, removed the chain from the door. Grabbing Samantha, she opened the door into a dark and moonless night.

"Come on—follow me. And run as fast as you can!"

THIRTY-THREE

MARY GRABBED SAMANTHA'S HAND and pulled her blindly across a scrub-filled parking lot, through a boggy, bad-smelling creek, then surprisingly, into pine trees. They pushed their way through soft branches as they ran uphill, their fingers growing sticky with sap as they slipped on the dead needles from the previous fall. Despite the hard going, Mary wanted to weep with relief. Woods she knew. Though she had no weapon and no real clue as to where they were in North Carolina or North Dakota, trees were trees and would, for her, level the playing field a bit.

Samantha felt less at home. "Can we stop just a minute?" She gasped. "I can't catch my breath."

"Okay," said Mary. "But for not long. We need to keep moving." She squinted into the darkness and made out a tall hemlock, its branches draping graceful as a skirt. "Come on."

They ducked under the leafy tent the tree offered. While Samantha crouched down and gulped deep breaths of air, Mary turned and looked back down the hill. They'd put about a hundred yards between themselves and the motel. The back door that they'd just unlocked remained open, spilling a rectangle of pale light on to the ground. In that puddle of light stood the white-suited man she'd seen in her room and two other men who were dressed in black. The two strangers cradled what looked like assault weapons, while the tall man held a single pistol the size of hand cannon. They conferred among themselves, their voices strident as they pointed into the woods. For one awful minute the Russian seemed to look directly at her, then he turned back to the men. From their sweeping gestures, Mary guessed they were probably getting ready to spread out like a grouse hunt, the assault rifles flanking the hand cannon, firing bursts to drive the two of them into his range.

"We need to get moving, Sam," she told the girl. "They're fanning out, to come after us."

"Okay," she said. "I'm ready."

Mary parted the hemlock branches so Sam could crawl out, then they went on, scrambling up the hill as quietly as they could. Mary figured the going would be easier at the top of the ridge; if they could get up there before the men caught up with them, they could circle around the motel and start looking for whatever road that led to this place. Once they found that, they could follow it back to some sort of civilization. For a while the idea buoyed her, then she glanced at the young girl beside her. Already Sam was breathing heavily again, struggling to keep up.

"I'm sorry," she wheezed when they were just yards away from the crest of the ridge. "But I need to stop again. My legs just feel so weak."

"Just for a minute," said Mary. "Sit down and I'll keep watch."

While Sam caught her breath, Mary turned to peer down the hillside. She thought she would have heard bursts of gunfire by now, but the woods had remained silent. Closing her eyes, she opened all her senses to the forest, but still she heard nothing. *This is not good*, she thought. *Everybody makes some kind of noise in the woods.*

She turned back to Sam. Her chest was heaving as she sucked in air. Mary frowned, puzzled. The girl was young, looked healthy. Why would climbing up a ridge turn her into an old woman? *Because she's been locked in a crappy room for two months*, she answered her own question. That old motel wasn't exactly a health spa. She knelt down, touched the girl's shoulder.

"I'm sorry," Sam said before Mary could speak. "I know I'm holding you back. I just can't get my breath."

"Then let's try a new plan."

"What?" the girl asked.

"I'm going to hide you."

Sam looked at her as if she'd gone crazy.

"I'm going to lead them away from you and get help."

"There's nowhere to hide. Just forget about me and get out of here yourself."

"No—it's an old bird trick," Mary whispered. "Lead the predator away from the nest." She smiled. "From now on, just pretend you're my little chick."

Before Sam could say anything else, Mary turned and started back down the ridge. She knew their hunters would head for the ridge top, just as she had. If she could find some kind of hiding place for Sam below them, then the girl would probably be safe, at least for a while. She saw what she thought was a fallen log big enough for Sam to hide beneath when a flash of bright light illuminated the woods a hundred yards to her right. The first loud clatter of gunfire followed, then tree limbs cracked and crashed to the forest floor. Above her, Sam cried out.

Mary raced back to her charge. She needed to get her quiet, fast. She found the girl crouched on the ground, her eyes huge. "I didn't mean to yell," she whispered. "It just scared me."

"Don't worry," Mary replied, grabbing her arm. "Come on!"

She pulled the girl down the hill, toward the log. As more gunfire sounded from the left, Mary wedged her under the downside of the log, invisible to anyone searching from above. For extra cover, she started quietly piling leaves and pine branches over her.

"Listen to me, Sam," Mary whispered as she worked. "You've got to promise to ignore whatever happens—gunshots, screaming, people saying they'll kill me if you don't come out. Don't move, don't cry, and don't make a sound—somebody will come and help you. It may take a while, but somebody *will* come. Can you do that?"

The girl nodded.

"Okay. You'll probably hear gunfire from sides of this hill; the guy in the white suit may come up the middle. It'll be scary as hell, but if you do as I say, you'll be okay."

Sam nodded again, then whispered. "If they catch me, can I use my shard of glass on them?"

"You can use it on anybody but yourself," Mary replied. She threw a couple more branches to hide Sam's blond hair, then she made note of a tall sycamore tree that stood about a hundred feet from Sam's log. *That will be my landmark,* she decided as she moved off through the trees. *If they don't bring in dogs, if Sam can keep a tight lock on her terror, then we might have a chance.*

If any part of her fragile little plan fell through, it would all be over. She and Sam would become just the two latest victims of Highway 74.

THIRTY-FOUR

GALLOWAY SCREAMED DOWN THE road in his green Mustang. He knew he'd gone rogue—should have followed standard procedure and checked in with Dispatch, but the chatter on the box was wildly focused on a 10-108 involving an officer on Kedron Road. The officer, he soon learned, was Crump, the lanky sergeant who'd once partnered with Gudger. Since the entire department seemed to be rushing to Crump's aid, he figured he would not be missed. Anyway, a Russian sex-trade operation was more important than Crump's sorry ass. More important than either of those was Mary Crow.

He pushed the car up to ninety. Just short of the Gaston County line, he skidded into the parking lot of a convenience store and grabbed the atlas of North Carolina topo maps he'd bought after he took the job here. Though his GPS had quickly shown Hubbard Mountain as an elongated green blob just north of the South Carolina line, he needed to know the topography of the place. Flipping on his overhead light, he looked at the map. The park was mostly woods, riddled with the broken lines that indicated hiking trails. Highway 74 rimmed its northern border; local two-lanes gave easy access to route 321 to the east. Ten minutes away lay South Carolina, should you need to dump a body fast.

"A perfect place," whispered Galloway. "In the woods, but close to civilization. Easy access to the interstate truck stops. And if you happen to be Russian, you're half an hour from Charlotte International Airport." He closed the atlas and shook his head. "That's where I would set up shop, if it were me."

He keyed Hubbard's Mountain Road into his computer, then headed back out to Highway 74. It was, he realized, a one-man search for the proverbial needle in a five-thousand-acre haystack, but he didn't care. The needle was Mary Crow, and that was all that mattered.

He drove east on 74, aka Jackson Highway, aka *la carretera del dolor*. Road of sorrows. Certainly it had proven so for Bryan Taylor and those two other girls Mary had come up with. He wondered— could Tiffani Wallace and Maria Perez have been part of this Russian sex ring? A hayseed teenage shoplifter and an illegal sweet potato picker? He shook his head as the highway lines flew by. "*Inocentes,*" he whispered. North Carolina, Georgia, Mexico. Predators preyed on the innocents everywhere.

He crossed over into Gaston County. Immediately, he slowed to the speed limit and turned his radio down low. He knew he should involve the Gaston County cops now, but that would take time and a lot of explanation. They would thank him for the tip and promise to let him know if they found anything. Then, in the way of cops, it would become their case and he would never see Mary Crow again. "Go on your own," he told himself. "Ask forgiveness instead of permission."

He passed through the little village of Mountain View, then turned from Highway 74 on to Sparrow Springs Road. If there was a moon out, it wasn't much of one—all he could see were lights from houses set far back from the road. He drove for several miles, until even the lights from the houses vanished. When the sharp aroma of pine suffused his car, he knew he'd begun to skirt the eastern border of the park.

"Okay," he whispered. "Here's the haystack. Now you've just got to find the needle."

Galloway slowed the Mustang to a crawl. It was hard to see in the darkness, but on a hunch he took an unmarked gravel road that veered off the main road to the right. His tires made a crunching sound as he rolled deeper into the woods, finally stopping when the road dead-ended at an old trash dumpster.

"Shit," he whispered in disgust as he turned the Mustang around. "Bad hunch."

He spent the next half-hour turning down every road he found. He'd given up approaching quietly—no more time for that—now he just barreled down all of them. Most just petered into paths the led into the forest; a couple were access roads to the park, with iron gates barring passage during the nighttime hours. None were wide enough to accommodate traffic from any kind of motel. He'd just reached a dead-end close to the southernmost point of the park when he decided that Gudger had been lying. He'd come on too strong, and the old bastard had just said the first thing that came into his head, just to get him out of his grille. Now, he'd lost Mary Crow forever.

"Jackass!" he muttered, viciously turning his car around. "*Caray!*"

He had no choice now but to call Gastonia and get them in on it. Flooring his accelerator, he headed back to the main road and a reliable cell phone signal. He'd just pulled out on to the road when a huge black car came roaring around the corner. Galloway slammed on his brakes, tires shrieking as he fish-tailed to a stop. He gripped the steering wheel, ready to receive a well-deserved finger from the driver, but no such gesture was made. The driver of the car kept going without a glance at Galloway, racing along the twisting road like a bullet in the night.

"Holy fuck!" whispered Galloway, turning to get a glimpse of the vehicle. It was a big Mercedes CLS sedan. The license plate was white with black numbers and a blob of something orange in the middle—maybe Florida or Georgia. His brief glimpse of the driver had given the impression of size—a great bear of a person who was streaking along this road like his ass was on fire. Galloway sat back in his seat, his adrenalin rush leaving him shaky. Who would be out here driving a hundred-thousand-dollar car like it was the Daytona 500? At this time of night? When there's nothing around here but a park that closes at sunset?

He took a deep breath. Something about that car was ringing a distant bell in his memory—but what? Something he'd seen? Something somebody had said? He closed his eyes, trying to remember—then suddenly, he had it! The peach truck kid. He'd gurgled something about a gorilla in big black car that had come and taken Gudger away.

"It's the gorilla!" whispered Galloway. "I gotta be close, and they must be scared about something. Nobody nearly gets T-boned without slowing down unless some serious shit is hitting the fan."

He turned his car to the right, continuing his circuit of the park. With an eye out for any more cars roaring past in the opposite direction, he searched for a road big enough to handle a moderate amount of traffic. He passed another trash dumpster, scaring a family of hunch-backed raccoons, then at a wide spot in the road that looked like a turn-around, he saw a birdshot sign clinging to an old tree. TOCHER HUNTING CAMP. PRIVATE.

He turned, rolled forward, his headlights flashing across the sign. To the left of it was a narrow road that coiled up into the woods. Though it wasn't paved, it looked freshly graveled and graded against any water runoff. Still, unless someone was looking for it, they'd never know it was there.

"Okay," he said softly. "It's not the Tick Tock Motel, but it's close enough."

He put his car in Reverse and doubled back to the last trash dumpster. He wanted to go back to the hunting camp on foot. No point in getting blocked in by the giant in that Mercedes. He grabbed his cell phone and a pair of cuffs, and slipped an extra ammo clip in the pocket of his jeans. *That,* he thought, *will give me thirty-two rounds of .40-caliber bullets. Surely I can stop the gorilla with that.* As an added precaution, he left his squawk box on. If the gorilla took him down, Campbell County could get a fix on his radio. At least they'd have that much on his last-known whereabouts.

He locked his car and ran back toward the hunting camp sign. The night air was humid and smelled of cedar. A few fireflies blinked among the trees, but only his footsteps broke the silence of the woods. He reached the Tocher camp sign quickly, and started up the heavily graveled road. It didn't climb like true mountain roads, but twisted like a corkscrew into the forest. With the thick trees and the moonless night, he felt like a blind man, navigating by feel and instinct.

He went on, listening for the sound of a car, watching for headlights slashing through the trees. None came. He decided that whatever fire the gorilla was driving to had not yet been put out.

He'd walked a good twenty minutes into the woods when he noticed a slight glow through the trees ahead. Not a real light—just a rise in the road that looked a shade lighter than dark-as-pitch.

He went on, but more slowly, now walking through the weeds instead of the noisier gravel. Knee-high thorn bushes tore at his pant legs; a tiny animal squeaked and rustled away in the grass. He reached the crest of the rise and there it was, nestled against acres of thick trees. Tocher Hunting Camp.

He flattened himself in the grass to get a better look. The place looked ancient—built of asbestos-shingled wings, joined in the middle by an office. The windows of the rooms were boarded up and he saw only two doors—one for the office, another at the end of the wing to his left. He would have thought the place was deserted, a prime candidate for the county demolition squad, except for the two white Mercedes sports cars parked in front and a ribbon of light that shone from the bottom of the office door.

"Bingo," he whispered.

He lay in the weeds, waiting to see if anybody was going to come out or if the gorilla was going to return to his friends. After a few minutes of seeing nothing but an opossum sniff around the edge of the parking lot, he drew his pistol. Now was the time to find out what the hell was going on inside the Tocher Hunting Camp.

He got to his feet. For a moment he considered going fast and straight to the office. But the gravel was noisy and he didn't want to alert whoever was inside. Instead, he crossed the driveway and walked through the weeds to the far end of the building. On a hunch, he tried the door, but the thing was locked tight. Pointing his weapon upward, he crept along the front of the boarded-up windows. Not a glimmer of light shown from any of them—all the action, whatever it might be, was going on in the office.

Mindful that the gorilla could return any moment, he hurried forward. Two more windows, then one, then he was on the little stoop that served as a porch. Carefully, he tried the front door; it was locked just as tightly as the other.

Moving past it, he inched up to the window of the office. Brownish-looking drapes covered most of it, but he found an inch-wide gap along one edge of the window. Bending down, Galloway looked inside; he saw a short man with oily dark hair pacing as he talked on a cell phone, crossing in front of a stunned-looking man who sat spraddle-legged in a chair, naked from the waist down. Galloway released the safety on his pistol and turned his ear to the slit in the drapes.

"Volk should be back with more guys any minute," the man was saying. "But you know—we don't need this kind of shit. I told Boyko that girl cop was bad news…"

That was all Galloway needed to hear. He backed up a step, looked away from the window, and fired. The window shattered, turning into a shower of glass chips that rained down upon him, the window ledge, the building itself. They were still hitting the ground as Galloway hoisted himself up and through what was left of the glass. The man on the phone stood there with his mouth hanging open, while the man who'd collapsed in the chair began to cry.

Galloway crossed the room, slammed the single office door shut, then pushed the phone caller into the wall, nestling his Smith & Wesson inside the man's right ear. "What girl cop?"

"I d-don't know what you're t-talking about." The man stammered, as the slightly metallic odor of urine wafted up from his trousers.

"One more chance," said Galloway. "Or you're gonna have a new .40-caliber ear canal right through your brain. What girl cop?"

"I don't know her name … she had dark hair, looked classy. B-Boyko thought we could make some money on her."

Galloway pushed the muzzle of the pistol harder against the man's ear. "Where is she now?"

"I don't know! She got loose. She went into the woods and took the blond kid with her. Boyko and his pals are hunting them now."

"Outside here?"

The man nodded.

"How many pals exactly?"

"Two with Boyko, now."

"But the ape's gone for reinforcements?"

Swallowing hard, the man nodded, sweat beading on his forehead as if he were standing in a sauna.

"Good boy," Galloway whispered. "You just saved your bare-assed buddy here the job of cleaning your brains up off this floor."

———

Galloway found a giant-sized role of duct tape in the bottom drawer of the desk and quickly subdued his detainees, taping wrists, ankles, eyes, and mouths shut. He confiscated the phone caller's keys and locked him in an empty motel room and the half-naked guy in a broom closet. After that, he called the Gaston County Cops.

"I'm not sure what the hell's going on here," he told the dispatcher. "Maybe a prostitution ring, maybe sex trafficking. I've got two suspects secured inside an old motel called the Tocher Hunting Camp. I understand that at least three more suspects are out hunting two escaped females somewhere on Hubbard Mountain."

"We've got a 11-80 that's got both lanes of Highway 74 shut down. It might take us a while to get there."

"Sugar, the governor's special prosecutor is one of the possible victims here, so I think it would be in your best interest to send every officer you've got ASAP!"

He clicked off the radio, disgusted. He knew he didn't cut any ice with the Gaston County PD, but if he didn't hear sirens in five minutes, he'd call in his own people, or even the SBI.

He rolled out the broken office window, his feet crunching the shattered glass on the ground. Outside, there was still no sign of the monster in the black Mercedes.

"Maybe he wised up and got the hell out of Dodge," whispered Galloway. It didn't matter. He would deal with the monster when and if he showed back up. Right now, he just wanted to find Mary Crow.

Suddenly, from the woods behind the motel, he heard shots—high-pitched, rapid-fire bursts that sounded like an old AK-47. He ran, keeping to the shadows, until he reached the back of the motel. Hugging the wall, he inched forward until he could look around the corner. He saw a man running across a trash-strewn parking lot, automatic rifle clutched in both hands, his eyes focused on some distant spot in the woods. He had the giddy look of a feral dog, about to fall upon some helpless prey. Without thinking, Galloway stepped from the shadows and called, "Hey!"

The man stopped, surprised. Before he could utter a word, Galloway pointed his gun at his heart. "Drop the gun now."

For an instant the man looked almost amused, then he started to swivel in Galloway's direction. Galloway did not wait. He aimed and clustered three rounds in the middle of the man's chest. The machine gun fell to the ground, as silent and useless as the man who'd just fired it.

THIRTY-FIVE

THE PISTOL SHOTS CAUGHT Mary's attention. She'd been running through the woods with intentional noise, trying to pull the men away from Sam, as the quick *rat-a-tat* bursts of the automatic rifles echoed through the woods. Then three deeper shots rang out, silencing one of the machine guns and sending the woods into a truce-like calm. She crouched behind a tree and listened. Before, the two machine guns had been as reliable as the corners of a triangle—one coming from the southeast, the other from the southwest, with the Russian walking up the mountain below and between the two. But something had changed all that. Now she heard just the one automatic firing short, almost plaintive bursts from the southwest, like some bird honking for its fallen mate.

It's Sam, she thought. *She got scared and broke cover, or maybe one of the machine gunners found her and she took him out with her glass shard. But who fired those shots? They sounded like a big handgun. Had the Russian turned on Sam? If so, then why was the remaining gunner still firing willy-nilly?*

Go back, she told herself. *If Sam is still alive, she'll need help.*

Mary turned and went back the way she'd come, only now instead of moving like a hungry bear, she slipped through the trees silently, a shadow among shadows. Though the remaining machine gunner kept up his distant patterings, he did not concern her. He advertised his location with every burst of fire. It was the white suit she worried about. He was silent, he was smart, and he was the one who wanted Sam.

She made her way to the top of the ridge. It was more exposed, but faster travel. And she needed to find the white-barked sycamore tree that she'd used to mark the place where Sam hid, down the hill.

She walked silently, peering through the darkness for the bleached-bone bark of the tree. Finally she saw it, a ghostly sentinel lifting branches into the night sky. She hurried on. When she reached the big tree, she stood against the side that faced the motel. Just to the left lay the fallen limb that hid Sam. It looked just as she'd left it—was it possible Sam was still there? She started to ease her way down the hill when a twig snapped behind her. She turned. Suddenly something hard jammed into the base of her skull. An instant later someone wrenched her arm back between her shoulder blades.

"I thought you might come back for your little friend," a soft voice whispered.

She didn't have to look to know the man behind her was Russian, no doubt with a pistol ready to fire a round into her brain

"I don't know where she is," said Mary. "We split up."

"Then why did you come back here? You were almost to the road."

"How do you know where I was?"

He laughed. "You think we have no forests in Ukraine? No night vision scopes in Moscow? You did well, though. For a little while, I could not find you."

The second machine gun gave a short burst of fire, then abruptly stopped. The Russian held the gun to her neck harder as another vast, vacant silence settled around them.

"*Chort*!" he said, under his breath. "Idiot!"

Mary turned to look at the man. With his shaven head and deep-seat eyes, he looked like a walking skull in the darkness. He frowned as he cocked his head to toward the trees, as if the breeze might bring good news. When none came, he looked back at her.

"Who's down there?"

She shook her head. She had no idea what was going on, other than that his two machine-gunning henchmen had grown strangely silent.

"There is wild card out here now," he said. "One of my men was killed a little while ago; I suspect the other just died as well."

Mary would have laughed had a pistol not been nudged up against her brain.

"So I am thinking someone has come to your rescue. You work for governor—important, no?"

"Very important," Mary said, hoping he wouldn't see through her lie. She couldn't imagine who would have come up here after her. Nobody knew where she was. And she was a laughably unimportant player on Ann Chandler's team.

"So we now have new plan. We are going to walk out of these woods just like this—my gun to your head, arm behind your back. We are going to walk in plain sight, around building to cars in front. If someone tries to kill me, you will die too. That I promise you."

"What about the girl?" asked Mary.

"Fuck the girl. Some deals just don't work out."

————

He wrenched her right arm higher up her back and stepped so close to her she could feel his slightly erect dick poking her hip. It repulsed her, but she couldn't move away. She and the Russian were now twins, conjoined by the pistol aimed at her brain. He pushed her down the hillside, matching her step for step. She glanced once at the log where she hoped Samantha still lay, then she veered to her right, once again steering the Russian away from the girl. They moved with difficulty, slipping on the same slick pine needles that she and Sam had negotiated on the way up. At one point she tripped over a root. As the Russian cried out, she heard something click on his gun. For an instant she thought she was dead, then he laughed as he jerked her to her feet.

"Better watch your step, Miss Governor Cop. My gun might think you want to get away."

He shoved her forward. As they left the darkness of the woods and entered the back parking lot, she risked a look around. She saw no one, heard nothing. If anyone was here trying to rescue her, they were certainly not making their presence known. *More likely one of machine gunners had turned on the other and is now drawing a bead on the Russian*, she thought, *wanting to cut his partners out of the deal for Samantha.*

They crossed the parking lot, walking fast. At first she thought they were going to go back through the motel, but at the last minute, the Russian changed his mind. He turned her, and they went along the front of the building, passing the boarded-up windows of the rooms. A cold sweat broke out on her forehead as she saw, in the distance, a white Mercedes parked and waiting. That was where he was going. But what was he going to do with her? Kill her? Take her as a hostage? Let her go?

She almost laughed at her own idiocy. This man would never let her go.

Okay, she told herself as he whisked her along the sidewalk. *Think. Get in that car and you're a dead woman—every kid in grade school knows that.* But there was no way she could struggle free—the arm that he'd wrenched behind her back had long ago gone numb, and the Russian was cleverly staying too close for her to get a good kick at his ribs or groin. Still, her left arm was free. If she could just figure out some way to connect with his eyes or throat, she might have a chance.

They sped up to a jog as they neared the office that stood between the two wings of the motel. She wondered if the Russian was going to stop and gather Yusuf and the other guy for his little expedition, but he made straight for the car without breaking stride. Her heart raced as she kept waiting for a new machine gun burst that would cut both them both in two, or a single shot from her unknown rescuer that would turn the Russian into a sack of dead meat. Neither thing happened—whatever drama had transpired between the machine gunners apparently had nothing to do with them. *What about Sam?* she wondered. Was she still up there, hiding? Or had she been caught in the crossfire?

Suddenly, the Russian pulled her roughly to a stop. "Tykho!" he whispered. "Slukhayle!"

She didn't know what he wanted, so she just stood there, trying to catch her breath. As she did, the faintest sound of siren came in on the breeze. It was far way now, but she could tell it was coming closer.

"Chort!" he cried. "Go!"

He pushed her toward the car faster, still holding the gun to her head. They were no more than ten feet away now. She went one step, then two, then he stepped on the heel of her shoe. It made her lurch forward, off balance. As he grabbed to keep her upright and moving, she felt his gun slip up and point into her hair rather than her brain. This was her chance!

She lowered her shoulder and swung her left fist as hard as she could. She pegged him, a glancing blow to his ear. He wobbled for an instant, then he straightened his arm and pointed his pistol directly at her head. "Now you die," he whispered, still holding her by her right arm.

She gulped, knowing he had her. But instead of fire and hot lead coming out of his gun, the thing exploded in his hand. Pieces of metal skittered along the ground while bits of his fingers splattered red against the white car. He screamed as blood spurted in long arcs from his wrist. Mary backed up, trying to dive for cover when suddenly, Victor Galloway leaped from behind the second car. He kicked the Russian in the jaw. The man fell, sprawling. He tried to crawl beneath the Mercedes, but Galloway was too fast, flipping him on his stomach, cuffing his mangled hand to the good one behind his back. As he took off his shirt to tourniquet the Russian's bleeding arm, he looked up at Mary and grinned.

"Galloway?" She was shaking so hard she could barely speak.

"To protect and serve, ma'am," Galloway said as he tied the tourniquet tight. "We Campbell County cops aim to please."

"And so you did," said Mary, collapsing on the ground, tears swelling in her eyes as a line of cars with flashing lights roared into the parking lot of the Tocher Hunting Camp.

THIRTY-SIX

– Eight months later –

"Remember what Ms. Morse is going to ask you about, Chase?" Mary smiled down at the little boy who sat fidgeting in a blue blazer and oversized tie in the Sligo County witness room. They'd moved Gudger's trial to the neighboring county—he had too many connections in Campbell for his case to be fairly heard.

"About how Gudger threatened to sell me. And how that gorilla came and beat him up." He looked up at Mary, pale brows drawn in a frown. "Sam told me that Volk killed her friend Ivan. And that gay guy, too."

Mary marveled at how much the little boy had grown. He was inches taller, and his straw-colored hair had deepened into a light honey color. "Bryan Taylor was going to do a movie about those other girls in the motel with Sam. Boyko found out and sent Volk to kill him. His fingerprints matched the unidentified ones in Mrs. Taylor's car."

"Then Volk was the real bad guy," Chase said softly, gazing at the old-school house clock that ticked away on the wall. "I mean, he did all the killing."

"They were all bad guys, Chase," said Mary. "Gudger, Crump, Boyko—they did terrible things to young girls and boys and they're all going to be in prison for a very long time."

"Everybody but Volk," he said, his voice cracking.

"Volk will be dead even longer," Mary said, wondering why the child was worrying about the giant Russian who'd died in the fiery car crash on Highway 74 that awful, long-ago night.

"I wish he were still alive," Chase said. "If he were in jail, they might have found out a lot more bad stuff he'd done. You know, maybe found some of those girls who've been missing for so long."

"That's true," said Mary. "But sometimes things just don't work out the way we want." She moved her chair closer. "So tell me about you, Chase. How's life in the eighth grade?"

"It's a lot better than the seventh," he said. "I joined the band. I'm learning to play the drums."

"That's great," said Mary.

"Yeah," Chase continued, lowering his voice as if he were embarrassed. "And Vicky Brewer asked me to the Sadie Hawkins dance."

"Whoa, Chase!" Mary lifted her hand for a high-five. "You go, buddy!"

Chase giggled. Mary was glad to hear it—she didn't want him obsessing over some dead Russian goon. She leaned closer and looked at the maroon-colored tie he was wearing. It was much too big and made his still-thin neck look even smaller. "That's a classy tie," she said.

"It was my dad's," he said proudly. "I'm wearing it for good luck. Dr. Knox helped me tie it."

"You like Dr. Knox?" Mary knew that the older, soft-spoken doctor whose testimony nailed Crump had become a regular visitor at Chase's house.

"Yeah, he's great. He's got all these cool books and he knows everything about the Civil War. He bought me a really neat bike, too."

"Does Sam like him?"

He shrugged. "As much as Sam likes anybody these days."

Mary had no answer for that. An ordeal like Sam's marked most people for the rest of their lives. Even though she had crawled out from under that log unharmed, she would carry the memory of those two months at the Tocher Hunting Camp to her grave. "Is she still friends with Alice?"

"Yeah, they talk all the time. They're both here today."

Mary thought back over the last eight months. The SBI had pulled Alice Reynolds off a Greek freighter, about to leave the port of Wilmington. She and Sam had both testified against the men who'd held them captive. At first the three defendants had sat silent and sullen, refusing to talk to anyone. But then Smiley had gotten so spooked by the girls' testimony that he'd ratted everybody out—happily naming names, giving dates, helping the FBI break up a trafficking operation that went the length of I-85—from Richmond to Montgomery. As a reward, Smiley had disappeared into the witness protection program. Boyko and Yusuf were both doing fifty years at the federal prison at Big Sandy, Kentucky. Crump had apparently sensed how his cards were going to fall and took a deal. He was now in for thirty-five of his own years at Central Prison, near Raleigh. Gudger was the last one left.

Chase fidgeted more, started flipping the end of his tie. "When do you think they'll start?"

"Pretty soon. Sometimes it takes a while to get through all the witnesses." Mary knew Penny Morse was hoping Gudger would take the modest deal she'd offered before Chase had to testify. But Gudger was apparently brassing it out. Perhaps he thought he could intimidate the boy with that hard glare of his. She had seen tougher witnesses than Chase come unglued on the stand.

"You know, Chase, Gudger's going to be in there the whole time you're testifying."

"Will he question me, too?" asked the boy.

"No. He can't say a word. He can't touch you. But he'll probably look really mean and try to scare you. His attorney might do that, too."

"I don't care," Chase said. "I'm still going to tell the truth."

She squeezed his shoulders. "I'm proud of you, Charles Oliver Buchanan. I know your father is, too."

Just then the door opened. A fat, florid bailiff stepped inside the room. "You're up next, young man."

They stood up. "Okay," said Mary. "Remember to speak clearly. And if you get scared, just look at me. I'll be sitting at the prosecutor's table, right beside Ms. Morse."

"Okay," said Chase, tightening his tie one last time. "I'm ready."

———

The courtroom was packed. Not only with reporters from Charlotte and most of the Campbell County Police Department, but with a vast array of victims and their families. Of all sizes and races, the mothers held their newly found daughters' hands while reunited siblings sat with their arms around each other. Most had testified against Gudger—he had stolen years of their young lives away from some; others had not survived at all. The lost ones were remembered by sad, single mothers who sat alone, holding pictures of their daughters in hopes that somebody in the courtroom might remember their faces, might tell them they were still alive.

Penny Morse called Chase as a witness. The little boy walked to the stand. He gave Gudger a single, cold stare, then he put his hand on the Bible and swore to tell the truth. Five minutes later, as he was recounting how Gudger poured hot sauce on his poison ivy blisters, the defense attorney asked for a recess to confer with his client. Fifteen minutes after that, the judge announced that the defendant had accepted the state's offer, that Ralph Newly Gudger would spend the next fifty-five years in Central Prison. A woman in a black T-shirt with *Dusty* sequined across it stood up, stuck her fingers in her mouth, and gave a shrill whistle of approval. Everyone else stood and clapped as two deputies escorted Gudger, head bowed and limping, out of the courtroom.

After the judge left the bench, Mary turned to Penny, who was beaming. "Nice job, counselor," Mary said, shaking her hand.

"If I had lost this case, I would have quit the law," said Penny. "Particularly after that sweet little boy put his hand on the Bible and swore to tell the truth."

"He did a good job," said Mary. "You coached him well."

"Was he nervous, back there with you?"

"I think Volk's still in his head, but he'll be okay." Mary smiled at Chase, who was enjoying a boisterous group hug with Sam, his mother, Alice, and Dr. Knox. "Both those kids have a lot of grit."

"Everybody in this courtroom had a lot of grit." Penny clicked her briefcase shut. "I just hate it for the mothers of the ones who are still lost."

"It breaks your heart, but like I told Chase, it's seldom that everything works out exactly like you want." Mary leaned over and gave the young woman a hug. "You're a good lawyer, Penny. Count this one as a notch on your gun."

"Thanks."

As Penny turned to talk to a reporter, Mary turned to leave. Since Chase and Sam were still surrounded by triumphant well-wishers, she just gave Chase a thumbs-up as she headed for the door. She'd gotten halfway down the courthouse steps when Galloway came up, dressed in a brand-new suit. He looked cocky as ever—dimpled smile broad, blue eyes bright.

"Detective!" she said. "How nice to see you. I thought you were deep in the throes of an internal investigation."

"Ended two days ago."

"They didn't mind that you shot two people dead? And threatened Gudger with a pulmonary embolism?"

"They *were* a little miffed about Gudger. But the dead guys were machine gunners who were trying to kill the governor's special prosecutor. And I shot them in self-defense, anyway."

"So one made up for the other?"

"I guess." He looked at her and grinned. "Like my new threads?"

"I do," said Mary. "Did they boot you upstairs? Are you now the police commissioner of Campbell County?"

"Actually, I'm not with Campbell County anymore."

"You're kidding. What are you doing now?"

Shyly, he pulled a new badge from his pocket. It had the seal of the state of North Carolina on it and read STATE BUREAU OF INVESTIGATION.

"You're SBI now?" asked Mary.

He nodded. "I got a nice call from the Honorable Ann Chandler herself. She thanked me for my service and said that if I ever wanted to take my talents to the statewide level, a position was waiting."

"Galloway, that's wonderful." Mary stretched to kiss his cheek. "Congratulations!'

"Thanks. I cleaned out my desk, and I'm heading east."

"To Raleigh?"

He shook his head. "Actually, I'll be in the Charlotte office." They fell into step together. "So where are you going?"

"Back to Asheville."

"The governor didn't fire you?"

"No, she gave me a raise."

"How come? Ecotron went to Virginia."

"She still got a hell of a lot of political mileage out of closing down an international sex trafficking operation."

"So North Carolina gay folks can now just twist in the wind?"

"No, she's still committed to gay rights. But I think she finally realized that you have to get the statutes changed first. Raleigh leads, everybody else has to follow."

"Campbell County won't follow willingly," said Galloway.

"Yeah, but that's not my problem," said Mary.

They walked on. Both had parked on the street, under a huge elm tree. Galloway's green Mustang was nudged up behind Mary's black Miata.

"Well," she said as she threw her briefcase in the passenger seat of the car. "I guess this is it."

"Only if you want it to be," said Galloway.

"What do you mean?"

"I mean Charlotte is one hundred and twenty-two miles from Asheville. Two hours travel time—unless you're an SBI officer in that Mustang, in which case it's about an hour and a half."

Mary raised an eyebrow. "So—you're saying you'd like to see me again?"

He took her hand, in a courtly, old-fashioned way. "Yes, Mary Crow. I, Victor Alejandro Galloway, would very much like to see you again. As soon as possible, in fact."

She looked at him. Though he was not the man she thought she'd wind up with, she couldn't help but remember what she'd just told Penny Morse. *It's seldom things work out the way you want.* Maybe in this case, things might work out for the better.

She smiled. "You doing anything this afternoon?"

He shook his head.

"Then follow me."

"Are you going on 74?"

"I am."

"I hear it has some nasty curves."

"It sure does," she replied looking at him over her shoulder. "But I bet you're the kind of guy who can figure out exactly how to drive them."

ABOUT THE AUTHOR

Sallie Bissell is a native of Nashville, Tennessee, and a graduate of George Peabody College. Bissell introduced her character Mary Crow in her first adult novel, *In the Forest of Harm*, soon to be re-issued by Midnight Ink. *Deadliest of Sins* is Bissell's sixth Mary Crow book. Bissell is a Shamus Award nominee and her work has been translated into six foreign languages. She currently divides her time between Nashville and Asheville, North Carolina, where she enjoys tennis and an occasional horseback ride.